Books by the same author

The Name of the Blade Book 1
The Night Itself

The Name of the Blade Book 2
Darkness Hidden

The Swan Kingdom
Daughter of the Flames
Shadows on the Moon
FrostFire

THE NAME OF THE BLADE
BOOK 3

FRAIL HUMAN HEART

ZOË MARRIOTT

WALKER
BOOKS

First published 2015 by Walker Books Ltd
87 Vauxhall Walk, London SE11 5HJ

2 4 6 8 10 9 7 5 3 1

Text © 2015 Zoë Marriott
Cover illustration © 2015 Larry Rostant

The right of Zoë Marriott to be identified as author of this work has been asserted by her in accordance with the Copyright, Designs and Patents Act 1988

This book has been typeset in Berkeley

Printed and bound in Great Britain by Clays Ltd, St Ives plc

British Library Cataloguing in Publication Data:
a catalogue record for this book is available from the British Library

ISBN 978-1-4063-4240-6

www.walker.co.uk

*This book – and this trilogy – is dedicated to
David Marriott, whose love of shenanigans,
badass heroines and unrepentant sarcasm
shaped not only his daughter's writing,
but also his daughter, far more than he ever realized.*

In search of the perfect costume for a fancy-dress party, Mio Yamato steals a priceless antique katana from her family's attic. Big mistake. The Nekomata – a cat-demon from Japanese myth – awakens and attempts to take the sword by force. Only the arrival of a mysterious warrior boy saves Mio and her best friend, Jack, from the monster's claws. Their saviour, Shinobu, has been trapped in the katana for the past five hundred years.

Foiled, the Nekomata kidnaps Jack's sister, Rachel. Shinobu calls for help from the Kitsune, immortal spirit foxes, who agree to fight by Mio's side. During a desperate battle with the beast, Shinobu sacrifices himself to save Rachel, and Mio bonds with the sword in order to destroy the Nekomata. Once it is dead, Shinobu's wounds heal. Mio is overjoyed.

But soon the Nekomata's dark mistress – Izanami,

Goddess of Death – sends an even worse threat into the mortal realm: the Shikome, monstrous winged women whose feathers spread a supernatural plague. With Jack infected and Rachel dangerously mutating as a result of the Nekomata's bite, Shinobu and Mio seek out answers from a sinister old man, Mr Leech, who tells them that the only way to end the plague and save Rachel is to imprison Shinobu within the blade once more. Mio also learns that her own father has known of the existence of monsters – and the sword's dangerous powers – all along, when he saves her and Shinobu from a swarm of the winged creatures.

As Shikome swarm on the hospital where Jack is being treated and Mio's father succombs to the plague, Mio has no choice but to sacrifice Shinobu to the blade. Jack, Rachel, and Mio's father are saved, along with all the plague's victims, and the Shikome are banished. But Mio is left emotionally devastated by Shinobu's death and determined to make the gods pay for what they have done…

CHAPTER 1

BROKEN

I couldn't see her.

The pearly white flames sheathing the katana illuminated dark streaks of fungus on the concrete walls of the storm drain, the fleeting red gleam of a rat's eyes further down the tunnel and the murky black water swirling and splashing at my toes. It also lit up a few things floating in the water that I didn't want to look at closely. But it didn't show me the one thing I had wanted and expected to see.

Rachel.

"Everything OK down there?" my dad shouted into the manhole over my head.

"I'm fine – hang on!" I yelled back.

I walked along the narrow edge of brick that ran down one side of the tunnel, trying to avoid the splashing water as I moved deeper into the darkness. I lifted the flickering light of the sword higher, squinting against the dark.

"You're very quiet," I whispered to the blade. "Nothing to say?"

The sword's energy jumped against my palm like an uneasy heartbeat, but the familiar, metallic voice remained silent.

I still felt the compulsion – a magnetic, physical attraction to the blade – twinned with a deep-down sense of responsibility to protect him, keep him safe. That was apparently hardwired into everyone in my family. It sat alongside my own rational awareness that allowing the sword's destructive power to fall into the wrong hands would be disastrous for the whole world. But the influence that the katana had exerted on my emotions, the silvery, persuasive whispering that had put such pressure on my mind that I sometimes thought I was going mad? It was gone. For the first time in what felt like forever, I was really and truly alone in my head.

I hated it.

"Rachel!" I called out. My voice bounced around the drain eerily. "It's me! You can come out!"

There were tiny skittering noises in the shadows as vermin fled from the noise and light, but nothing else. I strained my ears for any giveaway sounds: a splash, a footstep on the bricks, even a weak cry for help. This was where I'd sensed her, almost *seen* her, during my vision.

I knew I hadn't been mistaken. She'd been in this drain.

But not any more. I was too late, again.

"Shit."

Exhaustion pulled my shoulders down into a weary slump. With a sigh, I turned and went back the way I'd come. The dim blue disc of the open manhole appeared overhead. There was a circle of heads silhouetted against the dusky night sky. My father. Hikaru, our friendly neighbourhood fox spirit. And Jack, my best friend – Rachel's younger sister. They were all peering down anxiously at me.

"Well?" Jack asked. The word echoed around me, multiplying the single question into a hundred. I didn't have any answers.

"Make some room. I'm coming out," I called.

As they backed out of sight I reached over my shoulder and eased the katana into his saya – the lacquered wooden sheath – which rested against my back in its leather harness. As the blade entered the embrace of the saya, the prismatic white fire of the sword was slowly extinguished, plunging the storm drain into impenetrable shadow.

When the tsuba – the sword's guard – clicked home against the mouth of the saya, I let go of the katana, flexing my fingers experimentally. Not very long ago the simple action of replacing the blade in his sheath would have taken almost impossible effort. It would have left me

11

feeling shaken and bereft. The sword would have resisted all the way, beguiling me, tempting me, trying to convince me that I was only complete when I allowed him to wield me as if I was the weapon and he the fighter. I could hardly believe it was so easy now. It almost seemed like cheating – until I remembered the price I had paid for my free will.

I clambered carelessly up the metal rungs set into the wall of the storm drain until I could catch the edge of the manhole with both hands, then swung myself up and out of the hole in a jerky, abrupt movement. Crouching on the pitted tarmac, I grabbed the manhole cover, which we had found already pulled away from the opening in the ground, and pushed it back into place with a heave and a twist.

"She wasn't down there, was she?" Jack said as I straightened up. "Do you think you were wrong about what you saw – dreamed – whatever?"

"No." The deep white claw marks gouged in the grubby cement of the walls proved that my mental image of poor Rachel's desperate struggle down there, the way she had lashed out in her pain as she fought against the transformation, was real. But I couldn't exactly share that with Jack.

"She must have got herself out and away before we arrived. She didn't know we were coming to look for her."

"Why was she down there in the first place?" Jack

asked, pacing away and then back again. "What was wrong with her? What *happened* while I was in that hospital?"

"All right, there are a lot of questions to be answered, but the best thing we can do is head home..." my father began in his usual commanding tone.

Jack was too worked up to listen. She spun back to face me. "Are we in, like, immediate danger from anything horrible right this minute?"

I cast an apprehensive look at the royal-blue sky. It wasn't full dark yet, but the harsh orange glow of the streetlights behind the hospital made the shadows seem more intense, and my instincts were urging me to head for sanctuary. My parents' house, warded against supernatural attack by the London Kitsune, was the only truly safe place for us – the one safe place left in the city, probably. But we'd already seen, on multiple occasions, that darkness was no more dangerous than daylight. Plenty of creatures from the Underworld hunted equally well in either. And Izanami had just suffered a devastating defeat. She was surely going to need some time to recover from seeing her plans turn to dust.

Reluctantly, I shook my head. The bones in my neck creaked. My dad made an exasperated face and folded his arms.

"All right then, tell me what is going on with my sister," Jack demanded. "I know it's bad. She came to the hospital. She was talking with someone else's voice – it said it was the Nekomata's mistress – and her eyes were all black."

Well, shit. I rubbed my hand over my face wearily. "I didn't know that."

"Rachel was supposed to be with you, Mio. You were supposed to be keeping each other safe." The words were edged with an accusation that cut me more painfully than a knife in the gut.

"I tried my best. I did, Jack. She wasn't ... herself. The bite – the Nekomata bite – changed her."

"*Changed* her? What? *How?* Did you know that could happen?"

"Of course I didn't. When we left the hospital, she told us that she felt wrong. Different. She couldn't control her temper. Kept snapping for no reason. The tooth marks on her neck disappeared. She got fast and really strong. Stronger than me. Right after you called us she lost it. She attacked me and…" *No. Can't say his name yet.* "Then she ran off."

At her sides, Jack's hands trembled, then slowly curled into fists. "You let her go?"

Sometimes the only thing you can do is let go…

I flinched from the memory of his voice. "I couldn't stop her."

"You let her go and you didn't tell me. You didn't call me. I can't believe this. She's my sister. I had the right to know she's turning into some kind of monster!"

"She isn't turning into a monster," I said flatly. I could see that my lack of emotion was riling Jack up even more, but I didn't have anything else to offer her. I was so bloody tired. "That explosion of power that healed you and banished the Shikome? It fixed Rachel, too. She's OK now."

At least, as OK as anyone could be when their soul had been invaded by darkness and they only just escaped before the point of no return.

Relief and gratitude passed fleetingly over Jack's face. Then the anger was back. She took a step into my space, poking my shoulder. "Then where is she? Why should I believe anything you say when you've been keeping all this shit a secret from me the whole time?"

"Jack," Hikaru, his face chalky and drawn with tiredness, interrupted firmly. "I can tell you're upset but this isn't—"

"You stay out of it. You, too, Mr Yamato!" Jack snapped at my father as he opened his mouth. "This is between me and her. And you'd better not try to bullshit me, Mio, because I know you and I can see right through it. What the hell were you *thinking*?"

For the first time I looked Jack dead in the eye. She blinked, then took a faltering step back, suddenly uncertain.

"First I was thinking," I said quietly, "that my best

friend was in the hospital, dying, and her sister had just tried to carve my face off, and it was up to me to somehow figure out a way to save them both. A little while after that I was thinking about not getting swept off a rooftop or slashed to bits or dying of the taint when a bunch of Shikome ambushed me."

"Mio."

I ignored Dad's interruption, eyes still fixed on Jack. "Then I was thinking about how apparently everything I believed about my family and my father was a lie, because it turned out he knew about the sword and the monsters all along. And finally—"

"I didn't mean—" Jack began.

I rolled right over her without raising my voice, refusing to stop now that I'd started. "Finally, I was thinking about how in order to close the portal to Yomi, save London from the Foul Women, turn Rachel back into a human, heal you and stop my dad from dying at my feet, I needed to sacrifice ... sacrifice ... and watch him get sucked into an eternal prison of darkness. Again."

Hikaru, my father and Jack were all gaping at me now, wide-eyed and appalled. One of Jack's hands crept up to cover her mouth as her eyes fixed on my shoulder. I knew what she was staring at: the black-silk-wrapped hilt of the sword poking out of the baggy neckline of my dad's ruined old sweatshirt.

Jack had known *him* better than either of the other

two. She had been there when he first broke free of the sword, had listened when he described the endless dark horror of his centuries trapped in the blade. She looked stricken. Maybe I'd said too much.

"So. That was what I was thinking," I finished awkwardly.

"Mimi, I…" Jack stuttered. "I'm sorry… I didn't—"

"Forget it."

"But Shin—"

I flinched, cutting her off sharply. "Let's go home and see if Rachel's there."

Jack reached out. I avoided her as naturally as I could, and pretended not to see the hurt on her face or the warning look that my father gave her.

You must survive. You are the sword-bearer. You are the key to this battle.

I won't forget, I promised him silently, fingers stealing back to caress the grip of the katana. *I won't forget. Whatever it takes, I'll do it.*

I will end this war.

There was no sign of Rachel at the house. No sign she'd been there while we were gone, either.

The familiar rooms suddenly seemed too large, the space echoing with the memory of voices that weren't there, the shadows of people who should have been. I lingered in the doorway of the living room, my eyes trailing over the ordinary shapes of my home as if they were rare, exotic artefacts in a museum. Nothing seemed real.

"She hasn't called her own phone," Jack said fretfully, putting Rachel's mobile down on the coffee table. "Maybe she tried your house phone?"

She moved past me, back into the hall. Hikaru trailed after her, looking awkward. I realized it was the first time he'd actually been inside the house – in fact, it might be the first time he'd been inside a human house, full stop. I should probably say something to make him feel welcome. I should reassure my dad, too; he was sitting on the arm of his favourite chair, staring at me expectantly. But I didn't know what to say to either of them, or how to comfort Jack. It was like my little tantrum in the hospital car park had sucked out the last of my words and now I was empty. I felt distant from them all. I felt alone, even though they were right here with me.

I felt broken.

"Holy crap, there's more than a dozen messages on here," Jack said from the hallway. There was a loud beep as she hit the play button on the answering machine.

My dad's voice flooded the hall. *"Mio, why aren't you answering your mobile? I don't know exactly what is going on over there, but I've got an idea, and I'm coming back. Stay inside. Stay out of trouble. Don't do anything until I get there – do you hear me? Nothing."*

18

My dad rubbed his hand over his face, looking rueful at the echo of contained fury in his recorded voice. "I was ... worried."

The phone beeped again. "*Mio?*" My mum's voice now. "*Pick up if you're there, honey. No? Listen, Rachel called. Your father didn't give me the chance to talk to her, but I know something's happened. Are you all right? Please call me back as soon as you get this.*"

After the next beep I heard my mum's voice again, this time snarling. "*How* dare *you do this to me, Takashi? You had better have the best explanation of your damned life — no, I don't even care about explanations. Call me back as soon as you get there and tell me what is going on or I am getting a divorce, you bastard.*"

The next message from Mum was quiet and steely. "*Someone has to be there. Why haven't you called me? Why hasn't someone called me? Mio, Takashi, one of you pick up the phone. I need to know that you're both OK.*"

I spoke over the next message. "You have to talk to her."

My father's expression was artificially calm. "I know. But I don't know what I'm supposed to say."

I restrained the urge to throw something at him and scream *How the hell should I know?* "You say you're sorry. That we're both safe. And tell her she can't come home. No matter what. She can't come home." And that was it. I was done. I walked quickly towards the stairs and began the climb. "I'm – I'm going to my room. I need to rest. I need to think."

"Mimi!" Jack ran after me. "Are you...? Look, are you going to be OK? About what I said before—"

Various responses cycled through my head. I settled on, "I'm fine. Just tired. Don't worry about Rachel – I promise she's OK. But if she hasn't turned up by the morning, I'll come up with a new plan."

I went on up the stairs, leaving everyone behind.

I opened my bedroom door and stepped inside with relief. He had never been in here. I flicked on the bedside light and pulled off my leather sword harness with quick, efficient movements, removing the sheathed katana so I could check him over for wear, damage or dirt. Despite everything, the sword was still pristine. The one unchanging, perfect thing in my world.

After turning the light off again, I sat down on the edge of the bed, clasping the sword upright between my hands so I could lean my forehead against the silk-wrapped grip.

Are you ... are you there?

Are you there?

Nothing. I braced myself.

Shinobu?

The moment I let myself think his name the flash-back hit, tearing away my bedroom, dark and quiet, and flinging me back, back there—

The cold pavement under my knees. My father lies on the ground in front of me, rash turning black on his face. The fading rumble of Hikaru's lightning, and the stink of burned hair and feathers. Foul Women shriek and swirl overhead.

His face. Pleading, begging me. His lips still wet from mine. The faint resistance as the blade slices through muscle and flesh, the awful thud as the sword guard hits bone. That sharp gasp of agony, and his eyes, the eyes I love so much, too full of pain in that final moment to see me…

My stomach convulsed; bile rushed into my throat, burning like acid. I tumbled over the edge of the mattress, one hand thudding onto the floor to keep my balance as I threw up into the plastic wastepaper bin by the bed.

I knelt there, hollowed out and numb, until the arm which was holding my weight began to tremble. My other hand had kept hold of the katana. I still couldn't let him go. I could never let go. Because when I held the katana in my hand, I held not only the fate of the world – but the soul of the boy I loved.

Slowly, I hauled myself back up onto the bed. Then I curled up around the katana and closed my eyes.

CHAPTER 2

WHAT DREAMS
MAY COME

Back when he'd been obsessively reading The Chronicles of Narnia and *The Lord of the Rings* in the Great Library in his grandmother's palace, dreaming of a human life of freedom and adventure and change, Hikaru had never had any idea how confusing it would all really be. Take this, for instance. Gatecrashing a wild rave in someone's student house was very different to being invited into a friend's home – their family home – for the very first time. There were rituals for this, ways to make your respect and gratitude clear. But those were Kitsune rituals, designed to be performed in the spirit realm. Not for humans, in a human building in the mortal realm. No one seemed to expect anything of him right now anyway, and it was both liberating and terrifying.

All his life, people had pushed and pushed and pushed at him. No achievement was great enough, no amount of effort or talent impressive enough to meet everyone's expectations. But what was he, really? Nothing. Just an infant immortal of no significance. Painfully young and unprepared.

He didn't know what to do.

Mio's father was sitting in the armchair in the living room, lost in thoughts that looked unpleasant to say the least. He had a mobile phone clutched in his hand. Hikaru guessed that he was nerving himself up to call Mio's mother. Jack – lovely, funny, angry, sweet-smelling Jack – was still hunched over the hall table, her shoulders tense with strain, one of her strong, long-fingered hands clutching the edge of the table as she played the messages from the answering machine, hoping for one from Rachel. Her eyes kept straying back to the stairs. Personally, Hikaru wasn't sure if he wanted Mio to come back down right now so they could figure out a way to somehow help her, or if he preferred her to stay up there so he didn't have to see the dead, frozen look on her face again.

Hikaru had only known these people for a few days, but they had been pretty hellish days, and they had all been through a lot together. He had seen Mio Yamato fight, cry, freak out, seen her pushed to the absolute limit of what any person should have to endure. And through it all, she'd shone. There had been a light inside her, a sort of shining that made them all willing to follow her, even when the Underworld broke loose around them and it wasn't certain whether anyone would get through the next five minutes alive. Now it was as if that light had flickered out. Shinobu had taken it with him.

He already missed Shinobu. He couldn't imagine how Mio must feel. What had happened out there in those awful moments when Mr Yamato was dying and the Shikome were swarming on them? He had turned away to defend Mio and Shinobu with his lightning, only to look around and find Shinobu … gone.

What had Mio done in those desperate moments when Hikaru's back was turned?

And what had it done to her?

Hikaru had never had human friends before. He didn't know if they were always like this, so frighteningly fierce and fragile. But he did know that the less they expected from him, the more he wanted to give them.

"Nothing," Jack muttered, as the last of the phone messages ended. "Why hasn't the inconsiderate cow called? She must know that we're worried sick."

"She probably has a good reason," Hikaru said tentatively.

"A good reason? There *is* no good reason to run off and leave me freaking out this way."

Hikaru shrugged. "She might need a bit of time to get her head straight before she faces us again. She seems like that sort of person."

"That kind of… How would you know?" Jack demanded. "You don't even know her. You don't know any of us!"

He flinched inwardly. "Maybe. I know that Rachel loves you, though. She's going to come back." He met Jack's gaze, even though the sight of those lovely, dark, heavy-lashed eyes focusing on him made his whole body go tight. "She will."

Jack stared back at him defiantly for a heartbeat. Then she crumpled, hiding her face in her hands. Hikaru struggled with himself for a minute – *I could move in for a hug. That would be OK, right, not creepy? But what if she does think it's creepy? Damn, I over-thought. Now it's definitely creepy* – and settled on reaching over and lightly rubbing her shoulder.

"I'm sorry," she muttered. "I don't know what I'm doing. First I blow up at poor Mio. Now I'm having a go at you. I'm a hot mess."

"It's OK. Don't worry about it," Hikaru said. "We're all messes here."

Behind them in the living room, Hikaru heard Mr Yamato clear his throat. "Aiko?" he said into his phone. "It's… I'm sorry – let me… No, she can't come to the phone. She's… No, she's not OK. I don't know, Aiko. I … don't know what to do."

I had dozed off and woken, dozed and woken again. I was so tired that my whole body ached with the weight of exhaustion. But I couldn't give in to it. I forced my eyes open and stared down at the katana.

I know you're in there. I'm right here. I'm right here with you. You're not alone.

Can you hear me?

Shinobu?

Still no response. No spike of energy, no tingle in my skin, no voice in my head. Nothing. If Shinobu's spirit was cloaking the katana so tightly that the blade couldn't speak to me any more, then why couldn't Shinobu communicate with me in its place? He had before, on that first night, in the road outside Natalie's house, when I was dying.

Shinobu. Please. Please?

I had to hear his voice. Grasping the hilt more firmly, I slid the blade free of the saya. The distinctive black and silver ripples of metal glowed in the moonlight. I drew in a slow, even breath. And held it.

I visualized everything inside me – the dark, flowing shadows of my soul – reaching out, reaching into those flame-shaped markings, into the fibres and atoms of the folded steel. That was where Shinobu was. We were so close. He had to know I was there. That he wasn't lost and alone again.

I had to be able to reach him.

Shinobu. Shinobu. Shinobu.

My lungs burned, begging for air. Sparks burst across my eyes. The sword trembled in my hands.

Answer me!

My vision narrowed to the shining silver of the blade's cutting edge. I caught a glimpse of my own eye staring back at me, reflected in the polished metal. My dilated pupil seemed to open up like a black hole. It swallowed me.

I fell.

The warmth of the sun on my face. Long grasses whispering. A fleeting echo of laughter.

A low, rambling house, with a steeply pitched, thatched roof and yellow-brown walls, tucked into the curve of a forested hill. A clear stream dancing beneath ornamental bridges in a garden. Mountains beyond, blue and mist-shrouded in the midsummer sun. The sleepy scratching song of cicadas. A deep, commanding voice calls out:

"Hajime! Mae! Mae! Ato!"

The smell of warm, polished wood and fresh sweat. Long dust motes spiral in auburn rays of sunlight filtering through rice-paper screens fixed over large, round windows.

A man stands to one side, arms folded, his neat topknot and beard streaked with grey. His face is stern, his gaze keen, but crinkled lines around his eyes and mouth show that he laughs often, and deeply. In the centre of the room, two children – a boy and a girl, no older than ten or twelve – circle each other, holding bokutō, old-fashioned wooden practice swords. Both are dressed in plain black kendogi. The boy is tall and skinny, his back very straight, his limbs lanky in that funny puppyish way that means he'll probably be a giant in a few years. The girl is small, delicate, with wrists and ankles like fragile bird bones. Her hair is drawn severely back, but strands have worked free around her ears and forehead and are plastered to her warm, golden skin. The small, pointed face is taut with determination, but her large, dark eyes are shining.

She lunges forward. The movement is shocking, too fast, too fluid for a child. The boy responds just as quickly. As he turns, I catch my first glimpse of his face.

Shinobu.

The scene changes. I'm outside. The same girl – older now, more like fourteen or fifteen, but still tiny and bird-boned – stands in the shelter of a huge tree, one small hand resting on its pale, papery trunk. A heavy canopy of pink blossoms dances overhead, sending petals spiralling down into the girl's black hair and over her pale blue kimono. She is smiling. A boy walks towards her.

Shinobu *walks towards her.*

This is Shinobu's past. I'm dreaming his memories again.

He is taller now. His face shines, alight with happiness. He reaches out to pluck a cherry petal from the girl's hair, and then smoothes a silky stray strand behind her ear with a quick, practiced movement. The girl turns her cheek into his palm. They love each other. Anyone could see it. It makes the air around them seem almost to glow. It's beautifully bright, painfully beautiful.

My heart contracts with a mixture of yearning

jealousy and terrible sadness. He lost her before I was even born. Oh, Shinobu.

Who is she? Who was she?

The scene changes again. They are back inside the house. Time has leapt forward again – they are older. The girl looks the same age as me, and Shinobu looks the age I've always known him – seventeen.

Something is wrong. The girl's face is pale and streaked with tears. She stares at Shinobu as if she doesn't know him. He is still and grave. God, such a familiar expression, that shadow of anguish in his eyes.

The girl makes an abrupt gesture of repudiation with her hand, palm opening as if to fling something away. She speaks. The words are in Japanese, and I don't understand them, but they seem to tremble in the air. Shinobu recoils, his whole body jerking. He opens his mouth, but she has already walked away. She does not look back.

What did she say? What's happening? What's wrong?

I know I'm not really here. Even if this is "real" in any sense, it's still the past. Hundreds of years ago. I can't change any of it. But I can't help reaching out to him with my heart, trying to wrap some kind of comfort and love around his poor bowed shoulders.

Shinobu. It's all right. I'm here. I'm always here, Shinobu.

His back stiffens. Those beautiful dark eyes search the

room with an expression of disbelief. And just for an instant,
they meet mine.

A shrill, unearthly wail assaulted my ears, making me
gasp with pain.

The vision, Shinobu, the colours and warmth, everything disappeared as if someone had flicked off the light.

*I found myself on my knees in a dark corridor that stretched
out ahead of me as far as the eye could see. The walls were
glassy black, rough and jagged. And it was cold, so cold. As
cold as death. Clouds of vapour breathed off the warmth of my
skin. I could feel ice crystals forming around my eyes and nose.
My face and the tips of my fingers were already going numb.*

*A woman stood ahead of me in that long, narrow channel
of rock.*

*Her back was turned to me. She scintillated, burning with a
light that made my eyes sting. Every detail of her was as sharp
as if I was seeing her through binoculars. Glossy dark hair cas-
caded in a perfectly straight waterfall over her waist and hips,
almost to her knees. She wore a white and gold kimono, decorated with great swirls of intricate embroidery, each stitch as
tiny and fine as a grain of sand. She was very slender, and not
very tall. One hand, as delicate as a child's, rested on the rock
beside her, the fingers slightly curled.*

Her back shuddered. The faint sound of a sob reached me.

*I knew who this was. I knew. I was looking at the Goddess
of Death.*

You feel for him … so much. *The sweet, singsong tone sounded so eerie, so wrong, spoken with a grown woman's voice.* Such love. You ache for him. But you will do nothing for me. You deny me. You care nothing for *my* pain!

The icy air abraded my windpipe as I sucked in a ragged breath. "I – I can't give you what you want. I'm sorry."

A low moan of despair wavered through the corridor. Her loneliness, unbearable, ancient and cold, washed over me like a suffocating wave.

He promised me. He *promised.* I only want what I was promised!

"I'm sorry," *I repeated, the words hoarse with unshed tears.* "I'm so sorry. I can't let you destroy my world."

Her head jerked. I never wanted to hurt anyone. Crunch. Snap. Little white bones all poking out. I just want what he promised.

"I know. But you do hurt people. You've – you've hurt my friends." *I tried to speak as gently as possible. Her sorrow was like some kind of horrific radiation, so powerful it could kill. The cold of it gnawed the heart of my bones. My fingers were blue. I couldn't feel them any more. I couldn't feel my lips.* "You're hurting me – right now."

Slowly, she turned towards me. Just for a second I saw a flawless white profile – a delicate nose, soft full lips, a beautiful slanting eye fringed with thick black lashes. She looked so young. Years younger than me. Practically a little girl.

Then she completed her turn.

I shuddered, doubling up over my knees as I saw her properly for the first time.

Soft, pale skin hung in torn spiderwebs over the sharp yellow bones of her skull. Her left eye was missing, and the left side of her mouth and the flesh of her left cheek had been eaten away, exposing the teeth all the way to the roots in the spongy bone of her jaw. Worms and insects crawled through the gaps in her flesh. A thin black snake slithered out of the empty eye socket and coiled around her neck before disappearing into a gaping hole in the skin just below her collarbone. The clean white kimono seethed; the fabric was barely able to contain the movement beneath it. Ants, cockroaches, millipedes and gleaming beetles worked busily around the skeletal remains of her feet.

Give me what I was promised, or it shall be war… *the half-rotted face hissed. Maggots gleamed white on the pulpy black of her tongue.* And you will join me in hell, Yamato Mio. Soon. Soon.

Ssssoon!

Her voice rose into a hideous shriek that pierced my ears like a hot needle.

I snapped back into my body with a silent wheeze of terror, flying off the bed before my eyes were even fully open. My back slammed into the wall next to the window. I brought the katana up, ready to strike. Fighting for breath, heart palpitating wildly, I scanned the corners of my bedroom, searching every shadow for the awful pale gleam of shredded skin and exposed bone.

The room was empty.

Slowly, I let the sword drop. My sigh turned the air in front of my face white. When I looked down, I could see patterns of frost riming the back of my hands. My fingernails were blue-grey in the dim light.

It was nearly dawn. I had been out of it for a long time.

With Izanami.

She's coming after me. And she is angrier and more insane than ever.

Before I could begin to process everything I'd seen – the memories that seemed to be Shinobu's, Izanami's threats – I heard another scream. Not Izanami this time.

Someone human.

I swore and ran for the door, my unsheathed katana in my right hand, its saya clutched in the other.

The others were piling into the front hallway as I arrived downstairs. I realized they must have been sleeping in the living room when the sound woke them.

"What is that?" A bleary-eyed Hikaru demanded, rumpling his copper hair with one hand. He was wearing a white tank top, which revealed a slender but surprisingly muscular build with strong, wiry arms. His bottom half was clad in what looked like a pair of my father's pyjama bottoms.

"It wasn't me," I said in response to Jack's worried

look. She was wearing an oversized T-shirt and clutching her purple skull duvet around her.

"No, it came from outside," my father said, fastening his katana to his belt with quick, automatic movements. Like me, he was still fully dressed.

I stepped past him, put down the saya on the hall table and unbolted the front door. The street lay quiet under a thick blanket of sickly yellow clouds. The sun wasn't up above the skyline yet, but the streetlights had already winked off.

A woman flashed past the doorway. She was sprinting flat out, thin, pale legs flashing under the hem of her black coat. I had a blurred impression of a dead-white, terrified face as she whipped her head back to look behind her, hair streaming over her shoulders. She screamed again.

I couldn't see what she was running from at this angle. It didn't matter. Under my hand, the faint buzz of energy emanating from the katana's grip had become a fierce sizzle.

There was a monster out there.

I turned to look at my dad. He stared back for a second, his gaze searching my face. Then he nodded shortly, squaring his shoulders.

"You two stay here," I said to Jack and Hikaru. "We've got this."

CHAPTER 3

INCY
WINCY

My dad stepped out behind me and shut the door
on Jack and Hikaru's worried faces.

The woman stumbled to a halt, staring at us. "Can
you see it? Do you *see* that?"

I turned in the direction of her pointing finger and got
my first look at the danger that was causing the katana's
energy to growl.

The thing lumbered clumsily down the centre of the
road. Its massive, hair-covered abdomen seemed too heavy
for the thin, black-and-white striped legs that heaved it
forward. The body was black, marked with white zig-
zags, and had two segments. Mandibles bigger than steak
knives rubbed together with a dry, papery sound.

It was a spider. A spider the size of a Dobermann.

The creature's cluster of gleaming black eyes were
fixed on the woman. It was slow and didn't seem very

agile, but it never stopped moving and it never looked away. I wondered how long it had been chasing her. Long enough to send her frantic. Long enough to send anyone frantic.

"You see it, right?" she begged us. "Please tell me you're seeing this!"

"We can see it," I promised.

"Unfortunately." My dad's face had screwed up with revulsion. "I mean, my God, what's next?"

"Never ask that question," I advised. "Can you get her inside? I'll deal with this thing."

"Are you sure? Don't you want me to—?"

"I can handle it."

Dad hesitated again, giving me another of those searching looks. What was he looking for? What did he expect to see? Whatever it was, he obviously didn't find it in my eyes. When he finally nodded and peeled off towards the woman, his expression was tense and worried. I sighed, and made for the other end of the street, twisting the katana in slow figures of eight to limber up my wrist.

The spider took no notice of me at first, just pulled itself steadily along with arrhythmic lurching motions, as if I wasn't there. Then I stepped into its path – blocking its view of its prey. That got its attention.

The spider let out a weird sound, a series of oddly mechanical clicking noises. It reared back, and the top half of its body heaved up off the ground. While the front set of legs began to wave in the air, its back legs strained, lifting its body until the bulbous head was nearly level with mine. The razor-sharp jaws clashed together in warning.

An involuntary sound of disgust popped out of my lips. I was so busy trying not to gag, I almost failed to notice that the back half of the creature was curling up underneath it to point the sharp tip of its abdomen at me. *That can't be good.*

I jumped aside as a stream of greyish web-stuff splattered onto the pavement.

As a rule, I wasn't a spider killer. I preferred to catch them with a glass and a sheet of paper and put them outside. But this situation definitely called for an exception.

I ran around the side of the spider onto the pavement, tracking its awkward movements. It tried to turn and keep me in sight, but those crooked legs were just too slow. I struck from behind, two fast diagonal slices that made the blade flash in the pre-dawn light. Four of the spider's six back legs parted from its abdomen and slid away with papery rustling noises. The heavy body crashed onto the road. The creature cried out again – a series of dry clicks that rose and fell almost like a human voice speaking. More of the sticky web goo spurted out. I brought the katana down on the most vulnerable point of the spider's body: the join between the swollen abdomen and the upper carapace.

The blade severed the creature's exoskeleton neatly in half. Rusty liquid gushed out, mixing with the pool of web-liquid under the body. The spider collapsed onto the ground, front legs thrashing in its death throes. I waited for it to fall still, then turned to see if my father had come back yet.

There was no sign of him.

The street was deserted except for the running woman – who wasn't running any more. Standing motionless in the middle of the road about a hundred yards away, she smiled.

Dread dropped into my stomach like a ball of cement. The sword was still humming in my grip.

"Where is my father?" My voice was toneless. Flat. A killer's voice.

"He's gone. You're next." Her voice was different now, too: deeper and more resonant.

She wasn't a woman. She wasn't any kind of human. She was a monster in disguise.

Sparks crackled to life on the katana's blade.

Dad's all right. He has to be all right.

I won't lose him, too.

Her smile widened as she watched me approach, like a patron in a restaurant as the waiter rolls the dessert trolley to her table. In my mind I drove the hilt of the katana into her stomach, then brought my elbow down on the back of her neck, and finally applied my boot to her face until she told me where my dad was and that he was OK.

A second before I reached her she threw her head back. Mechanical clicking sounds rolled from her mouth. I staggered back as a swollen spider's abdomen burst out of the bottom of her black overcoat. It was dingy white, and the size of a hatchback. Six segmented white legs unfolded, lifting her from the road. The monster rose until her upper carapace towered six feet above me. Her human arms stretched and grew. Thrusting out of the sleeves of the coat, they reached the ground and then turned back on themselves. The jagged white limbs were each longer than my whole body and tipped with a curving, razor-sharp claw.

She bowed her head slightly, dark hair falling over her face in long, lank coils.

"They call me Jorōgumo," she said, with a hint of ceremony. "Mother of Spiders."

I darted forward, bringing my flaring blade sideways for a clean slice at her front leg. She twitched it away. I ducked under it and thrust up at the vulnerable joint of her body hidden beneath the remains of the overcoat. She was gone before the sword could make contact, skittering backwards onto the pavement with a lightning-fast, alien movement. Her taunting laugh echoed down the street.

"Where. Is. He?" I stalked after her. "What did you do with my dad?"

"What do you think?" she asked. Her tongue flicked out to caress her lips. "Were you listening when I introduced myself? I am a spider, after all."

No. No. She's lying.

There hadn't been time for her to kill him and suck out his blood. He would have fought her – I would have heard the struggle. He was too strong to go down that easily. She was just trying to shake me, mess with my head.

"Oh, I was listening." I drew near her again. "I've just sliced up one of your babies. How do you feel about that, Mother of Spiders?"

Her upper body moved in a jerky shrug. "Eh. I can always have more."

She lurched forward, one of the massive forelegs slicing at me. I dodged, and the claw-like foot smashed into the road, sending chips of tarmac flying. I reversed the blade to strike at the limb – and saw her abdomen curl up. I abandoned the strike, skidding to the left as a string of white web-stuff thicker than my arm squirted past me. The movement brought me straight into the path of her other foreleg, forcing me away from her again.

"Some mother you are," I sniped.

She bared her teeth at me. "Some daughter you are."

The spider-woman manoeuvred sideways, driving

me back. She was so much faster and more agile than the small one. I needed to concentrate if I didn't want to get skewered, but my gaze kept flitting past her, desperately searching for any sign of my father.

What had she done to him?

I won't let go again.

Something barrelled into my side. My knees went out from under me and I hit the edge of the curb with a bone-jarring thud, rolling instinctively. A striped black-and-white leg stabbed at my chest. I rolled again – and tipped into the gutter.

A spider the size of a Great Dane landed on top of me, its hairy abdomen crushing my legs. Chattering mandibles lurched towards my face. I thrust my katana up between us. The mandibles clamped on it, and the blade flared white-hot. The spider made an anguished clicking sound. It wrenched backward, trying to jump off me and drag the sword out of my grasp. The flames seared its face. One of the bulging black eyes popped with a loud snap, showering me in goo. The stink of its burning flesh was rancid.

Long legs thrashed around me as I jammed my hand up under its thorax, trying to push it off. It lifted a couple of inches – and I felt the abdomen fighting to curl up between us and spray me with web. Hurriedly I let its body drop and grabbed one of the legs. Bristly hairs abraded my palm as I twisted the limb up, trying to snap it off. I would rip the thing apart bit by bit if I had to.

I had to find my father.

A booted foot slammed into the spider. The sharp blow knocked the katana's burning blade free of the locked mandibles and drove it into the side of the monster's head. The spider shuddered. The boot kicked again, and the spider flipped off me and landed on its back. It curled up into a ball, legs twitching.

"Need a hand there?" asked a familiar voice.

I rolled to my feet, gaping like an idiot. It was really her, all in one piece, neat and tidy as ever. I couldn't believe my eyes. "Rachel! Are you OK? Where have you been?"

She gave me an *Are You Serious?* look. "How about we catch up later, Xena. Is that your *dad*?"

"Where?" I whipped around.

Relief made the world spin dizzily around me. It was him. He was alive and, judging by his expression, seriously pissed off. Several globs of web goo plastered him to the side panel of a van parked on the street. His whole right arm, one leg and his upper left arm were immobile. Another piece of web was stuck over his mouth, but he'd managed to get his left hand up and was working at it. His sword was still stubbornly clenched in his trapped right hand. I leapt forward to help.

He ripped the spiderweb gag off. "Look out!"

Behind me, Jorōgumo let out another clicking cry.

"Get him off there," I said urgently, giving Rachel a hasty push towards where he was trapped. "Quick."

I turned back to face the monster.

A tide of spiders crawled over the houses behind Jorōgumo, washing down onto the pavement. They ranged from house-cat-sized to nearly as big as the one Rachel had just nuked. There were dozens of them.

Way, way too many for me to hold off alone.

The katana seemed to tremble in my hand, energy throbbing. I could call on the power of the sword's first true name – Shinobu's name – but what if that broke the blade's intelligence free again? The baby spiders surged around their mother's legs and scuttled across the road straight at us.

Jorōgumo grinned.

My eyes flickered back to Rachel. She was sawing at the web with my father's sword. "Hurry up."

"I am *trying*," she snapped.

"Mio, run!" my father ordered. "Get back to the house. Rachel, you, too."

"I'm not leaving you."

"Me neither, so shut up and help me," Rachel told him.

The spiders kept coming. I braced myself.

The front door of my house flew open with a crash.

"Yippee ki-yay!"

Hikaru shot down the steps and into the road, his tail whipping at the air. A spray of lightning bolts zipped away from him and hit the first line of spiders. A large one popped, messily. Jack skidded out after Hikaru, slamming the door behind her. She clutched one of my mother's wicker shopping baskets in one hand, and there was a glass bottle in the other. Her arm went back like a cricket player's. She pitched the bottle straight at Jorōgumo.

The spider-woman dodged. The bottle hit the ground next to her and burst into flames. Jorōgumo shrieked as fire licked her legs. Several of the smaller spiders went up with a loud sizzle.

"Go get her, She-Ra!" Jack yelled at me.

Behind me, Rachel laughed. "It's Xena, Jacqueline. Xena!"

I saw Jack's face light up with joy as she heard her sister's voice. Hikaru whipped his tail again, driving the sea of spiders back towards their mother. His mouth was set in a mad grin of effort and elation.

OK, time to try something really stupid.

I charged Jorōgumo.

Spiders crunched under my feet as I leapt from back to back, picking up speed. When I hit the edge of the road, I jumped, putting everything I had into it. With a mad war cry, I flipped in midair and landed on Jorōgumo's back. The impact travelled through her body like a piledriver. Her spindly legs buckled.

Weird clicking sounds almost deafened me as I seized

the back of her overcoat to hold myself steady and brought the katana straight down in a powerful one-handed thrust, aiming for her waist – the narrow point where the torso met the abdomen.

The blade went through the spider-woman's chitin armour like a warm finger sinking into melting ice cream. I dragged the sword sideways to inflict maximum damage. She convulsed, legs jerking and flailing. I let go of the coat, spread my arms for balance and kicked. My boot thudded solidly between her shoulder blades.

With a *crack*, Jorōgumo's upper carapace separated from the hairy abdomen. Her human-looking torso toppled down onto the tarmac. The rest of her body juddered and then collapsed, almost throwing me off. Down in the road, the baby spiders let out shrill sounds as they saw their mother die.

I leapt away from the spider-woman's death throes. My landing crushed two of the smaller spiders, and I diced two more with a quick two-handed slash of the katana. To my right, Hikaru and Jack closed in, herding the spiders towards me with lightning and fire. My father was finally free, and was quite calmly instructing Rachel on the best way to use his sword to kill the monsters, even as he crushed them underfoot, punched them down and ripped off their legs with his bare hands. Overhead the sun was finally rising above the buildings, casting long fingers of light between the clouds and into the street.

Within five minutes, Jorōgumo's army was nothing more than ashes, twitching legs and splatters of goo staining the road.

"What now, boss?" Hikaru asked tiredly, looking at me.

When did I become the boss? A quick glance at the others showed them all – even my dad – staring at me expectantly, as if they were waiting for orders. I cleared my throat awkwardly. "Um. I think we're done here. Showers?"

To my relief, everyone nodded.

"You! You can make bacon sarnies to apologize for scaring the crap out of me," Jack said roughly, grabbing at Rachel and attempting to put her in a headlock.

Rachel fended her off with one hand, holding my father's katana carefully away with the other. "Euw, get off. Don't get spider guts on me!"

They headed for the house and I took a moment to sag, dazed with relief. We'd survived again. All of us, this time. We were safe. I had no idea how.

And I had no idea how long it would last.

CHAPTER 4

CONTROL
FREAKING OUT

The water swirling around the shower drain was an odd brownish colour. A mixture of amber Shikome blood from yesterday, a few dashes of rusty spider blood that had soaked through my clothes this morning and quite a bit of my own red stuff, which had dried in my hair and in long streaks down my neck and back. The wound had healed now, but I didn't need the diluted pink drips trickling over the white tiles to remind me of the Foul Woman's talons clawing open my scalp. I would never forget anything that had happened yesterday. Never.

No matter how much I might want to.

My chest felt tight – heart thundering, breaths rattling painfully in my throat as I fought the deluge of images and sensations that threatened to overwhelm me. Dad's chalky face. The stench of burning feathers clogging my nose. Shinobu's eyes…

47

I couldn't keep going back there in my head. I had to get it together.

Slowly, I managed to bring my breathing under control, tamping the flashback down into some abandoned dark corner of myself. My pulse still felt frantic and thready, and when I unclenched my hands I found that I'd crushed the bottle of bodywash into a mess of jagged plastic shards.

When I fumbled the water off and shoved back the shower curtain, my hand, reaching out for the towel, didn't look like mine. It was too big, the fingers too long, the wrist too sinewy. The sword's immense explosion of power yesterday had made me grow, again. Everything felt subtly off.

I didn't know my body any more. I wasn't sure I knew *myself* any more.

I dried off as quickly as I could. The bathroom mirror was misted with steam, and I didn't want the reflective surface to start clearing before I got out of there. Izanami seemed to like mirrors. After the last vision I was as clear as I'd ever be about her intentions, and I had a strong feeling that another chat might do me actual physical damage. She was getting stronger. Closer. Just like she had promised.

Mostly dry, I wrapped a bath-sheet around my chest and tucked it in to hold it in place, then picked up the katana from where I'd balanced him on top of the toilet cistern. A fine film of condensation had formed on the black lacquer of the saya. I wiped it gently dry with a fresh towel.

Shinobu? I still have you. I won't let go again. I promise.

With the katana under one arm, I stepped out of the bathroom – and nearly ploughed into Jack. She stood an inch from the door with one hand raised as if she'd been about to knock.

"Oh. Hey. Hi!" she said, just a shade too brightly.

"Hi, Jack." Once again I was surprised by the dead, flat tone of my voice. I cleared my throat and tried to add a bit more life to my next words. "Waiting for the bathroom?"

"Oh, no, no, no." She stopped abruptly and took an audible breath. "Um. I brought you some clean stuff. To wear. Your dad says nothing fits you since you got … you know, embiggened. Here."

She shoved a pile of folded clothes at me. I took them with my free hand, clamping the katana to my side with my elbow to try and keep the towel in place.

"This is great, thanks. But you do realize it's too late, right?"

Her eyes went wide with shock. "Mimi – look, I know I said some stupid stuff, but—"

"I've already seen inside your wardrobe," I interrupted. "What's seen cannot be unseen. I know your terrible secret … *neat freak.*"

She gawped at me for a long second. Then her head fell

back and she let out a helpless, relieved gurgle of laughter.

"It is no laughing matter, missy," I said, deadpan. "Our whole relationship is built on lies. I thought you were one of the normal slobs like me."

"As if you've ever been normal!" She snorted. Her arms shot out without any warning and suddenly she was hugging me, slipping towel, sword, bundle of clothes and all.

It was weird.

It was weird because up until a few days ago we never hugged – not like this – but suddenly hugging was a thing we did and I hadn't adjusted yet. It was weird because the last time she hugged me I broke down and howled into her shoulder like my heart was breaking, and she had held me and wordlessly comforted me until I could stand on my own two feet again. And it was weird because I was little Mio and she was big Jack, and yet now I was at least three or four inches taller than her, and she somehow felt small, and fragile, the same way she had looked when she was all huddled up in that hospital bed, dying of the Foul Women's taint.

With my arms full, I couldn't even try to hug her back, and a guilty part of me was glad. She was just … too close. Too much. *I have to keep it together.*

Thankfully it was over in less than a count of five. Jack moved back and then swiped her forearm quickly over her eyes.

"We're good now, yeah?" I said uneasily. "Cos, honestly, I'm feeling a little underdressed for this occasion."

"Whatevs, She-Ra," she retorted, grinning. "You know it's your secret dream to get naked with me."

"I think you're confusing my secret dreams with your filthy fantasies, perv," I shot back, turning towards my room with relief. *Keep it together just a little longer...*

"Mimi?" The tentative note in her voice stopped me.

I glanced back over my shoulder, trying not to let impatience or fatigue or just how close I was to cracking show on my face. "Yep?"

"I know I was a muppet before. I'm sorry."

Something – something soft and vulnerable – stirred inside me. It hurt. My hands curled into fists around my towel and the pile of clothes. *Don't. Please don't. I can't...*

"You don't have to apologize, Jack. I get it. It's OK."

"What about you?" Her dark, perceptive eyes – eyes that always saw more than people realized – were intent on my face. "Are you OK? I know that's a stupid question – you can't be OK – but ... I don't know what's happening in your head any more."

The forced smile felt unnatural, like a jagged break across my face. "I'm fine. Just tired."

I fled into my bedroom, closing the door, before she could catch me out in any more lies.

A severe-looking woman in a raincoat stood outside the familiar black door of 10 Downing Street. Other newspeople jostled around her, but she clung doggedly to her position as she stared at the camera.

"The strange wave of severe allergic reactions that swept through London like wildfire over the past forty-eight hours now appears to be under control, with a number of London Primary Care Trusts reporting that patients previously suffering with these mysterious symptoms have been discharged. But this brings us to a wider issue: currently most of London's hospitals are all but empty, after what experts are describing as 'an inexplicable spontaneous healing' affected thousands of patients with all kinds of injuries and illnesses. This extraordinary phenomenon has confounded medical science, and has already been dubbed 'a modern miracle' and 'an act of God' by religious leaders. We're here waiting for an official statement from the prime minister, who cut short his state visit to India to return to the UK following the hospitalization of Health Secretary Daniel Anders."

The programme returned to a studio set and a male newsreader at a desk. "Thank you, Diana. We will bring you an update as soon as the PM begins his statement," he said. "In the meantime, the BBC and the family of newsreader Felicity Tamworth would like to express their thanks and gratitude for the messages of support which have been pouring in since she was taken ill on air. Ms Tamworth is now fully recovered and at home with her family.

"In other news..." A slightly blurry picture of an ordinary street awash with vivid red liquid beneath a vast, black, mushroom-shaped cloud replaced the newsreader's face. "Meteorologists have been caught out by a series of highly unusual weather systems which have sprung up, apparently without warning, all across the wider London area over the past twenty-four hours. There have been reports of violent electrical storms, hailstones the size of tennis balls and even mini-tornados. The unusual weather is believed to have caused substantial property damage. Eye witnesses at one location have described a deluge of rain which was blood-red in colour and extraordinary cloud formations. Dr Janice Fincher, a senior member of the Royal Meteorological Society, has come under fire from the Bishop of York after describing the weather of the last twenty-four hours as 'like something from the end of days'..."

It's for their own good, I told myself firmly, as I crept down the stairs. The awkward conversation with Jack had just made it clear to me what I had to do. They wouldn't like it, but … it was the only option.

One of my hands reached back nervously to touch the silk-wrapped hilt of the katana in his sheath on my back. The other tightened around the short note I'd scribbled on Hello Kitty stationery in my bedroom. By the time they realized what had happened I would already be long gone.

I was almost sure they were all in the living room, gathered around the TV, but I paused for a second at the bottom step to make sure I could hear each of their voices, talking quietly over the morning news. Yes, the way was clear. As I sidled into the kitchen, the scent of coffee and bacon sandwiches made my stomach turn over uneasily. Hunger or nausea? Probably both. I looked around, then stuck the folded note on the breakfast bar underneath one of Dad's herb pots. There. They couldn't possibly miss it. I'd done all I could.

I made my break for the door.

My fingers had just made contact with the handle when someone cleared their throat, loudly and obnoxiously, behind me. I managed not to flinch, but my turn wasn't as slow and controlled as I would have liked.

Jack stood in the kitchen doorway, face stony, arms crossed over her chest. "Going somewhere?"

I met her gaze without blinking. "That's rhetorical, right?"

"Well, at least you're not trying to lie to me." She held up one finger as if to ask for a minute, then shouted, "Hey, guys! Mr Yamato! I think you need to come into the kitchen *right now*!"

"Jack!" I hissed.

"Don't even with the betrayed face," she snapped, folding her arms again as the others spilled out into the hall behind her. "You were about to ditch us and go off on your own like freaking Harry heading into the Forbidden Forest to give himself up to Voldemort."

"What?" Hikaru asked, bewildered. "Volde-who?"

"Don't worry, Hikaru," I said acidly. "She's talking Geek. Just ignore her."

"What's that?" Rachel asked, pointing at the breakfast bar. I leapt forward, but she was faster, snatching my note out from under the small terracotta pot and unfolding it.

"I'll take that," my dad said crisply.

Rachel passed it to him without a word.

"'Dear everyone,'" my father read aloud. "'I know you're going to be upset with me for leaving like this, but it's for the best…'"

"Dad." Mortification squirmed through me. "Don't read it like that."

"Why not? I assume you left it here for us to read," he said calmly, not looking away from the pink notepaper. "Where was I? Oh, yes: '… it's for the best. This morning just proves that. I've already put you all in so much danger and I can't stand losing anyone else. I started this and I promised that I would finish it, but none of you need to be involved. Please stay in the house and be safe. I will come back if I can. Take care, love, Mio.' Well, isn't that touching?" He crumpled the note into a small pink ball and threw it across the room, where it bounced off the wall and landed neatly in the kitchen bin.

"Mio," Hikaru said, genuinely shocked. "You were really going to try to go up against Izanami alone?"

"Damn straight she was," Jack said. "I knew she was planning something stupid. This is why you couldn't look me in the eye earlier, isn't it?"

"I'm looking at you now," I said evenly. "And, yes, Hikaru, I was leaving. What I said in the note is true. I'm responsible for this mess. There's no good reason for any of you to be endangered further."

"Except that we chose to be," said Rachel.

The soft words hit me like a sandbag in the face.

If you love me, do not take that choice from me. That had been Shinobu's last, passionate plea. The last words he had ever said: *You have to let me go.*

I didn't even realize that I'd taken a step back until the handle of the door dug into my hip. My face must have done something really awful, because Jack's tense shoulders suddenly slumped, and Hikaru looked like he was going to cry. The urge to wrench the door open and flee was strong – but my dad's fierce expression had changed now, too, and his unfamiliar look of … of *understanding* … held me still. He stepped forward. I hesitated, fingers clenching on the handle behind me, as his hand came to rest gently on my shoulder.

"Maybe it would be easier for you to be alone out there," he said softly. "Maybe you'd feel less guilty, less conflicted, less afraid. But it's our city you're fighting for,

Midget Gem. Our lives. Our world. And we have a right to fight too, if we choose to. You can't take that from us. Not to keep us safe. Not even to keep your heart safe."

You have to let me go.

That agonizing warmth tried to unfold inside me again. Tears wanted to come. I crushed it all down. If I broke, even once – if I let one single emotion out – I would shatter and be useless. I had to hold it together until this was done.

But did that mean I needed to do it alone?

"You really are so much like me," Dad said, the words quiet enough that it felt as if he was talking to himself more than anything. Unlike the last time he had told me that, when I'd wanted to punch him in the face, this time I knew – accepted – that it was true. Being a control freak ran in the family. At least neither of us was as bad as my grandfather.

Shinobu had been right. If you love people, you have to let them make their own decisions. Sometimes all you can do is let go.

I shuddered, let out a shaky breath and nodded. "OK," I said tiredly. "Message received."

There was a collective sigh of relief. Rachel gave me a small, approving smile, Hikaru stopped giving me anime princess eyes and Jack strode forward and punched me lightly on the arm.

"Ow. Crap. What is your arm made of these days,

cement?" she muttered, shaking her hand out. "Listen, I'll give you a freebie on this one, since I was an ass earlier and you let me off. But no more self-sacrificing bull, Mimi. I don't care if you do have the Power of Grayskull, I can still take you. Probably."

Looked like I still had … what? Backup? A team? I had no idea what to do with them, and I couldn't exactly feel *good* about it, but … I didn't feel terrible about it, either. That was probably the best I could hope for.

Between them, Jack and my dad herded me back into the living room and pretty much force-fed me a bacon sandwich and a mug of tea. Then Jack sat down in the middle of the big sofa with Hikaru on one side of her and Rachel on the other. My dad took the armchair by the fireplace and turned the volume on the TV down. I sat alone on the other sofa, finishing my tea while all of them stared at me like I was a time bomb that might go *boom* at any moment.

You want to stick with me? Fine. You can get used to me playing dirty.

"Rachel," I said. "Sorry if you've already explained, but – what happened to you? Where've you been? You're OK now?"

It worked. Everyone's anxious faces suddenly zeroed in on Rachel instead of me. She shifted uncomfortably, staring down into her mug.

"I don't really know what I did or where I went after

58

I ... ran away. It's all jumbled up and confused. Cat-thoughts. Instincts. Wanting to hunt. Kill."

Her voice trailed off and she shivered. I felt a tiny pang of guilt for putting her in the hot seat.

"I don't remember going to the hospital. I just sort of ... woke up there. Staring down at Jack. And Jack was having one of those awful fits. I didn't know if I'd hurt her, done something to her. I ran away again and hid in the sewer. After – after I..." She knotted her hand into a fist, then gently uncurled the fingers as if in release. "When the pain stopped and I thought – felt – that I was OK, I just had to get out and get away. The university wasn't far, and I had my student pass in the pocket of my jeans. I always leave spare clothes in my locker at the swimming pool, so I went in, cleaned up, changed and then..." She shrugged sheepishly. "I went to the library."

Jack let out a choked laugh. "Oh my God, that is typical. Completely typical. Were you worried about missing an assignment deadline?"

"Shut up," Rachel said, smiling a little. "I just wanted to be quiet and alone – get my head around everything. Make sure I was really back to normal. I drank hot chocolate and ... waited. I even slept for a bit. When I was sure nothing bad was going to happen, I came home. And, you know, found Mio nearly being eaten by a giant spider."

"What? I didn't see that!" Jack yelped.

"You were too busy grabbing the firebombs," Hikaru put in. "I saw it, though. Rachel clocked it in the side and knocked it right off. It went flying."

I gave Rachel a questioning look.

She shrugged again and put down her mug on the coffee table. Picking up an empty metal serving plate with her right hand, she poked it sharply with the index finger of her left. There was a rending noise, and Rachel's finger popped out of the bottom of the plate.

"I'm pretty strong," she said, with what I thought was epic understatement. "But I can control it now."

Seeing the alarmed expressions on Hikaru and my dad's faces, I quickly said, "The king – your king, Hikaru – told me this could happen. If people recover from the Nekomata's bite, they have gifts. Seeing in the dark. Speed. Strength."

"Let me get this straight," Jack said slowly. "My sister is Catwoman now?"

"I suppose that makes you the Joker, then." Rachel reached out to mess up Jack's spiky hair.

Jack squeaked, trying to bat Rachel's hands away. "Not the hair!"

"Oh, please. Try that on me when you don't have an inch of roots."

Hikaru leaned out of their way, looking confused and not sure if he should try to intervene. I could sympathize. Siblings were odd.

Children, please. Must I separate you?

The echo of Shinobu's voice in my memory was so real. It was as if he was right next to me. My hand clamped down instinctively over the katana's hilt, and I struggled to keep my expression blank as I breathed through the aching sense of emptiness.

Shinobu? Can you hear me? I'm here. I've got you.

I realized I'd let my eyes fall shut and hurriedly forced them open, hoping no one had noticed.

Only Hikaru seemed to have picked up on my weirdness. He glanced down at where my trembling fist clutched the sword hilt and raised his eyebrows. I had to look away.

"So, what's the plan now, sword-bearer?" he asked. "I mean, I'm guessing you were sneaking off *to* somewhere, not just running away…"

I cleared my throat and launched into a carefully edited account of my visit to Mr Leech at the nexus/bookshop the day before, finishing with, "He's the only person – being – I've met since all this started who really seems to understand what's going on and *isn't* trying to kill me. I think he knows a lot more than he had a chance to tell yesterday."

"Then why are we still sitting here?" Jack surged up off the sofa so quickly that Hikaru and Rachel slid together. They pushed apart hastily, with mutual expressions of discomfort. After everything that we'd been through together it was odd to think that those two were actually still virtual strangers. Hikaru scrambled to his feet and, after a moment's hesitation, offered Rachel his hand. She stared at it with narrowed eyes, then deliberately stood up on her own, without his help. She brushed herself off as if she thought he might have left fox hairs on her or something. Hikaru sighed, slumping a little.

Oh, wonderful. More drama.

We'd all started for the front hall when my father's throat-clearing stopped us. "Where do you think you're going?"

Jack and I exchanged wary looks. Parents pretending to be stupid was usually a sign that they were about to try to be – eugh – funny.

"Out, Mr Yamato," Rachel said patiently, falling for it. "We're going to walk to this nexus place. Aren't you coming?"

Dad got out of the armchair and stretched fluidly. "Yes, but I'm not walking it. I assume you're up for a ride in the Dad Taxi?"

I might be a barely functioning, emotionally shattered control freak, but I wasn't an idiot. The next word out of my mouth was "Shotgun!"

The others groaned.

CHAPTER FIVE

RETURN TO AVALON

If there was one advantage to two gods turning our city into a battleground, it was that the traffic was really light. Only a handful of brave or stupid travellers shared the road with us that morning, and the pavements were completely deserted. Everywhere I looked there were smashed and boarded-up windows, buildings with long black scorch marks that showed someone, or something, had tried to burn them. We drove past four or five abandoned cars, a couple of which had their doors still open as if the driver and passengers had fled without looking back. In several places the roads, pavements and walls were splashed with dark red stains. I really hoped those were from the blood-rain that the news had mentioned, but when I saw a distinctive pattern – handprints and drag marks – on one white-painted wall, it made that hope a lot more difficult to cling to.

This couldn't go on. Shinobu had given his life believing that I had the power to end this terrible conflict. I had to be worthy of that. Before the whole city fell apart.

Dad parked illegally at the curb right outside the Avalon bookshop. There was a metal shutter rolled down over the large shop window today and a closed sign on the door, but unlike the cafe on the corner, where a similar metal shutter seemed to been have pried up by some immense force until it belled out over the pavement, there were no signs of damage.

I battered on the door, ignoring my dad's anxious looks as the noise reverberated down the road. If there was anyone in the flats above to hear us, I was pretty sure that after the events of the past couple of days they wouldn't be likely to turn all Neighbourhood Watch. Not even if they heard screams and gunfire down here.

"Mr Leech!" I bent to push open the post flap in the door. "It's Mio. Mio Yamato. We need to talk. Let me in."

"Even if he's home, he might not be able to hear us," Rachel said, tipping her head back to look up at the curtained windows of the apartment over the shop. "He might still be in bed."

"He can hear us. I know you can hear me, Mr Leech! Come on, open up."

"Why don't we…?" my dad began, only to swallow the rest of his sentence when I threw up a hand for silence.

Crouching down, I pushed the post flap open again

and strained my ears. There it was again. A faint muffled noise.

Hikaru stepped closer, his eyes narrowing as his sharp Kitsune ears picked it up too. "Someone's shouting for help. We have to get inside, now."

He shouldered past me to the door. I got out of his way, catching my dad's arm to pull him a few cautious steps to the side.

"What's he doing?" my dad demanded.

"I'm guessing he's breaking and entering, Kitsune style," I said.

Jack caught on and ushered Rachel aside, too. "Trust me. I was there the last time he broke into a place. You don't want to be too close."

Hikaru's tail, which had been tucked inconspicuously under the back of his hoodie, whipped free and began making complex swirling motions in the air behind him. He laid his hands on the painted wood, feeling out the seal between door and frame with the delicacy and respect of a bomb-disposal expert examining a bunch of multicoloured wires sticking out of a large ticking object.

"It's warded. Mega warded," he said. "This is going to take a bit of subtlety. Don't interrupt."

Dad and Rachel both opened their mouths to make – I could see from their expressions – sarcastic remarks. I shushed them with a finger on my lips and a stern look.

Hikaru began to make a low, eerie crooning noise in the back of his throat. The strange, beautiful tune sent a prickle of excitement raking through the fine hairs on the back of my neck. Sparks of lightning flickered and danced up and down the luxuriant copper brush of his tail, coalescing on the silvery white fur at the tip. Identical sparks began to form around the hinges and handle of the door. Long filaments of electricity flowed around the doorframe.

Nothing happened.

Hikaru's crooning song took on a lower, rougher pitch, almost like a growl. His tail flicked hard. White light flared around his hands on the door. Something inside the wood clunked loudly.

The door still didn't open.

Hikaru's growl began to sound less like a song and more like a series of muttered swearwords. He shook his head. "Oh, stuff it."

He brought both hands down on the wood with a sharp smack.

Lightning crackled over the whole surface of the door. Thunder boomed, shaking the front of the building until the windows rattled. My ears popped.

Hikaru spun sideways and plastered himself to the wall. "Make a corridor, people!"

The door blew out of its frame in a trail of glowing sparks and smoke. It rattled across the pavement and crashed down, narrowly missing the boot of Dad's car at the curb. The shop bell pinged off and landed with a discordant jangle by my foot.

"I give it a six out of ten," Jack said, poking a smouldering piece of wood with her toe. "Excellent opening. Lacked finesse in the finish."

Hikaru's cheeks darkened and he folded his arms. "Did you want to get in there or not?"

I was already climbing over the door and rushing into the shop, pulling the sheathed katana from my back as I entered. The others followed more cautiously, goggling at the vast space, the mesmerizing sea patterns painted on the ceiling and the huge glass aquariums filled with dozens of different types of jellyfish.

"*Jellyfish?*" my father said, as though it ought to mean something.

Hikaru nodded thoughtfully.

"Mr Leech?" I called out. "Are you hurt? Can you tell me where you are?"

We all heard the feeble voice echoing down from somewhere above us.

"He must be in his flat. Come on," I said.

I led the way to the back of the store, and we trooped up the rickety, rusty old staircase together, making it shudder under our tromping feet. The door at the top was unlocked.

Beyond, Mr Leech's tiny flat was shrouded in darkness.

Tiny, brittle things crunched and snapped under my feet as I stepped inside. My hand patted at the wall in search of a light switch. "Mr Leech?"

"Over here…" His rich, fruity voice sounded alarmingly ragged. Where on earth was he? How could it possibly be this dark in here? He only had lace curtains at the windows.

I stubbed my toe on something. The impact set off a mini-avalanche. There was a sliding noise and then a crash. Mr Leech let out a little grunt. *Screw this.* We needed light. Tightening my grip on the sword's hilt, I pulled him free of the saya and shoved the sheath into the harness on my back. Then I lifted the blade above my head. *Burn. Burn. Burn.*

The bright silver crescent of the blade's cutting edge flared with sudden brilliance, the flame-shaped ripples in the metal seeming to shift as they caught fire, sending out rainbow-edged curls of living white light.

"Whoa," Jack breathed behind me.

The flickering light of the blade revealed nothing but wreckage. The tiny flat had been filled with what Jack would have called "Old Lady Bling" – overly large, dark furniture, doilies, occasional tables and shelves crammed with knick-knacks, plates, bowls, figurines. Now everything was smashed. I mean, *everything.* The furniture had been thrown around and torn into chunks. The knick-knacks and figurines had been crushed to dust. The walls were pocked with holes deep enough to expose brick, and the flowery carpet had been ripped up from the floorboards in long, ragged strips.

And the windows were gone. Vanished. It was as if they'd never been there. That was why it was so dark. For some reason that realization made nausea churn in my stomach. Mr Leech had been left alone here in total darkness.

"Mr Leech? Can you keep talking to me, please? I'm trying to find you." There was no response this time. The nausea wriggled slimy tentacles in my gut. "Mr Leech?"

"What happened here?" Hikaru whispered from the doorway as I advanced cautiously into the ruins, trying not to set off another avalanche.

"It looks like an earthquake hit the place," Rachel said.

I caught sight of a battered brown-leather shoe poking out from under the debris. "He's buried under all this. Help me!"

My dad muscled through the mess, sending off mini-landslides in the wreckage. The overhead light finally snapped on. Rachel had found the switch. I slid the katana quickly back into his saya and bent to grab the smashed-up remains of a giant Welsh dresser that was lying on top of Mr Leech.

"Don't let anything else fall on him," I said, getting my fingers under the splintery edge of the dresser and preparing to lift. My dad crouched down, ready. I took a deep breath, then heaved up the massive chunk of wood. Things crashed and smashed all around, but my dad slid into the gap, sheltering Mr Leech's body with his own. I got the dresser upright, then pushed it back away from both of them. Dad painstakingly brushed off pottery shards, flecks of wood and shreds of carpet to reveal Mr Leech's crumpled body.

He was curled into the foetal position. His golden skin, delicately crinkled with age, had a disturbing grey cast, and his mouth was set in a thin, straight line that told me his teeth were clenched together.

Looking at him brought back a sickening rush of memories of my grandfather's collapse. I had found him after school, lying unconscious at the bottom of the stairs. Ojiichan had been a complex man with a lot of hidden motivations, and I'd accepted that I had never truly known him while he was alive. But he had been the lodestone of my childhood, and I would always love his memory. I would never get over the fact that he had died all alone in a hospital bed, and I hadn't had the chance to say goodbye.

"No ambulances," the old man said suddenly. "Trust me. I will be quite all right. Can anyone see my cane, at all?"

I let out a ragged sigh of relief.

"Where does it hurt? Do you think you could bear to let us move you?" My dad's voice was gentle. He looked at the towering heaps of debris all around us. "I don't think it's safe down here on the floor."

"Can anyone see my cane?" Mr Leech repeated, perfectly calmly, as if Dad hadn't spoken.

"Concussion," Rachel whispered, peering over my shoulder.

"What if he has a spinal injury? He should probably lie still," Jack said.

"We can't leave him lying there like that!" Hikaru protested.

"I haven't regressed back to childhood, thank you," the old man said crisply. He opened his eyes and gave me a look that held a trace of the forceful personality I had met the day before. "I just want my cane. Will someone please find the blasted thing? Quickly, if you don't mind."

Maybe it wasn't concussion after all. I looked over my shoulder at Jack, Hikaru and Rachel. "The cane is dark wood, with a silver cap, I think."

"Is that it?" Hikaru asked. He waded through a pile of smashed china and heaved a nondescript walking stick out of a mess of what looked like broken table legs. "This is it, right?"

In answer, Mr Leech feebly lifted one arm, his twisted fingers making a painful beckoning motion. Hikaru passed the stick across the wreckage to Jack, who handed it to Rachel, who handed it to me. It felt like ordinary wood, a little heavy at the top because of the silver cap. I put it carefully in Mr Leech's hand.

The instant the old man closed his fingers around the cane, it began to glow. Shimmering, blue-green light – the kind you'd see if you lay on the bottom of a clear ocean and stared up through the waves towards the sun – undulated along the dark length of wood. Suddenly it was hard to look at it, or at Mr Leech. I turned my face half away, squinting. Was the cane a long silver-white icicle? A twisted piece of translucent turquoise sea glass? Was Mr Leech holding a cane at all, or a handful of pulsating mercury-like liquid that spilled between his fingers and soaked into his skin? For a second I even thought the walking stick looked like a long, slender wooden fishing rod.

Then the light faded, and the cane in Mr Leech's hand was just a piece of plain, dark wood again.

He let out a long, deep exhalation of breath. His skin had regained its healthy golden tinge, and his eyes were sharp and twinkling once more. "Oh, that's so much better. Thank you."

"That bastard Izanagi did this to you, didn't he?" I growled.

"I'm afraid so," Mr Leech confirmed breathlessly as my dad and I each took one of his arms and eased him to his feet.

Rachel and Jack had already unearthed an old leather

armchair and were setting it on its feet. It was battered and missing a few strips of its upholstery, but otherwise seemed solid. Hikaru hastily dusted about an inch of dirt and debris off the seat and back, and then we helped Mr Leech down into it.

"Why did you stay here?" I asked. "You must have known what he'd do to you."

Mr Leech sighed heavily, planting his cane down firmly on the bare board by his foot. "I really had no choice, my dear. I cannot … ahem. Let us say that I am…" he hesitated, his mouth working as if the next word was difficult to say. "Stuck."

"You can't leave. You're bound to the nexus!" my father said in tones of dawning discovery.

Mr Leech didn't answer.

Dad seemed to take the silence as confirmation. "Did Izanagi bind you?" He folded his arms, staring down at the old man. "Tell me, Mr Leech, why did he go to such trouble? Why didn't he just kill you?"

"Dad!"

Mr Leech shook his head. "No, it is a good question. I assure you, Mr Yamato, he would have, if it were within his power." He paused, eyes expectant.

"I knew it," Hikaru said, his tail whisking excitedly. "You're a Kami."

Mr Leech beamed at Hikaru. "Care to hazard a guess as to which one?"

"I don't need to guess," my father said dryly. "The name would have given the game away, even if you hadn't filled your shop with jellyfish. You're Ebisu, aren't you? Patron of good fortune for humans in general and fishermen specifically, and of the health of children. Izanagi's oldest son, the one he called—"

"Leech-child," Mr Leech finished softly. A flash of something dark and wild passed behind his eyes and then faded into his usual calm twinkle. "But you, please, will call me Ebisu. It feels good to hear my own name again."

"He bound you to this place. And ... this form?" Hikaru's voice was grave and respectful.

The old man, the bound god, nodded. "A punishment."

"For what?" Jack asked, appalled.

Mr Leech made a tiny shrugging movement, lips pressing together, but his eyes fixed on mine, as if he was waiting for something.

"I don't know much about Izanagi," I said, "but I do know that he's a coward. If he bound you like this, it's because you threatened him somehow. He wanted you out of the way. But he couldn't kill you?"

"No more than the wind or the moon or the sky can be killed," Ebisu said. "In a sense that is all any of us are, we who call ourselves gods. Just little pieces of nature's capricious will that woke up one day and became self-aware."

I paused, sidetracked. "What about Izanami? Your ... your mother," I said hesitantly. "I've seen her and she definitely looks – um, I'm sorry – dead."

"Does she?" he asked sadly. "When was the last time you saw a dead person get up and walk, and wail, and mourn?"

"Then why is she trapped in the realm of the dead? Why is she...?" I let my voice trail off. I didn't want to describe his mother's rotting form to him.

"She does not live. But she is not dead in the sense that mortals understand death," Mr Leech said. "That is the great tragedy. My mother loved her family. Too much. She gave up all her strength, all her powers, in her desperation to save her youngest child. It destroyed her. Left her in a state of undeath, ruined and rotting. She cannot ever truly die, yet she is barred forever from life."

"Wait," Jack chimed in again. "Mio told me the story. After Izanami... Well, after she went to Yomi, didn't Izanagi kill the baby? The baby that Izanami gave everything to save?"

"He tried. In his rage, he chopped the child into small pieces and scattered them. But though it was only a newborn, even he, father of the gods, could not destroy it. Each mutilated piece – even the drops of blood that fell from the blade of his sword – eventually grew into a new god. That is why he did not bother to try to kill us, you know, my defective sister and me. He did not want our ugliness to multiply. He intended us to sink to the bottom of the sea, where we would choke and flounder for an eternity, helpless and trapped in the dark. That way he would have been rid of us and the shadow of imperfection that our existence cast upon him, and we would have been justly punished. That was to be our fate. If our mother had not intervened."

There was a long moment of quiet as we all absorbed that.

Finally Jack grunted, her gaze catching mine as one corner of her lips tugged up into a twisted little grin. "I've said it before and I'll say it again: that guy is a class-A dick."

A tiny giggle popped out of my lips, and just as suddenly I felt myself choke up. I covered my eyes for a second, then wiped my hand shakily over my face.

Jack nudged me with her elbow, her smile transforming into an expression of concern. "OK there, Mimi?"

Clearing my throat, I took a deep breath and nodded. "Yes. Yeah."

I was just so grateful that Jack had caught me before I managed to sneak out of the house and leave her and the others behind. What had I been thinking? I had been an idiot to believe I could walk out on them and do all this alone. I needed my friends. I needed my dad.

And I was so glad they were with me right now.

CHAPTER 6

THE TIES
THAT BIND

Stiffening my spine, I turned back to the old man and looked him in the eye. "Mr – um – Ebisu," I began. "When I came here before, you offered me something. A sword. A wakizashi. You wouldn't – couldn't – tell me what it was for, or why it was hurting … *him*. So I refused it, and you made it disappear."

I could feel the others staring at me in shock. Yeah, I might have left that bit out when I was telling them about my visit here. *Oops.*

Mr Leech waited, his eyes huge and dark in his small, wrinkled face.

"That sword was really important, wasn't it? Do we need it now? To end the war between the gods?"

Mr Leech's face went tense with effort – I could see the muscles around his jaw standing out. He managed a minuscule, painful inclination of his head.

"Where is the wakizashi now?"

Nothing. He didn't even twitch.

"You can't tell us?" My father leaned forward.

"What? Can't you even give us a hint?" Jack put in.

Rachel propped her hands on her hips. "This is weird. You offered the sword to Mio before, but now you can't even talk about it? What's changed?"

Ebisu's twisted, arthritic fingers were clenched on the handle of his cane, twitching. The lines around his eyes and mouth had deepened, his shoulders rounding as if he wanted to curl back up into a ball. This was actually hurting him.

We were hurting him.

"Stop," I said hastily. "Just … give him a minute."

We all waited in silence until Ebisu let out a little sigh and slumped slightly in his chair.

"Thank you. I'd managed to work … things … a little looser, over the years. Now it's all tighter than ever before."

Hikaru slapped himself on the forehead. "The binding physically stops you from saying things Izanagi doesn't want you to talk about."

"My old lungs aren't as strong as they used to be," Mr Leech said, nodding, which I figured was as close as he could get to confirming. "The ticker gives me some trouble too, if I'm not careful."

"Wow, that's horrible. It must be like walking about

with a boa constrictor wrapped around you," Jack said sympathetically.

"His body is the boa constrictor," Rachel said, and for a moment her eyes went somewhere far away. She must know, better than any of us, what it was to feel that your body was a monster, working against you.

"We'll have to try to work around the bindings. In a non-hurty way," I said firmly. "Maybe we can guess, and you can just … blink twice for yes, or something."

Ebisu nodded, a hint of relief in his expression. "Let's go downstairs, shall we?"

"Do you think you can walk?" my dad asked.

"Why don't you let me carry him?" Rachel suggested. "It'll be safer and probably more comfortable. What do you think, Mr – Ebisu?"

"When a beautiful young lady offers to get close, only a fool would decline," he said, twinkling at her. She rolled her eyes at him, and bent to scoop him into her arms.

Hikaru rushed to hold open the door of the flat for them, and they proceeded down the stairs ahead of us. It was a strangely stately procession, even with the stairs making their worrying groaning noises. When we reached the shop, Mr Leech asked Rachel to set him down by one of the large double-sided bookcases that divided the shop space into three wide aisles.

"Just give me a moment. I think that this will help make things a little clearer for you." Leaning heavily on his stick, Mr Leech tottered over to the end of the middle bookcase. For a minute or two he stared at – or through – the books, his eyes going unfocused. Then he nodded, apparently satisfied, and lifted his cane to give one of the shelves just above his head a sharp tap.

I had been expecting him to offer us some kind of a clue, maybe direct me to a book that could tell us more about the wakizashi, or where to find it. I was not expecting what happened next.

The books began to shake, and the bookcases rattled in place. A deep groaning noise echoed through the shop, coming from somewhere beneath the floor. Mr Leech stepped back hurriedly – Rachel steadied him – as the front half of the seemingly solid bookcase split in two, each part swinging out to the side like a pair of automatic doors.

Behind them, where logic and a basic knowledge of the laws of nature told me the other side of the bookcase should be, there was a doorway.

It was a looming arch, at least eight feet tall and framed with white marble. On each side, a little higher than my head, a statue of a woman's upper body emerged organically from the stone, as if in the process of melting into it, or maybe trying to escape. Long hair streamed back from their faces and swirled around their shoulders. The one on the left had both hands clasped together at her breast, her expression set in stern sadness; the hands of the one on the right were raised in supplication, her eyes wide and pleading. Tears shone on their carved cheeks. Both statues had a cloudy moonstone the size of my thumb in the centre of their forehead. I realized with a churn of uneasiness in my stomach that the carvings bore more than a passing resemblance to my vision of Izanami – or at least, to what she must have looked like before half her face rotted away.

The opening between the carved pillars had no door, only a shimmering curtain of silvery light.

I couldn't help myself. Apparently neither could Jack, or my father. As one, we all scrambled around to the other side of the bookcase to stare disbelievingly at … nothing. It was just a bookcase, shelves and all. We scrambled back. A doorway. Jack poked her hand into the silvery light and then brought it back out. She wiggled her fingers.

"No books," she confirmed.

"What is this, the Three Stooges?" Rachel asked. "Haven't you all been through portals before?"

My dad raised his hand. "I haven't."

Jack snorted.

Hikaru tried to hide his laughter with a cough, then leaned in to sniff at the doorway. "It smells … wet. Not damp. Wet."

Mr Leech – Ebisu – reclaimed our attention. "This doorway leads to London Under London, the city that this city is built on. There are miles of sunken buildings, abandoned Underground stations, sewerage and maintenance lines down there. Most of them are flooded. I draw strength from water, and I needed strength to make this opening and the portals beyond it."

"Did you hide the—?" my father began.

"Shh!" Hikaru hissed, cutting him off.

Dad pulled a face. "Right, bindings, sorry."

"Can you tell us what this doorway leads to, *other* than the sunken city?" Rachel asked carefully.

Ebisu smiled. "It leads to the one place that no god, not even I, may enter. Gods do not sleep. Gods cannot dream. This place is forbidden to us."

"What – you mean – the realm of dreams?" Hikaru looked like a toddler who had been presented with an ice-cream van and a spoon and told to go nuts. "Even my grandmother's never been there. I can feel something beyond this doorway, but it's like no portal I've ever come across before. It's like … soap bubbles. Flickering and popping and floating. One minute it's there, the next it's gone."

"That is the nature of dreams, isn't it?" Ebisu said. "I am not an expert, but from what I have read, people do not fall into them headlong, all at once. They drift, slowly, deeper and deeper, never truly realizing when reality ends and the dream begins."

"The realm of dreams would be the perfect place to hide … something … that the gods want." I carefully didn't look directly at Ebisu as I spoke, not wanting to accidentally trigger the bindings again.

"Yes," he agreed gravely. "But even so, invoking the gateway underground, in a flooded location where I may draw upon my greatest strength to shield it, seemed prudent."

"I don't suppose there's any kind of a map?" my father asked, sounding resigned.

"Sadly, no," Ebisu said, partly apologetic and partly amused. "I believe that the dream realm changes constantly – each person who visits it finds something different. What you encounter on the other side of the portal will be formed by the unique dreamscapes that you each bring with you. I can tell you that the world of dreams has a powerful guardian who may choose to help or hinder you, and who may place obstacles, trials or tests in your path as you travel. These too will be shaped from the stuff of your own dreams and nightmares. But if you keep the thing you seek paramount in your thoughts, and keep moving forward, eventually you should be guided to it."

"Kind of like a Choose Your Own Adventure book," Jack said. "So if this place is made up of dreams, doesn't that mean nothing that happens there is really real? Dreams can't hurt you, right?"

The twinkle in Ebisu's eyes dimmed and he shook his head, completely serious. "In *this* world dreams cannot hurt you. But just as when your mind is inhabiting a dream it is impossible for you to tell the dream from reality, so a body present in the dream realm will be unable to distinguish any injuries suffered there from the real thing. Once you are on the other side of the portal, your dreams will have the power to wound you. Your nightmares may have the power to kill."

On that bombshell, the familiar notes of "I'm Too Sexy" by Right Said Fred began to play.

"Sorry! Sorry," my dad mumbled, mortified, as we all stared at him wrestling his phone out of the pocket of his jeans. When he saw the display, his expression went from embarrassment to dread.

"It's your mother," he said to me. "I'd better take it."

He moved away, putting the phone to his ear as he finally silenced the stupid ringtone.

"Hi. What? Wait – *what*? Where are you calling from? … I can't believe this… I told you not to… No, I can't – Mio needs me. Look, just please, *please* stay put when you get there. I will send someone. Just don't go anywhere by yourself. This is *important*, Aiko! I mean it. Be careful, OK? … Well, I suppose I'll see you soon. I love you."

I felt a creeping tide of horror sweep over me as I stared at the back of his head. *Please, no.*

The look on his face when he turned round told me exactly what I didn't want to know.

"This cannot be happening. This is a nightmare." My voice came out as a moan. I put both hands on my knees and bent over at the waist, taking deep, slow breaths. *Don't hyperventilate. Don't freak out...*

"What? I don't get it." Hikaru's eyes darted from me to my dad. "What's happened?"

"Mio's mum is coming back," Jack said hollowly. "Mr Yamato, I thought you said you took her train tickets and everything?"

"She went to the embassy for help and managed to get on a flight out of Paris. They're about to take off. She'll be at London City Airport in less than two hours." My dad shoved his phone back into his pocket so hard I was surprised it didn't rip straight out through the bottom.

"You have to go and get her," I said.

"I can't."

"The city is at war. Anything could be out there; anything could come at her! She wouldn't even see a monster until it was already too late. *You have to go.*"

My dad took a step closer to me, his face grim with determination. "Listen up, young lady. You are about to walk through a wormhole into a completely unknown realm where your own dreams can kill you. There is no way I am letting you go down there without me. The sword may be yours now, but I am still your father, and you are *my* responsibility. I'm not going to abandon you again."

I gaped at him. "Dad. Dad that isn't… Look, it's OK. I'm—"

"Do not tell me that you are 'fine'," he said quietly. "I'm not stupid, Mio. You may not choose to confide in me, but please don't lie. You are light years away from fine."

There was a silence that buzzed with unspoken words as we stared at each other. Then Mr Leech cleared his throat. "I hate to interrupt, but we don't have an infinite amount of time to make this decision. What do you want to do?"

"Dad, please—"

"You're not going anywhere without me. Either we both go and collect your mother, or we both go after the wakizashi. There's no third option."

I opened my mouth, not even sure what I was going to say.

"I'll go," Rachel said suddenly.

"Huh?" I blurted out.

"I can drive. I passed my test ages ago. I'll take your dad's car, fetch your mother from the airport and bring her back to our house, where she'll be safe. Mrs Yamato's known me since I was a kid – she won't mind me picking her up. Plus, I can probably bend steel bars into pretzels with my bare hands now, which, you know, is … useful. You're OK without me, right, Jack?"

For a second Jack looked stricken. Then she squared her shoulders and nodded. "Sure. That's a great idea. I don't think your mum can do any better than Catwoman as a bodyguard. If our mother was coming home right now, I know who I'd send to get her, Mimi."

"Are you sure?" my dad asked Rachel, cautious but hopeful. "We don't know how dangerous things are out there. Wouldn't you rather stay with your sister?"

"Yes," Rachel admitted, giving Jack a little shove on the shoulder. "But I know there's no way to talk her out of going with Mio, and no matter what happens she'll have all of you looking out for her." Rachel pushed her trendy hipster glasses further up her nose and looked directly at me. "You saved me. Then you saved Jack. Then you saved me again. I owe you. Let me do this."

I hesitated, a part of me resisting because I didn't want to delegate this way. Splitting up, just when I'd decided we ought to stick together, felt wrong. But I knew Rachel was more than capable of protecting anyone who needed it, especially my mild-mannered, sweet-tempered mother. And someone did have to go. So I nodded jerkily.

My dad let out a relieved sigh and pulled his car keys from his pocket. "Look after my baby," he said, straight-faced. "And make sure my wife's all right while you're at it."

Rachel took the keys with a smirk and then quickly grabbed Jack for a hug. "Don't let Mio blow up anything important while I'm gone."

"On it. Don't let London fall into the sea while I'm busy."

"On it."

They held onto each other silently for another minute.

"Right. Well … good luck." Rachel cast us one last look that glittered with determination – or maybe unshed tears – pointed a stern *I'll Be Watching You* finger at Hikaru, then walked away. The door slammed shut with a jaunty jangle from the shop bell, and we all stared after her, caught up in our own thoughts.

"Hey," Hikaru said suddenly, breaking into the quiet. "How did the door get back on its hinges?"

"Self-repairing wards," Ebisu said. "And it's time for you to go now, I think."

"Wait a moment. Is there anything else we need to know about this place before we leave?" my father asked Ebisu. "Or about … the thing that we're looking for?"

Ebisu frowned, and then nodded. "The realm you are about to visit has no fixed physical form. While the sword that Mio carries seems more … restrained now than it was the last time I encountered it, it still has a great deal of destructive power. That power may warp the dream landscape in unpredictable and dangerous ways. I would advise you to keep the blade sheathed at all times. The thing that you seek has similar qualities. The same caution applies. And finally, although my powers are weak to non-existent in that realm, if you are in desperate danger and can see no other way to escape, as a last resort, try to find your way to water and call my name. I might be able to pull you out. But bear in mind that there is no guarantee I will succeed, and that even if I do, such an abrupt exit would not be without risk. Nor will I have the strength to send anyone back again. You have one chance only."

"Game over," Jack said grimly. "Gotcha."

I shrugged my shoulders to loosen them up and looked around. "OK. Everyone ready?"

Subdued nods all around. We were going to be risking our lives to regain possession of an ancient, battered old wakizashi that we didn't even know the true significance of. It was crazy and reckless – and we didn't have a choice.

I marched through the glowing curtain of light into the realm of dreams.

CHAPTER 7

ONWARDS AND DOWNWARDS

Passing through Ebisu's doorway wasn't like step-ping into one of the Kitsune's ruptures. There was no darkness. No muffling, claustrophobic Between. I felt an intense tingling, almost a fizzing sensation as the light enveloped me – like walking into a lukewarm shower, the water needling at my skin through my clothes. As I went to take my next step, the floor fell away, but instead of dropping I found myself floating – adrift in a sea of shining, shifting light. There was an echo of laughter, all around me and yet far away, and a strong feeling of unseen, curious eyes peering at me.

"Interesting. We shall see, then..." a voice whispered. *"We shall see."*

My foot hit the ground and I stumbled a little as the light and feeling of weightlessness disappeared abruptly. I was on the other side of the doorway now, at the top of a narrow, spiralling staircase made from massive blocks of sandy-coloured stone. Wrought-iron brackets held torches that gave off a flickering orange light and a faintly sickly, fatty smell. I needed to get out of the way or the next person through might push me right down the stairs. I started downwards cautiously, footfalls ringing strangely off the stone steps.

Almost immediately I heard another set of footsteps – quick and light, probably Jack's – start after me, followed by a slightly heavier, more cautious tread. That would be my dad. Finally Hikaru, almost soundless, only betrayed by the tiny scraping of his boot soles on the rough stone.

"You guys all get through all right?" I called.

Three answers came back to me, all variations on "yes". None of them sounded too traumatized, but the steps were too narrow and winding for me to see any of them. If I stopped, I'd probably cause a pile-up. So I kept going. And going.

A couple of minutes later Jack's slightly breathless voice asked, "Any sign of an end to these stairs yet, Mimi?"

"Not yet," I called back.

"The smell of water's getting stronger," Hikaru chimed in from the back.

"I hope that's not all that's down there," said my dad. "Shockingly, I forgot to bring my water wings."

As he spoke I caught a faint sound from below: the distinctive noise of water moving, lapping against something solid. My feet sped up without my volition, and in a minute I was at the last step.

The stairs culminated in a narrow stone dock. The rocky platform stuck out about six feet into water the deep green of mint jelly. I walked along it, staring at the ornately carved stone columns rising from the water to support a vaulted roof dappled with reflections of the shifting pool below.

"Wow." Jack hopped off the last step and moved up beside me. My dad and Hikaru were close behind her. "This is a Medieval water cistern. I saw one like it on holiday in Italy when I was a kid."

Hikaru's mouth was a wide "O" of surprise. "I've got to admit, after all the talk about abandoned sewers, this is a nice surprise."

"I'm just glad the stairs didn't end up being endless," my dad said. "I have that dream all the bloody time."

I bit my lip. Was this a part of the sunken London that Ebisu had described, or were we already dreaming, or half-dreaming? Maybe this was Jack's dream of the place she had seen in Italy. Surreptitiously I scuffed my foot over the dock. It felt solid and made a pretty normal sound. But then, dreams always did seem real…

"Is that for us, do you think?" Jack asked, nodding down at the water. I turned and for the first time noticed the boat. It was shallow and flat-bottomed, with a boxed-in section at the back for someone to stand on. In place of seats, dark green cushions lined the bottom. The sides were painted the same dark green. It almost faded into invisibility against the water.

"It must be, unless we want to swim for it," I said. "Does anyone know how to drive one of these things?"

Jack and Hikaru shook their heads emphatically.

My dad sighed. "I suppose I can figure it out."

The boat was tied to a cleat on the side of the dock. My dad knelt down and pulled the boat in closer so that it floated parallel to the dock. Getting the idea, I went down next to him and grabbed the other end of the little craft to hold it steady. Jack skipped off the dock and sat down on one of the cushions easily enough. Hikaru hesitated, put one foot out, wobbled, made distressed foxy noises, and finally stepped into the punt, where he stood uncertainly, waving his arms around as if he was trying to balance on marbles. His antics made the boat rock, and Jack rolled her eyes at him.

"Sit down, Furball. Capsize this thing and I promise there will be a slow and hideous revenge."

Hikaru collapsed next to her, panting. "Sorry. I've – er – never been on a ship before."

"It's a boat, not a ship. Don't be a baby."

He pulled a mournful face. "You are so mean to me."

"Oh, you love it." Jack elbowed him in the side, which made the boat rock again. Hikaru let out a tiny whimper.

My father ignored them pointedly. "Could you pull a

couple of those lights off the walls before you get in, Mio? They might be handy later."

I obeyed him, handing the flickering iron-bound torches to Hikaru and Jack. "Don't set fire to anything," I said firmly as I climbed in.

The movement of the boat reminded me of standing up on the bus. I sat down in the middle section, holding onto the cleat in an effort to steady the boat as my dad took up a standing position on the flat part at the back of the little craft.

"Can one of you hand me the pole, please – without tipping me off this thing?" he asked.

"I see it. Hang on." I unhooked a long, polished wooden stick from under the rim of the punt and carefully lifted it upright so that my dad could grab the end. Then I sat back and waited.

Dad gave us all a look of terrible patience. "Someone also needs to untie us. Once again, without tipping me off."

"Oh, right! I've got it." Jack jammed her torch into a little bracket in the side of the boat and clambered over Hikaru's knees. She was practically sitting on his lap as she unknotted the rope from the dock. Hikaru's eyes rolled back in his skull and his expression wavered between guilty bliss and seasick terror as he held his torch up out of Jack's way.

When Jack had finished with the rope, my dad

cautiously pushed the punt out from the shelter of the dock. Straight away the little craft began to drift, heeling to the left as it headed for the gap between two of the stone pillars. My dad's eyebrows snapped together with concentration as he used the pole to nudge us away from the left pillar so the boat didn't scrape into it.

"There's a very strong current here," he said. "I don't think I can move this thing against it, so cross your fingers it's taking us in the right direction."

"It ought to be," I said. "Ebisu said as long as we keep moving forward we'll be guided where we need to go."

"Personally, I think Ebisu's a bit too helpful," Hikaru mumbled as he fitted his torch carefully into the bracket on his side of the boat.

"What?" Jack frowned. "What do you mean?"

Hikaru cleared his throat. "I just mean ... he's so *nice*, isn't he? All jolly and endearing. A bit like – what do you call him? – Father Christmas. Not so much like a Kami."

"Well, he's been trapped in human form for a long time. He might've picked up a few things. Plus, he's a god for children, right? Maybe he's just naturally nice," Jack argued.

"Or maybe," my father suggested as we drifted between another set of pillars, deeper into the cistern, "he's desperate to be freed from his bindings, and he thinks that helping Mio is the best way to make that happen."

Everyone looked at me again. Why was I always

supposed to have all the answers? I sighed. "Izanagi threw Ebisu away like trash. Whatever other motives the old man might have, I think his main ambition is to see Izanagi's plans ruined. Which is exactly what we want, too. The difference is that we want it to happen without any more mortals getting hurt, or our world being fried in the process. I don't know if Ebisu ultimately cares more about the mortal realm or his revenge, or which he'd choose if he had to. So we find the wakizashi and we get as much information out of him as we can, and then we make our own decisions. And we remember that Ebisu might look like a harmless old man, but he's not. He's a god. We're insects to them. We need to make sure we're never in a position where we can be crushed."

There was a short pause as that sank in.

Jack looked a little shocked. "When did you get so cynical?"

"The fate of the world *is* at stake," I said, faintly defensive. "Not a great time to be laid back about stuff."

"Well, I can see I shouldn't have worried that you were being too trusting," Hikaru said. "Never mind."

But they were still all staring at me, especially my dad. I didn't know what else to say, so I pretended not to notice them looking and turned to study our surroundings. We had passed through a final set of pillars, leaving the cistern behind as we floated into a dim, narrow tunnel. The walls were brick, dirty and crumbling, and the roof was low. My dad ducked, tucking the pole under his arm.

"There's something up ahead," he said. "I can see more lights."

Hikaru tilted his head to the side. "Do you hear that? Sounds like a river."

"It had better not be white water," my dad said. "I am not equipped for that."

The strange tunnel widened out even more, the inexorable flow of the water taking us through a massive jagged hole in the brickwork that looked as if it had been caused by an explosion. The sound of rushing water was audible to us humans now, too. We drifted under more shattered walls – stone this time – and then my jaw dropped as I took in the tall Gothic arches, stonework windows and the ceiling that swooped away above us. The arches of that ceiling, revealed by the golden flicker of our torchlight, were painted with flaking pictures of angels. Giant angels, with richly coloured robes and cloud-like wings.

"It's a church!" Jack exclaimed.

"A cathedral, I should think," my dad corrected. He pulled the pole up – probably the water here was too deep to use it – and rested it on the wood between his feet. "An old one, too. Looks pre-Reformation."

Whatever coloured glass once filled the panes of the tall church windows had long since disappeared.

Spectacular silvery streams of water crashed through the intricately cut stone, cascading down the walls and foaming into the river that flooded the old cathedral and rose halfway up the walls.

"Human churches are cool," Hikaru said, staring wide-eyed.

"Yeah, no. The waterfalls aren't a normal feature," Jack said flatly. Her grandmother insisted on dragging Jack, Rachel and their mother, Beatrice, to church with her on most of the principle feast days. Jack hated it, but there was only one person in the world that she feared more than her mother, and that was Granny Rassin. No one messed with that old lady. I'd rather fight the spider-woman again, alone, than get on her bad side.

Something rushed by my face with a sharp whistling sound. I jumped, scanning the air around me, but I couldn't see a thing. The katana's energy was a calm, even hum against my back – no warning of danger. Had I imagined it?

Jack let out a yelp. Her flaming torch jerked up out of its bracket and sailed over the side of the boat. It landed in the water with a fizzle, fire instantly extinguished. Suddenly the looming space of the cathedral was a lot darker, and its shadows a lot deeper.

"What the—?" Jack looked around her wildly.

"Hikaru, grab that torch!" my dad snapped out.

The whistling sound came again – from two different

directions this time, seeming to cross in front of my face. Hikaru grunted with pain as an invisible force knocked him sideways. The flickering light in his hand lurched up. Hikaru yanked it back down into its place in the bracket, and was repaid with another impact that snapped his head back like a slap.

Jack knelt up, flailing her arms. "Leave him alone! Stop it!"

More rushing and whistling surrounded us. The boat rocked wildly. I struggled to keep my balance, my hand flying to the grip of the sword as I jumped to my feet.

"Mio, don't!" my father cried. "Remember what Ebisu told us. Everyone get down."

I curled down over my knees. Jack did the same. In a fluid movement, Dad raised the punt pole and began twirling it around his head and body, swapping it from hand to hand as if it weighed nothing. He swept the pole one-handed over the top of the punt, twirled it and swept again. The whistling sounds were immediately joined by deep growls that rumbled all around us, coming from everywhere and nowhere.

"Dad, I think you're making it worse—"

It was already too late. The pole suddenly stuck in the air, as if he had smacked it into wet concrete. Then it wrenched sideways, yanking him with it. His foot skidded. I shot up out of my crouch and grabbed hold of him with both hands. We collapsed into the bottom of the boat, along with a few bucketloads of water as the punt nearly tipped over. The pole went spinning away into the white foam of one of the waterfalls.

Hikaru let out a strangled cry as the torch catapulted out of his hands and hit the water.

We were plunged into darkness.

CHAPTER 8

CLOSE ENCOUNTERS

Aiko Yamato tapped her short fingernails on the armrest of the passenger seat in her husband's Mercedes. The small noise was like a drumbeat in the silent interior of the car.

In the driver's seat, Rachel Luci, whom Aiko had always considered such a nice, responsible young woman, stared straight ahead at the traffic jam that they had driven into about ten minutes outside the airport. Rachel's face gave nothing away, but her hands flexed on the steering wheel, bunching into fists, then relaxing, then bunching up again. Aiko ran through the facts in her mind.

Rachel was the one who had been left in charge at the house to take care of Mio and Jack.

Rachel was the one who had unexpectedly called Aiko's husband in Paris a mere two days into their second honeymoon and told Takashi something so shocking that his face had turned the colour of rice pudding, and he had started packing before he even got off the phone.

Rachel was the one who had come to pick her up – driving Takashi's precious car.

Therefore: Rachel was in this up to her neck.

Aiko had heard enough chatter at the British Embassy in Paris to know that there'd been an outbreak of some weird illness in London, and she'd had a small panic attack about that before Takashi had finally phoned and promised her that none of them had caught it. A subtitled news bulletin playing at the airport had assured her that whatever the mystery illness was, it was under control now with no fatalities, and it had helped that the first thing Rachel had done, after finding Aiko and taking her bag, was to assure her that everyone was fine. So clearly that wasn't what had sent Takashi running home. But for some reason after that Rachel had clammed up like a … well, a clam. Takashi wasn't answering his phone any more, and neither was Mio. No one was *talking*.

Aiko opened her mouth—

"Why don't we listen to some music?" Rachel said, her voice just a shade too loud and cheerful. She punched the button for the radio, and the car was flooded with the sound of a whining cello and a throbbing piano. Takashi must have left it tuned to Classic FM. Personally, Aiko preferred Radio One.

She folded her arms.

"Rachel…"

"That was 'Mediation from Thais', played by Yo-Yo Ma and Kathryn Stott," said a plummy male voice. *"And now Sandy Fisk, bringing us our news bulletin."*

"Thank you, Steven." A woman's voice, slightly breathless, filled the car. *"I'm here in London this morning, where there is panic in the streets after—"*

Rachel's hand shot out so quickly that Aiko jumped in her seat. The radio clicked off.

"So! How was Paris?"

"I didn't get the chance to see too much of it. Although the waiting room in the British Embassy was really nice. Outstanding carpets. Just what you would expect of the French."

Rachel cleared her throat. "And how was your flight?"

"You've already asked me that, dear. Now—"

"Well, I'm sure you can't wait to get home! Even short flights are so tiring. You'll probably just want to rest when you—"

"I'm not tired," Aiko interrupted firmly. "For heaven's sake, what is the big secret? Mass murder? International espionage? What the heck have you all been up to?"

Rachel coughed out a short burst of laughter. "Good one, Mrs Yamato. But you know me – boring. Bit of cooking. Homework. Catnapping. Ha ha. Nothing to worry about."

The car in front of them inched forward about half a

foot. Rachel suddenly became extremely concerned with disengaging the handbrake and moving the Mercedes forward to close the gap. She crunched the gears slightly, and both of them winced.

"Look, I've been driving for twenty-two years and I still have to practically beg to get behind the wheel of this car. There's no way Takashi would lend his precious to a beginner driver unless there was some sort of earth-shattering emergency. So what was it?"

Rachel gulped audibly. "I don't – um…"

"Spill the beans. Cough it up, kiddo."

"Mrs Yamato, I think this is personal business between you and Mr Yamato and, no offence, but I'm not getting in the middle of it."

Rachel's restless hands went still on the wheel as Aiko let out a short scream of frustration that almost seemed to rock the car. "Rachel Louise Luci! I have known you since you were seven years old and I know when you are lying to me. You are already in the middle of it, and I am fed up to the back teeth with being the only bloody person who has no idea what is happening to my own family! Tell me what is going on!"

Aiko felt the strange trembling sensation rock the car again and thought, *I'm even angrier than I realized.*

But Rachel didn't seem to be listening any more. She was sitting bolt upright, her eyes riveted on the windscreen. There was a muffled shout – almost a scream – somewhere up ahead. A moment later Aiko saw someone in the other lane of stopped traffic shove open their car door and run, abandoning the vehicle right where it was.

The car shook again, shifting palpably on its wheels.

"An earth tremor?" Aiko was momentarily distracted.

Rachel undid her seatbelt, flung open the door and hopped out of the car. Her neck craned back as she stared up at the sky. Aiko put her window down and poked her head out. The sky was empty, dull and grey with low clouds. What was she supposed to be looking at?

Up and down the road the cars shuddered in place. Aiko heard the Mercedes' suspension squeak. Other drivers were responding to the tremors now: leaning out of their windows, opening doors.

"We have to go," Rachel said.

Aiko watched in disbelief as Rachel reached back into the car, turned off the ignition and snatched the keys. "What in the world – we can't just leave the car! Takashi would cry like a baby! And my luggage is in the back."

"I really don't think Mr Yamato will care about the car. Forget the luggage. Come on."

"Come where? If it's an earth tremor, we can't outrun it."

Rachel had already slammed the car door and was zipping around the bonnet to Aiko's side. She wrenched the passenger door open so forcefully that the hinges groaned.

The car bounced on the spot, wheels hitting the tarmac

with a thud as it came down. The long grey strip of the road seemed to ripple, and Rachel clung to the door to keep her balance. *Actually, this is getting a bit alarming now,* Aiko admitted to herself.

Rachel glanced over her shoulder once, shuddered and then fixed serious eyes on Aiko's face. "Unbuckle your seatbelt and get out of the car now, or I'll do it for you. I'll carry you if I have to."

There was no temper in her voice, and no panic. Just a simple, calm statement of fact. It got through to Aiko in a way nothing else could have. She hastily undid the seatbelt, grabbed her carry-on bag and stood out of the car.

"What are we running from here, Rachel?"

The road leapt underfoot. Aiko staggered. And about ten cars ahead, a sleek silver Jaguar flipped up on its side like a Tonka Toy in the hand of a giant, invisible child.

The Jaguar's engine screamed. Its wheels spun. The driver's door flew open – Aiko could see someone frantically trying to climb out. Before they could, the smooth bullet shape of the car crumpled. Then it rose into the air and *flew*.

Aiko felt her mouth drop open in horror and disbelief as the vehicle sailed over her and Rachel's heads and crashed down thirty feet behind them, ploughing into two parked cars in a glittering explosion of glass and shrapnel.

Panic broke out. Screams and wails filled the air. Doors shot open everywhere and people stampeded away from their vehicles. Aiko whipped her head round to stare at the place where the Jaguar had been.

A massive form was shimmering into view there, rippling and drifting at the edges as if she was squinting at it through a heat haze. Blocking the road completely, the shape towered above the cars. It had a humanoid body, leathery red skin and the head of a bull. In addition to the two white horns on each side of the skull, a third, black horn sprouted out of the centre of its head above the eyes. A giant potbelly jutted over a ragged loincloth – the only piece of clothing the thing wore. In huge hands that had only three fingers each, it held a spiked iron club the length of two cars.

The creature threw its head back and let out a wordless animal roar of fury.

"Oni," Aiko whispered, awestruck as fairy tales from her childhood came washing into her memory.

In the next instant, she was plucked from her feet and hefted up over someone's shoulder like a sack of potatoes. She choked back a scream, realizing incredulously that her abductor was Rachel, making her earlier threat a reality. As Rachel darted between the parked cars, surging past fleeing drivers and passengers and leaving the monster behind, it no longer seemed like a threat at all. More a rescue.

"Is it real? Is that thing real? Where did it come from?" Aiko yelled.

"From Yomi, most probably! But we're not sticking around to ask. I promised Mio I'd keep you safe, and that's what I'm going to do!" Rachel yelled back.

"How did my daughter know that there would be a – an ogre loose on the bloody A10?"

"There are a lot of things loose in London right now, Mrs Yamato. Bad things. Mio's working to fix it."

"Mio? *My* Mio?"

"I promise I'll tell you everything later, but right now I really need to concentrate, if you don't mind."

Aiko shook her head dazedly. "OK, but ... sweetie, please put me down! This can't be good for your back!"

Behind them the Oni roared again. Another car flew overhead and crashed down to the right of Aiko and Rachel in a spray of shattering glass, landing upright on its front bumper. It spun like a coin, cartwheeled sideways and slammed onto the roof of a nearby blue hatchback. More glass flew as it flipped over. Aiko watched in slow-motion as the car teetered and began its descent – directly on top of Aiko and Rachel. The black mechanical underbelly of the vehicle sailed towards them like a falling hammer.

All she could think was, *This isn't how I want to die, I need to see my girl again, I need to see Takashi, I can't go like this—*

She felt Rachel's muscles bunch.

Then they were airborne.

Aiko stared down while they flew up – effortlessly,

impossibly, miraculously – over the place where the wrecked car had just crashed to a halt. She heard its deafening shriek and the sound of rending metal and saw the SUV next to where they'd been standing cave in under the impact.

They landed lightly on top of a black city cab.

Aiko let out a confused babbling sound. There was a lot of "how" in it, but it wasn't really a question because her words seemed to have stuck to her tongue.

"Don't worry, Mrs Yamato. I've got you."

Rachel sprang off the cab roof, landed squarely on both feet and kept running.

I froze, my fingers tightening around the silk wrappings of my sword's hilt as I contemplated ignoring Ebisu and drawing the blade.

Jack swore savagely.

"Jack? Are you all right?" Hikaru asked anxiously.

"I'm fine," she said, voice tight. "I just … really, really *hate* the dark."

"Shh, listen," my dad said.

The high-pitched whistling noises were fading away, replaced with a soft rumble remarkably like a cat's purr. Given my recent experiences with cats, that realization instantly sent a shiver down my spine. But the sword's energy still wasn't reacting. It was as if there was no danger.

A glimmer of brightness danced through the shadows. It was peacock green. I tried to track it with my eyes, but was distracted by another movement, a soft fluttering like a moth's wing that left a faint trail of fluorescent pink.

Slowly the lightless space of the sunken cathedral filled with luminous colours. The crashing waterfalls shone pale blue and deep purple. The walls and ceiling were lit with complex patterns of yellow. The wake of the boat glowed vivid green. I could see the others' faces again.

And in the air around us there were creatures. Dozens of creatures, with long, slender bodies, delicate little paws, tiny round ears and pointed, clever faces. Their long, fluffy fur shimmered with colours – pink, blue, orange, purple, red, green – that seemed to trail behind their sleek bodies like comets' tails as they zoomed through the air.

Jack let out an incredulous huff of breath. *"Ferrets?"*

"Kamaitachi." Hikaru and my father spoke together, in hushed tones.

"What?" I said.

"Invisible weasels," Hikaru said, a sudden grin splitting his face. "Great and little gods, they're invisible weasels. I thought they were just a story for children!"

"They're so … cute," Jack said uncertainly.

"Are they going to attack us again?" I asked, still edgy.

"They didn't attack us in the first place," my dad said,

a laugh trembling in his voice as he stared at the creatures gambolling through the air. "They're famed for having claws like knives, and ripping strips off people who annoy them. They just wanted us to get rid of our lights. They live in the dark. We must have hurt their eyes."

Jack let out a startled laugh as one of the little animals did a loop the loop around her head, brushing her cheek. She raised her hand tentatively, and the weasel rubbed against it and made a purring *chirp* before zooming off again.

"No wonder they dragged the pole away from me," my father said. "Did I frighten you, little ones? I'm sorry."

Two of the weasels closed in on him and began doing barrel rolls round his shoulders, making flirtatious noises. Hikaru had managed to get one to twine around his forearm and was sending it into ecstasies by scratching the back of its neck.

One of the Kamaitachi circled me, deep blue radiance drifting away from its luxuriant fur like tiny stars. It hovered before my face, its head tilting to one side as it peered curiously at me. Long whiskers tickled my nose, and a laugh bubbled up in my throat. I reached out tentatively to touch one delicate ear. The weasel let out a *meep*, and I felt the rough lick of its tongue on my fingers.

Unbidden, the thought sprang into my head: *Shinobu, you'd love this.*

For an instant I felt as if he was sitting beside me, as if all I had to do was turn my head to see his smile, hear the sound of his laughter.

But he wasn't here.

He wasn't waiting for me somewhere, just around the corner. His smile and his laughter were gone, forever. He was gone. Yawning, sickening emptiness swallowed every good feeling and left nothing behind but grief.

I almost threw up over the side of the boat.

My hand dropped away from the little creature as if it had burned me. I shut my eyes, trying to force back the nausea churning in the pit of my stomach and the tears that wanted to squeeze out from under my eyelids. My fingers clenched until I could feel my nails digging into the tendons in my palms.

I can't afford to break like this. I have to hang on.

I won't let go.

I won't let go again.

Opening my eyes, I saw that the little blue weasel who had tried to befriend me was gone. Jack, Hikaru and my dad, engrossed in the wonder of what they were seeing, hadn't noticed what had happened. *Good. Good. That's ... good.*

I wrapped my smarting hand around the hilt of the katana, flexing my fingers on the silk wrappings as I made myself think about other things. The katana had failed to react to the weasels' assault on us. Was that because the little animals weren't really a threat? Or had our entering the dream realm somehow made the katana go dormant? If that was the case, then I couldn't rely on the sword's energy to warn me of danger.

It was just me and my instincts from now on.

CHAPTER 9

SOMEBODY FORGOT TO BRING TOTO

The current carried us inexorably forward. The Kamaitachi gradually left us, dispersing to fly about their own business with soft farewell chirps. We left the waterfalls of the cathedral behind, and the yellow glow of the walls began to fade. New sounds – echoes and dripping noises – reached my ears. The darkness became total, oppressive.

I heard Jack's breathing speed up, and her valiant efforts to control it. "Hey, Hikaru," she said, voice shaking a little. "I know you're, like, too young for fox lights, but I don't suppose you could hit the ceiling with some lightning bolts or something? Just to show us what the place looks like?"

Hikaru was silent for a long moment. "I'm sorry. I'm just... I can't control my lightning well enough to risk it. If I misjudged, I could bring the roof down, or electrocute you. I'm really sorry."

There was real distress in his voice. My dad shifted uncomfortably.

"It's OK," Jack said. "Don't – I mean, don't stress out about it."

"I wish I could—" Hikaru cut himself off with an angry growl.

"Listen, seriously," Jack said more forcefully. "I shouldn't have asked. This right here is amazing therapy for me. By the time we get home I probably won't even care about the dark any more."

There was a gentle rustle of fabric. I pictured one of them – who knew which one? – slowly reaching out to the other. Jack's breathing began to even out.

A moment later, Hikaru said, "There's some light above us now. It's coming through a crack in the roof."

"Actually, I can kind of see it," Jack said, sounding relieved.

Shortly, I could make out the difference between the rough, dark cavern walls and the dark water lapping around us.

"There's an opening ahead," Hikaru reported.

The boat bumped into something, jolting hard enough to send us all sliding forward. Worrying grinding noises came from the hull as we scraped and dragged along the bottom. Finally we came to a halt.

"Dry land?" Jack asked hopefully.

"There's a ledge – see?" Hikaru said. "That rock out-cropping just above us. And above that there's a crevice with light coming through it. I think that's our way out. If we're careful, we should all be able to climb up through it."

"And if we're not careful, we get a spontaneous swimming lesson," my dad said.

"Just FYI," Jack put in matter-of-factly, "the hideous, lingering revenge is still on the table. So nobody had better bump me at the wrong moment."

With a lot of nervous shifting around and some panicky swearing, we all managed to get out of the punt and onto the rock ledge. The crevice that Hikaru had spotted was very bright and very obvious once we were up there. It was also extremely narrow and shaped like a sickle. There was enough space for us to slide through in single file, but once inside, it was impossible to fully straighten your legs or back. The only way to move was to lean your shoulder blades into the curve of one wall, press your hands to the other and scuttle sideways like a crab.

"You think when Ebisu said 'eventually' we'd be guided to the waki-doodah, he actually meant any time this century?" Jack asked. "It feels like we've been here hours and there's still no sign of it."

"How long *have* we been here?" Hikaru asked.

"An hour? Maybe an hour and a half," I said, assuming Jack was exaggerating.

"No way!" Jack's voice was incredulous. "It's been nearly a full day!"

"Hmm. Is anyone hungry? Or thirsty? Does anyone need to pee?" Dad asked.

"Er … no, now that you mention it," said Hikaru.

"This makes sense, I suppose. There's generally no sense of the passing of real time while you're asleep," my father said, sounding concerned. "We have no way to tell how long we've been here – and no way to know how much time has gone by in the mortal realm, either."

"Everyone just concentrate on what we're here to find," I said firmly. "It's a wakizashi blade. A Japanese short sword, usually twinned with a katana. It had a plain black-lacquer saya that was kind of battered and scraped up and rubbed black silk wrappings on the hilt."

"So – you got a pretty good look at it," Jack said hesitantly. "You know, you've never really told us what happened…"

Instantly my brain nailed me with a painfully vivid image of Shinobu's face as he gasped for breath on Mr Leech's flowery carpet, the feel of his hand clasped in mine and the smell of blood, his blood, smeared on my palm.

I was trying to save him. Didn't work.

I blinked a few times, incredulous when I realized that my eyes were trying to well up *again*. I scrubbed my forearm roughly over my face.

"Midget Gem?" my dad said softly. His hand slid on the rock, as if to touch me. I swiftly pulled away.

"I'm…" *Don't say fine.* "OK. I just tripped." I shuffled sideways again, trying to put a little distance between me and the others.

I picked up the pace as more light flooded the narrow gap in the rock. The next shuffle carried me out into a space where I could finally straighten up. I felt weird twanging sensations in my lower back and neck as I stretched vigorously and looked around.

We were in a roughly oval-shaped cave. It was about the size of a tennis court, with straight walls that soared away overhead to some great distance I couldn't measure with my eyes. Irregular shafts of bluish light criss-crossed the space above me, revealing something extraordinary about the walls: they were painted.

I moved closer to stare at the strange markings that covered the rock. The artists had used the natural swirling formations in the stone to suggest landscapes – hills, mountains and valleys, plains, rivers and forests. Animals cavorted across the painted world, sketched with simple, powerful strokes that somehow suggested more to my eyes than careful details could have. Elegant deer, lumbering bears and shaggy wolves seemed almost to move, their white-dappled, red-brown and silvery-grey pelts rippling under an imaginary sun. In contrast, the humans in the pictures were spiky and black – determinedly two-dimensional. Small settlements were sketched out with steeply pitched roofs and faint wisps of smoke. The style of the paintings was primitive but beautiful, like prehistoric art I'd seen in school textbooks. But there was something hauntingly familiar about the scenes depicted, about the shape of the mountains, the dark shadow of the forests and the curve of the rivers. I turned slowly, watching the progression of the images as they travelled across the curved walls.

Here a tall, dark figure marked with golden swirls fled into the forest, pursued by deformed, twisted creatures that bristled with fangs and had too many limbs. The dark figure carried something – a shining green light. Further along the wall the same figure emerged from the woods and came to a small group of houses nestled between the woods and the mountains. In the next image, he and the green light he carried vanished into the little village.

A swirling catlike creature slunk out of the trees and attacked the village under the light of a full moon.

Then the dark figure reappeared, this time pointing towards the forest – a forest that now glowed red and gold with the colours of autumn. Another, smaller figure – a boy – went into the woods. He fought the cat-creature there, with a blade in each hand. The cat-creature transformed into a blur of grey swirls and became a lump of rock, and the boy fell.

The black-and-gold figure loomed over the fallen boy. Green light swirled in his hands, and gold and white energy seemed to boil all around them. In the next painting, both the boy and the light were gone, and the dark figure seemed to be exulting as he held something new – a shining, silver crescent. A blade. A katana. The image that followed showed the dark figure handing the silver blade to a tiny, faintly feminine person, even smaller than the boy.

But that wasn't the end. The next painting showed a fourth figure, as tall as the black-and-gold one had been, but coloured a soft bluish green. Holding a long staff in one hand, the figure walked into the red forest. Then that same figure was standing in the clearing where the cat-creature and the boy had fought, and fallen. In its free hand was another object. Something black, curved like a blade. A wakizashi.

The tall blue-green figure straightened, its head tilting back and its mouth gaping wide. It swallowed the wakizashi, and the blade disappeared.

"This place is amazing," Jack said. I jumped violently and turned my head to see her spinning in slow circles as she tried to take everything in. "God, I wish I'd brought my phone so I could take pictures."

"I wish we'd brought that rope from the dock." My father's voice was grim. "Because this seems to be the only way out."

He wasn't staring at the walls, but at the floor in the centre of the cave, where there was a large, round hole in the ground. I moved closer to examine it. Its walls were smooth pale blue rock, with a series of metal rungs set into one side. There was no way to tell where the ladder led.

"Can you smell or hear anything?" I asked Hikaru.

Hikaru crouched and sniffed a few times, closing his eyes. "Well, this is boring, but it just smells of more water. And maybe … fish? It's pretty quiet down there."

I chewed on my lip, then tucked my hair back behind my ears. "OK, here's what we'll do. I'll climb down first—"

"Why you?" my dad interrupted.

"Because I'm the strongest one here – if there's a problem with the rungs, I can probably get myself back out. And if there's trouble at the bottom, I've got the katana. For emergencies only," I added, when he opened his mouth again. "I'll check it out, and if everything's safe, you can follow me."

"Maybe you should take Hikaru," Jack suggested. "For backup. He's got lightning – that's at least as good as a katana."

"I'd rather know Hikaru's here looking out for you if something nasty slithers into this cave while I'm down there."

Before anyone could argue, I swung myself into the hole. The rungs felt solid under my weight, but I bounced and tugged a little to be sure. The walls were completely smooth to the touch and offered no grip for climbing. I'd just have to hope that the "ladder" went all the way to the bottom of the shaft.

"Be careful," my dad said, leaning over the opening as I started down.

"Shout if you need help," Jack added.

After a few rungs the light faded away and I was reaching for and finding each new rung by feel. Jack wouldn't like this. With my next step, I found my foot dangling in what felt like empty space. I lowered my other leg and let both feet kick out, feeling for toeholds. Nothing. The shaft had either ended or opened out. In any case, there were no more rungs for my feet. Using just my arms, I lowered myself down the last few rungs until I was hanging from the final one. Arm muscles straining now, I kicked out again. My feet still found nothing. I peered downwards, but all I could see was darkness.

I would be mad to try to go any further when I couldn't even see what awaited me. It could be a hundred-foot drop onto metal spikes. It could be water filled with man-eating sharks. It could be an endless black hole.

My dad yelled from above, his voice echoing tinnily. "Are you at the bottom yet? What can you see?"

"Not sure. Hang on!" I shouted up, my brain working rapidly.

If I climbed back up and admitted what I'd found, they'd never let me go down there. But this was the only way forward into the realm of dreams, which meant the only other option was to go back. Back through the crevice, back into the punt, back to Mr Leech. Game over. That was not an acceptable outcome.

I counted to three, then let myself drop.

I fell in darkness for a heartbeat. Then light flooded my eyes and I landed lightly in a half-crouch. There was solid sandy rock beneath my feet, and when I looked up, the bottom of the hole was little more than three or four feet overhead. There had never been any danger at all. I had a strange sensation, and it took me a moment to realize what it was. Disappointment.

Wow, I'm even more messed up than I knew...

I mentally slapped myself and began to examine my surroundings. It was a low-roofed space at the end of what seemed to be a sea cave. The walls were covered in small bluish shells like barnacles, and there were streaks of that green sea slime everywhere. The cave opened up ahead and beyond that—

"Mio?!" Dad's voice echoed down the shaft, fainter than ever. "Are you all right?"

"I'm at the bottom! It's a short climb and then a really short drop at the end. You can come down."

I quickly moved out of the way so that no one would land on my head, then kept walking until I had enough room to stand upright and stare out at what awaited us.

This wasn't underground any more. But it wasn't exactly outdoors, either. In fact, I had no idea what it was, except that we had clearly left London Under London behind.

Ahead there lay a seemingly endless expanse of water – maybe even a sea. Motionless and glossy, black as oil, the water was interrupted by a short path of white stepping stones that started practically at my feet. At the end of the path, a structure thrust out of the liquid in sharp spears, like diamonds glittering in the light: a white palace floating on a dark ocean. An iceberg, or a glacier. And beyond and above that, a sky that wasn't a sky at all but water: vivid turquoise, rippling and shift-ing constantly.

"Hooooly crap…" Jack whispered behind me.

"Yeah," I said. "I think it's time to start looking out for the flying monkeys."

Wordlessly, we all trooped out of the cave. I was careful not to look too closely at the dark water as I hopped onto the first stone – an ocean that still and dark probably had something nasty hiding in it. Knowing my luck, anyway.

The stepping stones led to an opening in the side of one of the glittering iceberg's white walls – a long, narrow split that started high up as nothing more than a blue line in the ice and gradually widened out until it was around the same width as a normal door.

"Geronimo?" Hikaru asked as we made for it.

I managed a quick smile for him. "Save it for a special occasion."

Jack quickly nipped in front of me and Dad pushed in to my left, and we entered the iceberg all bunched together. The tunnel beyond was wide and low. My dad's head nearly brushed the ceiling, but there was room for us all to walk side by side.

The quality of the ice around us was strange: glass-like and highly reflective, it formed extravagant eddies and bulges and whorls, like a raging river that had been frozen solid in an instant. The ice glowed, lit from within by a deep sapphire radiance.

"It's beautiful," Jack said.

Itssssss beautifulllll ittttttsssss beautiffffffffulllll itsss itsss sssssss…

Her words echoed up and down the glowing ice corridor in a sibilant rush, as if the frozen river had stolen them to give its unmoving currents a voice again. Our reflections warped and flowed around us as we walked – blurred ghosts jumping and jerking through the frozen water. As the tunnel curved to the right, something – some alien flicker of movement – made my gaze snap to the right.

A face stared out of the ice at me.

"Ojiichan?"

I barely whispered the word. But the frozen river

seized the breath as it left my lips and rolled it up and around the walls and ceiling, the way a kid rolls a sweet around and around its mouth and over its tongue. The face faded back into the ice.

Behind me, Hikaru jerked. "Did you see that?"

Sssssseee see see thaaaa seeeeeeethaaaaseeeeeseeseee...

"See – *what is that*?" Jack spun around, staring at the ceiling. Her face was stricken.

Seeseseeeeeesssse whaaaaa issssssssss thattttttttttt...

The echoes of our voices blended together, rushing through the corridor like water. We all staggered, buffeted by waves of sound that had somehow become more than sound. My dad made a slashing motion across his throat and held his finger to his lips. *Be silent!*

Jack and Hikaru froze, fixing their eyes on him. I slapped a hand over my mouth to hold in any further noises – and the faint sound of my palm hitting my skin echoed through the corridor like a gunshot. Dad jumped and whipped round to stare at the ice behind him. He fell back, and I saw his lips move. "It can't be..."

Caaaaaantbeeeeeeeeebeebeeee beeeeeee...

I reached out to him, unable to keep silent. "Dad?"

Dddaaaaaaadadddaaaadaaaaaadaaaaaaaa...

It wasn't my voice any more. There were other voices now – strange, weeping, mad voices, wailing voices, voices no human should have to hear. A woman stirred in the ice-glass wall beside me. She had red hair, blue eyes and a friendly smile. Blood dripped in thick clotting rivulets from a gaping hole in her neck. *Sssaaaave mmmmmeeeeee...*

Tooooo llllaaate... A homeless old man slumped to the ground in front of me, clutching at the terrible wound in his chest. His other hand groped for me, fingers warping the ice.

Ojiichan's face glared at me from the ceiling, angry and disappointed. *Seeeecret Mmmmmio! Prooooomissssssecretttt...*

The reflections were everywhere – doubling, tripling as faces loomed out of the glowing blue walls, ceiling, even the floor. The voices rose like a tsunami until they were deafening, unbearable. I clapped my hands over my ears, trying to block them out – but they wormed into my ears and my head.

Miomiomiomio... Shinobu walked towards me through the ice, robes and hair rippling around him, bringing a tide of darkness into the corridor like storm clouds blotting out the sun. His dead, white face shone in the shadows, and his eyes were black holes of anguish. *Mmiiooo Mio why why whywhywhyMioooo...*

"No!" I screamed. The sound echoed back to me, piercing my eardrums like needles. I couldn't see or hear Jack or Hikaru or my father. I couldn't hear my own thoughts. I was on my knees, drowning in the faces and voices of everyone I'd failed. I was going mad.

Then I heard singing.

It was a deep, powerful voice belting out the unmistakable lyrics to one of Lady Gaga's greatest hits. *I know that voice. I know it… Jack? Jack.*

I squeezed my eyes closed, hiding from the terrible images in the ice, and turned my head blindly, seeking the direction of the singing. Slowly, falteringly, I crawled towards the sound of Jack's voice. The skin of my hands burned as I scrabbled across the ice. I hit a wall with my shoulder and bounced off, but I didn't dare open my eyes. The tunnel still echoed painfully with an overwhelming wail of pleading, accusing, dying voices. But none of the echoes had the warm, living vibrancy of Jack's voice – they weren't real, and they couldn't fool me while she was singing.

My voice shaky and thin, I began to join in. My higher-pitched voice provided a counterpoint to Jack's. The echoes around us became less distinct, less distracting, as a third voice – a light tenor that had to be Hikaru's – chimed in, too.

My groping hand found the rounded toe of a Doc Marten boot. Eyes still firmly shut, I climbed one of Jack's long legs, grasping handfuls of her coat to help me get upright. Jack's hands steadied me, and then one arm linked through mine, and Jack's voice got even louder.

My dad was singing now, too – humming and mumbling most of the words, but providing plenty of noise in his deep baritone. A hand suddenly closed around my wrist, clutching hard enough to bruise. Not my dad's hand. It must be Hikaru's; yes, his voice was right there, as close to me as Jack's. I managed to get hold of his arm. I wanted to call out to my dad, but the song was working and I didn't dare break whatever spell it was that was keeping the madness at bay.

Come on, Dad, come on…

I could hear his voice getting slowly closer. He was hitting more of the words now as he picked up the lyrics. Closer. Closer. Hikaru let out a little hiccup, as if someone had walked into him. Then fingers latched onto the back of my shoulder, winding into the leather strap of the sword's harness.

We were all together again.

Slowly, stumbling and hesitating, we began to move forward. Was it forward? Maybe it was back the way we'd come. There was no way of telling, and right then I didn't care. I just wanted out. We hit a wall again, adjusted, still hanging onto each other desperately, still singing at the top of our lungs, and shuffled on.

It took three more full repeats of Lady Gaga – complete with *whoooa oohs* and *la la las* – before we finally fell out of the ice tunnel. The echoing phantom voices cut off so suddenly that the quiet seemed to punch my ears. Jack's slightly hoarse voice went silent with a sigh. The rest of us slowly trailed off around her. We stood, still holding one another, our heads bowed close together, panting.

"I just might get that song tattooed on my butt," Jack said finally.

My dad let out a strangled bark of laughter. "I wouldn't tell Beatrice about that plan if I were you."

I forced myself to let go of Jack's arm before collapsing down onto the ground. The others followed suit.

"What *was* that?" Hikaru asked soberly.

"One of those tests Ebisu talked about, I guess," I said, not wanting to get into discussions of what any of us had heard or seen. "Which we'd have flunked completely if it hadn't been for Jack."

"Yeah, you crazy genius," Hikaru said. "How did you know that would work?"

"I didn't, really," she confessed. "I just remembered a song from when I was a kid – about how when you're afraid you should whistle a happy tune? I can't whistle, so I sang."

My dad shook his head in disbelief, then reached across and ruffled Jack's multicoloured hair affectionately with one hand. "We're incredibly lucky you were with us."

"Aw, shucks, Mister," she said, her grin tinged with shyness.

CHAPTER 10

SEAFOOD SURPRISE

We sat at one end of a bridge beneath a huge dome that reached its rounded apex at least a hundred feet overhead. The dome was constructed of translucent panes of what I guessed must be ice, coloured in every shade of blue, green, turquoise, jade and purple. The panes had been fitted together to form stylized shapes: stars, moons, galaxies, strange planets. At the very top of the dome was a sun, with thin, waving amber rays radiating out from its golden centre.

The bottom of the dome – which was about the size of a football field – was flooded. The water was as clear as uncoloured glass at the surface, but it went down, down, down, gradually deepening to an opaque blue that seemed bottomless. The thin bridge, made of pure white ice, stretched across the pool, from where we were sitting to the other side of the dome, where there was an opening in the wall that I assumed led deeper into the iceberg. The bridge was exquisitely carved in lacy fairytale arches that made it look like a sugar decoration from the top of a princess's wedding cake, and supported by four thin columns which plunged down into the clear water, getting thinner as they went. By the time they disappeared from sight, none of them looked any thicker than my wrist.

And the air was full of fish.

They swam soundlessly through the coloured well of light above the bridge. Glittering shoals of tiny silver minnows darted and danced between the mantles of graceful manta rays, fat golden fish with drifting fins like angel-wings and the sinuous green-gold ribbons of eels. The only creatures that were in the *water*, as far as I could see, were tiny jellyfish. About the size of a fifty-pence piece and almost completely see-through, they looked like bubbles of cellophane decorated with fine orange or pink spots and short, delicate streamers in the same shade.

"I need a new word for 'wow'," Jack announced. "It's starting to sound repetitive."

Hikaru stared at the ice bridge dubiously. "How about 'yikes'? That thing doesn't look like it can take much weight, and I had a big breakfast."

"Well, I wouldn't go into that tunnel again if you paid me a million quid. And Ebisu told us to keep moving forward. So it looks like we're chancing it." I got to my feet.

The ice bridge was steady under my weight, but no wider than both my feet if I stood with them together. That meant I had to walk like a model on the catwalk, placing each step precisely. I don't think I could have managed to stay upright on it if the ice had been slippery, but there was a fine coating of crunchy frost that seemed to offer some grip. After about a metre I stopped and waved the others on after me. Soon we were all strung out along the bridge, leaving cautious spaces between us, just in case.

Flooding down out of the glowing coloured lights of the dome, a cloud of silver fish broke around me, brushing curiously through my hair and tickling my face and hands with their delicate fins. Jack made an incredulous, nervous noise. When I glanced back, I saw a manta ray circling her in a tight corkscrew spiral, begging to be stroked, just like the weasels earlier.

A low, mournful call filled the air and a large shadow glided overhead, staring at us with curious, wise eyes as its massive tail waved gently in the air. I knew it was some kind of whale, but I didn't recognize the sleek grey shape until my father whispered, "A humpback..."

Meanwhile, at the back of the line, Hikaru was trying to fend off a couple of mischievous eels that were nibbling on his long burnished-copper hair.

In the middle of all this I might have missed the splash if a fine spray of water hadn't blown into my face. We were only about three feet above the pool at that point on the bridge, and when I looked down I saw the jellyfish dancing in agitated patterns below, and the water rippling. I came to a halt, raising my hand to stop the others.

"Something wrong?" my father asked.

"I'm not sure."

There were drops of water on the bridge ahead of me. Something must have come out of the water just now. Had it swum overhead? The drops of water grew and spread into puddles as I watched. An almost imperceptible shiver travelled through the largest puddle.

The curious fish, even the whale, had fled up into the dome above us.

"Back up," I said, keeping my voice steady and soft with an effort. "Slowly."

"Why—?" Hikaru began.

"Just do it," my father ordered.

I took a cautious step back, then another, feeling behind me for the bridge with my feet. My hand crept upwards, longing to touch the hilt of the katana. There was no warning buzz from the blade, but I hadn't expected one. I knew I was right. We were in danger.

There was a shift in the light ahead of me – a movement somehow *beneath* the view of the bridge and the far wall of the dome. I froze, struggling to track the distance and size of ... whatever it was. My fingers gently brushed the silk wrappings of my sword's grip.

Something else moved. I looked down to see a fat tentacle, the exact same silver-ice shade as the bridge, curling around my boot. The moment the suckers made contact with the leather, dark streaks began to form across the tentacle. Leather-coloured streaks.

I sucked in a panicked breath. "Shi—"

The tentacle pulled. I flew off the bridge.

The icy water hit me like a concrete slab. Breath erupted from my lungs in a cloud of bubbles. My eyes and nostrils burned. Jellyfish scattered around me as I flailed, breaking the surface.

"Mio!" My dad was kneeling on the bridge, staring down at me, with Hikaru and Jack behind him. Their faces bore identical *WTF* expressions. "What happened?"

"Squid!" I managed to choke out. "Giant squid!"

Something slapped against my back with a faint sucking noise.

The katana!

My hand clamped onto the hilt. A slimy tentacle coiled around my fist and yanked, dragging me down under the water again.

I cartwheeled through the pool, tossed around like an ice cube in a cocktail shaker as the squid tried to tear my fingers from the hilt of the sword. I forced the sword down into its saya with every bit of strength I had. More tentacles whipped out at me, stretching thin as they wrapped around my body, drawing me downwards away from light and air and help. I struck out desperately with my left hand and managed to latch onto one of the delicate ice pillars that held up the bridge, anchoring myself in place.

In the thrashing chaos of bubbles and boiling lungs and *don't let go don't let go don't let go*, I caught my first proper glimpse of the creature that had hold of me. It was huge – its mushroom-shaped hood at least as big as an armchair – with glaring yellow eyes the size of dinner plates. It was now exactly the same colour as the deep blue water around it, but against clouds of white bubbles it stood out as clear as day.

The squid's limbs pulled at me, trying to peel me away from the bridge. I kicked out. My boot hit the monster in the left eye, knocking it sideways. I kicked again – this time it reared back to avoid the blow. My ribs felt as if they were tearing into shreds, my heart as if it was about to burst inside me. I had to breathe!

Something black flashed by. My father fell on the squid's back and wrapped his arm around its body. He plunged his sword deep into its vulnerable eye.

The squid's convulsion ripped me from the bridge. Even under water, I could hear the monster's roar. It shook me again, then bashed me into the pillar, driving the last bit of air from my lungs. My vision blurred – and my hold on the katana loosened, just for a second.

The hilt jerked upward, half freeing the blade.

Power exploded. The shock wave turned the water into an impenetrable, churning sea of bubbles. I felt the energy hit the ice at my back and the squid that still held me at the same instant.

The pillar disintegrated. The squid's tentacles quivered and then relaxed, falling away from my skin with a faint sucking sensation. I slammed the katana back down into his sheath and struck out for the surface.

My head broke through. Water streamed out of my mouth, eyes, ears and nostrils as I gasped for air. I blinked frantically, clearing my eyes – just in time to see the bridge, its central pillar now nothing but a melted stump, begin to crack and fracture under Hikaru and Jack's weight.

"Get off the bridge!" I screamed.

My dad's head popped up beside me. "Are you—?"

Seizing his shoulder, I dived, forcing him under with me. Jagged shards of ice lanced down into the water all around us as we swam deeper, out of range of the deadly missiles.

My father gripped my arm and pointed. There, below us, the body of the giant squid drifted in a dark trail of its own blood. Thousands of the tiny jellyfish were swarming around it. I stared in disbelief as I realized that they were attacking it, hooking themselves onto the body and stripping the flesh away in savage, circular wounds to get at the blood. The monster was already a ragged mess, half its tentacles gone. My father shook his head, sending his hair floating around his face, and then drew one finger across his neck in a slashing motion. If my father's sword or the katana's energy wave hadn't killed it, these harmless-looking creatures would have finished the job. Thank God the squid hadn't drawn blood on me or my dad...

The rain of ice had stopped. We swam back up again, bobbing to the surface like corks. I was already looking for the others when I heard Hikaru's yell.

"Help!"

I whirled round in the pool and saw Jack and Hikaru struggling to tread water by one of the smooth, curving dome walls. The pool was boiling around them. They were beating at the water with their arms, clearly trying to fight something off. As Hikaru lifted one of his hands, I saw a trio of the jellyfish clinging to his skin – feeding from him. His skin was streaked with blood.

We swam furiously towards them, cutting through the dense swarm of jellyfish creatures that seethed in the water. I could see dozens of the little monsters coating Jack and Hikaru from neck to foot, attacking any exposed skin. I expected to be bitten, but they paid no attention to me or my father at all.

"Get them off!" Jack shrieked. Blood poured from a shallow slice above her eyebrow. "Get them off me – ow!"

"It's the blood – they're attracted to it," I said. "We have to get you out!"

Kicking at the clouds of jellyfish and scraping them away from her where I could, I muscled Jack a few feet across the pool towards the closest wall. The ice was straight and as smooth as glass, but above us, where the ice bridge had broken off, there was a shallow dent in the surface – hopefully deep enough for a foothold. I pushed her at it. "Climb!"

She scrabbled at the wall, soaked boots sliding off the ice and sending her slipping back down into the water. I grabbed a double-handful of her backside – she squeaked – and gave her a boost. She shot upwards out of the pool and managed to dig one foot into the shallow dip. Clinging to the ice with her other hand, she began clumsily tearing the jellyfish off, crushing them between her hands with noises of furious disgust.

"Hikaru, quickly!" I reached out for him.

"Get out of the water," he growled. Blood trailed down the side of his face too. I could see a pinprick of burning white light in the centre of each of his pupils. His expression was terrifying.

My dad shoved me towards the wall of ice. "Discretion is the better part of valour, Midget Gem. Out we go."

Jack, jellyfish-free, shuffled sideways, making room. Dad and I clawed our way up the wall, struggling to fit one foot each onto the narrow foothold. I ended up leaning into Jack's back, squashing her into the ice, while my dad squashed me into her. My wet fingers stuck to the ice and went numb, but I managed to find another barely adequate handhold and hang on.

The second the three of us, sodden, dripping and exhausted, were up on the ice, Hikaru began to croon. The sound was deep and rumbling, like a far-off storm. I saw his tail thrash under the water, displacing dozens of jellyfish which simply drifted back and attached themselves to his fur again.

Big mistake.

The copper brush of Hikaru's tail sparked, then flared with white light that shattered into lightning. Bolts radiated from him in every direction, striking the underwater walls of the pool again and again, leaping from the water to crawl along the ice of the dome, shooting up to hit the sun-shaped peak. The water frothed. The ice let out a series of sharp, frightening cracks. Thunder shook the air. I closed my eyes, ducked my head and waited.

Finally the noise died away.

I opened my eyes, faintly surprised to see that the dome was still standing, even if it was riddled with cracks and breaks which had destroyed the intricate coloured patterns. The flying sea creatures had disappeared to who knew where. And the surface of the pool was clogged with the floating bodies of thousands upon thousands of dead jellyfish.

Hikaru flopped onto his back with a splash and drifted in the water, arms and legs limp. His hair and clothes were steaming. But there were no savage fish stuck to him any more.

"So. You're completely immune to lightning, then?" I asked, trying to sound matter-of-fact about what I'd just seen.

"Uh-huh. My own, anyway."

"Ooookay," Jack drawled. "Remind me not to annoy you. Like, ever."

Hikaru gave a strained snort of laughter. "*Nrrgh*. I'm freezing. And my head hurts."

"That's what you get for showing off. Think how the jellyfish feel," Jack said. I could see her preparing to slide out from the dog pile of me and my dad and drop back into the water with Hikaru.

"No, Jack, don't!" my father warned urgently. He was staring past my shoulder into the pool.

We followed his gaze. The electrocuted fish were moving. At first I thought they were somehow coming back to life, but then I realized that a whole new crop of the tiny, ravenous creatures was rising up from the bottomless depths of the pool. Some of them were feasting on the dead bodies of their unfortunate cousins – but a lot more were already beginning to converge on Hikaru.

"Come here right now," Jack ordered Hikaru fiercely, trying to reach down for him.

"Huh? What? Oh, *shit*." He thrashed towards us.

There wasn't enough room for four people on the tiny ledge – there was barely enough room for three. I shoved back, dumping me and my dad down into the water again as a tide of the tiny fish surged around the weakly struggling Hikaru. The explosion of lightning had taken pretty much everything he had – he was about twelve stone of floppy deadweight. Even with me and my dad working together, we could barely get enough leverage to shove him up out of the water – and we couldn't lift him high enough to get his feet on the dip in the ice. He kept slithering back down, and every time he did, more fish attached themselves to him. He let out a choked yelp of pain as one latched onto his neck. When he yanked it away an alarming torrent of blood streamed down his throat, driving the fish into a fresh frenzy.

"Come on!" Jack reached down frantically, trying to catch one of his flailing arms. Her grip on the ice failed. She teetered off her precarious perch and bellyflopped back into the pool. The jellyfish swarmed on her instantly and she screamed.

If you are in desperate danger and can see no other way to escape … try to find your way to water and call my name…

"Call him!" I yelled, choking on the tide of icy water her landing had displaced. "Call Ebisu!"

"No – we're not leaving you!" Jack shrieked. "Get off – *argh!*"

"You're being *eaten alive*," my dad bellowed. "Do it! Call him – call him *now*!"

"Ebisu!" Hikaru shouted. "Ebisu, help! Please!"

"Oh, *hell*. Fine. Ebisu! Help!" Jack yelped.

For a long, breathless count of ten, I thought nothing was going to happen. Then shimmering blue-green light burst around them, nearly blinding me. I flung one hand up to shield my eyes, involuntarily letting go of the back of Hikaru's top. Jack shrieked again – high-pitched and helpless – and her voice was joined by Hikaru's. For a count of two breaths, both of them were screaming, non-stop, at the top of their lungs, and I couldn't even open my eyes to see why. Then the sound twisted and blurred, like a corrupted digital recording, and cut off.

When I lowered my hand, they were gone.

Dad and I were floating alone in the icy water, and the swarm of jellyfish was already dissipating.

"Well," my father said croakily. "Nice to know that it works, anyway."

"If it did," I whispered. "If he got them safely. He said he *might* be able to pull us out. He said it was risky. What if it went wrong? What if—?"

"It worked. He pulled them out. It worked. They're fine." Dad's voice was firm, but he didn't know any more than I did. He was just more hopeful. Jack and Hikaru could be caught in some awful magical limbo for all we knew. They could be dead.

No. No, I can't think like that. I have to keep it together.

We both trod water in silence for a moment, trying not to stare at the empty space Jack and Hikaru had left behind.

Finally, I gave in to the urge, braced one hand against the wall of ice and reached back to pull the sheathed katana from his harness on my back. I wanted to draw the blade, check him for water damage, wipe the metal down. But besides the fact that the shattered bridge and dead squid proved what a very bad idea that was, the saya and the silk wrappings were both dry as a bone under my cold, wet fingers. The water hadn't even touched the katana, let alone hurt him.

"I think I'll keep him in my hand from now on," I muttered. And if that was for comfort as much as for safety, no one needed to know but me.

CHAPTER 11

FLESH WOUNDS

Hikaru and Jack arrived on the floor of Ebisu's shop in a cascade of water. They clung to each other mindlessly, shuddering with the sizzling pain of the transition.

Is this what being hit by lightning feels like for mortals? Hikaru wondered, before Jack's breath, laboured and hot in his ear, distracted him. He wanted to open his eyes and check on her, but the attempt forced out a choked grunt as a spasm of agony seemed to move right through his skull, and his eyelids squeezed even more tightly shut in response. He could feel her trembling, mashing her face into his shoulder. His fingers curled into the back of her top, and he drew her in against his body, as if he could somehow protect her from the pain.

Slowly – very slowly – the sensation that every atom of his body was trying to rip its way free of all the others began to fade.

It might have been a few minutes or an hour later that a familiar voice near by made Hikaru jump, forcing him to open his eyes at last.

"You two look like something the cat coughed up."

Ebisu. The old man was perched on a tall stool by his till, cane in one hand, a steaming cup of green tea in the other. At first glance he looked the same as when they'd left him, but a second, closer look revealed that the tea was shaking in his grip, the green liquid threatening to slop over the rim, and his fingers on the silver head of the cane were white-knuckled.

"Thanks," Jack croaked, pushing clumsily away from Hikaru. She tried to sit up, but ended up flopping limply onto her side instead. "You're looking a bit peaky yourself there. You OK?"

"As well as could be expected. I'm afraid we – you – almost didn't make it," Ebisu confessed, gently placing his tea on the counter. "Are you both … er … in one piece?"

Hikaru stared down at himself in sudden alarm, then at Jack. There weren't any missing bits that he could see. "I think so?"

"Good, good. That's … good." Ebisu sighed, his bent frame seeming to crumple a little more. "Two at once was rather more difficult than even I had guessed."

"But we did make it," Jack said urgently, trying to sit again, and this time succeeding. "So you'll be able to get Mio and her dad back, right?"

"I hope so," Ebisu said.

Hikaru couldn't help feeling that was quite a bit less reassuring than a *Yes* or even an *I think so*. Jack's expression said she was having the same misgivings.

"If things play out the way I hope they will, they may not need my help," Ebisu said, more firmly. "We shall cross that bridge when we get to it. They most likely have a long way to go yet."

"I guess," Jack said, rubbing water – and some blood – out of her eyes with a shaking hand. "Um, sorry about the mess."

Hikaru finally forced himself upright, and looked around. They had washed up right in front of the massive stone doorway into the sunken city. But where before there had been a sort of curtain of light, now a sheet of gently rippling water hung between the arched stone lintel and the floor. It was silvery and highly reflective – like a living mirror.

"A scrying pool," he said, recognizing it. "My grandmother has one."

"You were watching us?" Jack's expression flashed with alarm, and Hikaru remembered the discussion they'd had about Ebisu while they were floating in the cistern.

"Scrying pools only show images," Hikaru told her, with a quick, reassuring wink. "There's no sound, but the pictures can be seen over great distances, even between dimensions. My grandmother can use hers to look a short way into the future sometimes."

"I hope she's not wasting her time on that endeavour right now," Ebisu said. "All there is to be seen is shadows and blood, blood and shadows. Anything could happen over the next twenty-four hours – and I mean anything. The only constant is young Mio. Mio is the key. Her choices will save or destroy us all. And if she falls, we all fall with her."

Jack and Hikaru stared at the old man in appalled silence. He blinked and seemed to shake himself. "Where are my manners? You need to dry off and do something about those nasty bites. Why don't you head upstairs and use my bathroom? There's antiseptic and plasters in the cabinet, and clean towels and so forth hanging up. I'm afraid your entrance disturbed the scrying spell, but by the time you're finished up there I should have it tuned in again, and we can check on how Mio and Takashi are doing."

In the greater pain of their abrupt re-entry into the mortal realm, Hikaru had almost forgotten about the damage the jellyfish creatures had done – but once the old man had pointed it out, the wounds immediately began to throb again. He offered his hand to Jack and together they heaved themselves to their feet and headed for the stairs.

Ebisu's bathroom was mostly untouched. The only signs of Izanagi's rampage were a few long cracks in the walls, and a handful of shattered tiles that had fallen into the olive-coloured bathtub. Hikaru grabbed two towels from a rail under the bathroom cabinet, and handed one to Jack before sitting down on the toilet-seat lid and pulling off his wet hoodie.

The towel was a strange orange colour, but it was fluffy and smelled fresh. He put it over his head and went to work on the heavy, dripping strands of his hair, watching out of the corner of his eye while Jack peeled her sodden jacket and the sweatshirt underneath away, then stripped off wet boots and socks too. In just her damp purple T-shirt and jeans she rubbed vigorously at her arms and neck with the towel. As she started work on her hair – which was taking on a strong resemblance to a pink and purple dandelion clock – Hikaru noticed she was favouring her right hand a little. There was a particularly deep bite wound there. It looked raw, and it was still bleeding.

"That's a bad one," Hikaru said.

"Yeah, the little buggers got me all right. But you're a lot worse off than I am. We need to find some plasters for your face."

Her hip nudged his shoulder as she rummaged around in the medicine cabinet above his head and emerged triumphantly with a box of plasters and a tube of ointment. "I'll put this on the back of your arms where you can't reach," she offered as she turned round. "And you can do mine."

Hikaru hastily forced his eyes away from her jean-clad bum, which was directly level with his face. He felt his cheeks starting to get hot. *Oh, great and little gods, please don't let her have noticed...*

Jack backed away from him slightly, and a quick glance at her face confirmed that he just wasn't that lucky.

"I'm sorry," he said quietly.

"Sorry? For what?" She busied herself with opening the box of sticking plasters, apparently riveted by the process of picking out exactly the right ones. Unfortunately that just brought his attention right back to the nasty wound on her hand. He winced.

"For letting you get all bitten up like that."

Apparently that was the wrong thing to say. She put the plasters down with a smack and looked him in the face. "What? Why is that your fault?"

"Because ... because if I were a better Kitsune, I could have stopped it. I could have ... made a lightning wall to protect you, or used an isolation net, or—"

"In the water? Wouldn't that have fried me? Or Mio and her dad?"

He slumped down miserably, not even attempting to stop his tail from drooping over the side of the toilet seat. "Not if I had proper control. It's the same thing as the fox lights. They look so simple, but whenever I experiment, things end up exploding."

"Well..." Jack said slowly, sitting down on the edge of the bath. She reached for some toilet paper and wet it under the cold-water tap. "You're only twenty, right? Other Kitsune can't make fox lights till they're a hundred, Araki said. Why should you be able to do something no one else can do?"

She's so nice. She's far too nice. He sighed as he made himself confess. "I should be able to do that stuff. I'm supposed to be – you know – *special.*" He emphasized the word bitterly. "But I'm not. That's why I spend more time hanging around in your world than my own. It's just easier. People don't know me here. No one expects anything from me."

Jack shoved the wet paper at him. "Here. Get the blood off."

Hikaru stared at the wad of wet tissue for a second, then took it and hesitantly started dabbing at his face with it. He could feel gloopy, half-clotted blood smearing across his cheek and forehead. "This is human medicine?"

"Not if you do it like that," she said, grimacing. "What are you even…? Never mind – let me."

She stood up again and grabbed the tissue, then leaned over him to carefully swab at his face. Hikaru stared at the frankly amazing view of Jack's chest for half a second – OK, maybe a full second – looked down – legs, fantastic legs in very tight jeans – and then unthinkingly snapped his eyes shut. His cheeks flushed hot again.

What are you, five? Closing your eyes doesn't mean she can't see you!

Shut up, he told the critical voice, keeping his lids firmly closed. *It's just safer this way, OK?*

"So..." Jack began. He felt her take the paper towels away and then a gentle dabbing that came with a medicinal, ointment smell. "Why don't you explain all this to me? You know, why you think you're not special enough?"

He opened his eyes to see her determined face and nearly sighed again. It was all so complicated and stupid and just ... just horrible, really. But there was no way to explain it without ... explaining it. *Eugh.*

"Do you know how Kitsune reproduce? I mean, traditionally?"

Jack bit her lip, eyes going wide. Her voice wobbled a little bit as she asked, "Ah ... is that, like, the foxy missionary position or something?"

He gave her an annoyed look. This was hard enough without stupid human jokes. "I'm talking about babies, Jack. The reason there are so many stories and legends about the Kitsune among humans is that fox spirits have traditionally *mixed* with humans. A lot. Get it?"

"Ooooh," she breathed. "Yeah, I get it. But why?"

"Kitsune aren't fertile. When male and female foxes mate ... they hardly ever have kits. For thousands of years we only avoided extinction because a) we live for a very long time and b) we have the ability to interbreed with mortals. Foxes would head out into the human realm, take the form of a man or woman, and find human mates. Most of the time the children would be human, and the fox would stay with their human mate and live a mortal life with them, keeping their fox nature hidden—"

"Hang on," Jack interrupted, grabbing a plaster. "First of all, didn't the humans notice that their husbands and wives had tails? And didn't their families notice that they never got any older?"

"We have ways of hiding our tails if we choose to," Hikaru told her. He hesitated for a second, his heart suddenly louder in his own ears, then carried on, "And if a Kitsune falls in love with a mortal, they can choose to surrender their own immortality. To age at the same rate as their human beloved."

"Wow. OK, I know this makes me sound like Mio, but that's really ... nice. Romantic, even." She leaned in again to press the plaster carefully over the wound on Hikaru's forehead, then straightened and reached for the next one.

"Not really." Hikaru's voice came out flat. "There was an ulterior motive. Once or twice in every generation one of those foxes or their human mate would bear a child that wasn't human. A child that was Kitsune, with Kitsune characteristics: the immortality, the tail. When that happened, the law said that the Kitsune parent had to leave their mortal mate and any mortal children and return home to the spirit realm with the child. Then they had to either leave it there to be brought up by the other Kitsune, or abandon their human family forever to raise it themselves. That's why some of the Kitsune – like my Aunt Midori and that annoying maid of hers, Miyako – are especially angry and bitter towards humans. They were left behind in the spirit realm by parents who chose to return to human families. They feel that the humans stole their Kitsune mothers or fathers – even though they wouldn't exist without their human parents."

Jack stopped in the middle of pressing the next plaster onto his forehead. "Jesus. That's pretty messed up. Why did the law have to be so – black and white? Why couldn't people choose what to do for themselves?"

Hikaru forced himself to shrug matter-of-factly. "There were good reasons for it. A Kitsune kit can't keep to one form – they change constantly. Some of them are even born as foxes. They can't control whether their tail shows or not; they can't control their lightning. They could accidentally hurt their human family. And they'd pretty much destroy their Kitsune mother or father's secret identity. In years gone by some kits and their parents were killed by their communities. The humans were convinced they were unnatural or possessed or evil. But ... but it was a hard law. Too hard. The practice has almost completely died out now. Kitsune don't have children with humans any more. Which means, most of the time, they don't have children at all. You didn't meet any Kitsune under the age of two hundred in the spirit realm, right? There aren't any. We're a dying race."

"I met you," Jack pointed out.

He laughed without meaning to. The sound was humourless, and both Jack's eyebrows went up. "That's the really fun thing. That's why I'm ... different. Why I'm supposed to be oh-so-special. I'm not just the first kit to be born here in this country. I'm the first kit in hundreds and hundreds of years to be born to two Kitsune parents. They were both over five hundred years old and I was a complete shock. So much of a shock that my mother died having me. My father left me and went back to the old country, leaving my relatives to raise me here. There's only one other like me, one other 'pure-bred' Kitsune, in Europe. The king. My great-great-great-great-great-grandparent. The most ancient and powerful Kitsune we have. That's why I should be able to control my powers, why fox lights and isolation nets should be a doddle for me. Everyone keeps expecting me to wake up one day and be … extraordinary. They say the king could make fox lights before her tenth birthday. Sometimes, when I lose my temper? I strike myself with my own lightning. That's like … like a cat who's scared of mice, or a dog who can't bark. I'm a complete loser, Jack. I'm not worth—"

He broke off suddenly and swallowed hard. He couldn't make himself meet Jack's eyes. *You took it too far. Shut up now, before she thinks you're even more pathetic.* "Anyway. Yeah. So, I'm sorry."

There was a short pause. Jack moved to crouch down at Hikaru's feet. "That is bullshit."

He shook his head miserably, still refusing to look at her.

Jack grabbed his hands, her fingers cold and clammy, and gave them a little shake. "You *are* special."

He couldn't stop his hands gripping hers back, but he

also couldn't hold her gaze for more than a second. "You just think that because you don't know about Kitsune. It's nice of you, but—"

"Don't call me 'nice' or you'll piss me off," she said sharply, squeezing his fingers. "I don't know your relatives, but if they're anything like Midori and the king, then they're too busy manipulating everyone around them to be really honest with you, or anyone. You know that! You warned us about them yourself. They've messed you up with all this shit. Don't let them tell you what you're worth. You're not a failure. You helped us; you *listened* to us when any other Kitsune would have just shrugged and walked away!"

"That was selfishness. Anything to distract me from the endless, crushing weight of disappointed expectations."

"Oh, yeah, right. And when you stuck your neck out with the king and all the other Kitsune, and put yourself on the line to force them to fight alongside us? Was that selfish, too? What about at Battersea? Hiro and Araki were both killing themselves trying to open that loading-bay door, and even together they couldn't do it. Then you came along and opened it in two seconds flat, on your own, so we could get in there and save Rachel. She would have died without you. A lot of people would have died. You came to help Mio and Shinobu, against the king's orders, when you knew the Foul Women were about to swarm, when you knew their taint could kill you. You knocked about a thousand of them right out of the sky with your lightning. You've done so many amazing things, Hikaru. Your problem is that you're so busy expecting yourself to be a screw-up that you don't even notice how awesome you are."

"But—"

"Listen. Really listen to me, right? I don't have a dog in this race. I don't have a reason to lie to you. You're so much more powerful than you realize. You don't give yourself any credit at all. But even if you *were* a Kitsune loser, even if you couldn't hit the side of a bus with your lightning, you would still be an awesome person. A brave, funny, kind person. You would still be my friend."

Hikaru's eyes – which just a moment before had flinched uncontrollably away from Jack's face – now lifted irresistibly to stare at her, as if mesmerized. He couldn't look away. She meant it, he could tell. She really did. He blinked dazedly. Then he felt a reckless smile slide across his face. He squeezed her hands back. "Jack…"

CHAPTER 12

CRACKS

My dad and I swam rapidly through the clouds of jellyfish to the other side of the pool, clambered up onto the outcropping of ice which was all that remained of the shattered bridge on that side and left the dome behind with relief. I was pretty much expecting something awful to happen to us straight away, but the opening in the wall led to a plain old cavern – a vertical split in the glacier's fabric, wide enough to drive a bus through at the bottom, but gradually narrowing as it climbed through the ice overhead. Muffled cracking and groaning noises echoed through the space, sending flurries of snow drifting downwards. The walls were the palest possible shade of blue and glittered like crushed topaz. They were marked here and there with carved symbols as tall as my dad. The zigzagging markings reminded me vaguely of the Japanese writing systems – hiragana and kanji – but my dad, who could read both, couldn't make sense of them any more than I could.

"They're probably nonsense," he said. "Like the flying sea creatures or those blood-drinking jellyfish. Real jellyfish don't even *have* teeth. And the fact that we're soaking wet and walking through a tunnel made of ice, but neither of us is showing signs of hypothermia. This is a realm of dreams – it seems to run on dream logic."

"Hmm." He was right. I was definitely a bit goosepimply and uncomfortable, but my teeth were chatter-free and I felt no urge to shiver. My fingernails were even pink. I'd been colder than this in the geography classroom in the prefab building at school. "At least it's some kind of logic, I suppose. That's better than our realm has to offer most of the time."

Even I could hear the flat, weary tone of my voice. Dad gave me a questioning look which I avoided by trudging on. For a short while the only sounds were of ice crunching under our feet and the faintly mournful groans and snaps from the walls, and I hoped that I'd managed to get away with it.

"Do you think…?" he began.

The tentative tone made my ears scrunch up around my shoulders. *No, please, anything but more attempts at Talking About Our Feelings.* Maybe I'd managed to project that thought telepathically, because he paused and didn't go on. We walked in silence for another few minutes.

"You know, your mother and I almost didn't get married," he said.

I gave him a sidelong look of confusion. "What?"

"We broke up a couple of times, actually," he went on, as if I hadn't spoken. "It was ridiculous because from almost the first time we met, I knew that she was special. Honestly, Aiko taught me how to be really happy for the first time in my life. I wanted to be with her more than anything. Yet I came from such a profoundly dysfunctional background and I'd barely managed to unpick half the ways that I was messed up. By God, it showed."

I fixed my eyes on my stomping feet, torn between the expected embarrassment at hearing my dad talk about my mum in this lovey-dovey sort of way and reluctant fascination *because* it was my dry, sardonic father talking this way. "What happened?" I asked quietly.

A crack rang out above us, and a light powder of snow shifted down, silvering my father's hair.

"Your mother broke up with me – twice. Both times she said I was pushing her away and she wasn't going to have a relationship where she was constantly walking on eggshells. I tried to work on it, and when she saw that got back together and got engaged. But then I … got scared." He stopped, swallowed, as if pushing the words out had been painful. "The fact was, Aiko couldn't possibly understand what she was letting herself in for with me. My family. And I couldn't explain. So I broke up with her less than a month before the wedding."

I blinked at that. "Jeez. That's … that was a pretty awful thing to do."

"I'm aware." A few more crunching footsteps.

When it didn't seem like he was going to go on, I prompted, "You guys never told me about this."

"For your mother, the past is the past. The woman doesn't know the meaning of the word 'grudge'."

"What about you?"

"Oh, I can hold a grudge all right," he said grimly. I heard the echo of Ojiichan's voice in that grimness. And my own voice, too. The Yamato family legacy wasn't just meitou and magic. It was festering anger and desperate unhappiness.

"I hated myself," he confessed softly. "For what I'd put her through, for being selfish, for being afraid. I went into this … this spiral of self-loathing and depression. I nearly dropped out of uni."

"But it didn't end there," I said. "You got her back, right?"

He shook his head. "I got a phone call from a police station one night. Your mother was there."

"Was she mugged or something?" I asked, shocked.

"She'd been at a peaceful protest rally when some troublemakers gatecrashed. Your mum got into a fight. I've no doubt that she gave as good as she got, but the sight of her all bashed up like that scared the life out of me. All I could think was that I should have been there. I could have taken those punches for her." He shook his head, eyes determinedly fixed on the ice ahead of us. "Anyway, she needed someone to bail her out and take her to the hospital. She chose me, said she'd known she could call me for help, even though we weren't together then. It was basically her way of forgiving me. I broke down completely. Begged her for another chance."

"And she gave you one?"

"Not straight away. She told me she'd never stopped loving me, but she wasn't going to be the pincushion for my issues any more. I didn't get to push her away, or walk away. Either I made my mind up, right then, to be with her and work things out, no matter what, or I could do her the very great favour of pissing off so she could find someone better." His face lit up with a reminiscent smile.

"So you promised?"

"Yes. But I made another promise to myself that I never told her about, and it was just as important. I promised myself that I'd take the punches from then on. If my past jumped out and started swinging again, I'd make sure the bruises didn't end up on her. The Yamato family weirdness would stop with me."

My dad dragged his gaze away from the cavern and looked me dead in the face. The intensity in his eyes nearly knocked me off my feet. "I broke that promise.

I failed. Aiko's out there right now, dealing with everything I swore to myself I'd shield her from. I've loved very few people in my life, Mio. You and your mother are at the top of that list. I've let you both down."

"Dad—"

"I don't need you to reassure me, or say that it's not my fault, and everything's OK. I know those things aren't true. You've changed. I can see this ... darkness in you that was never there before, and it scares me, because what's looking at me out of your eyes is the same thing I used to see in the mirror. I'm frightened for you. I didn't ever want to see you in the place where you are right now. Aiko could pull you out of that hole, but she's not here. I'm all you've got. And I might not have shown it in the right way, I might have messed up, but I love you every bit as much as she does, Mio, I promise. Tell me what happened to you. Tell me what happened to Shinobu. Tell me."

"It was my fault." The words sprang out of my mouth unbidden, and I clapped my hand over my lips in a reflex that came about a second too slow.

A deep groaning noise echoed through the cavern, followed by a series of shuddering creaks. The powdered ice fell in fat flakes. We had stopped walking without me even noticing.

Dad whispered. "What was your fault? What did you do, sweetheart?"

I swallowed, my throat making a dry glunk as I let my hand fall away from my mouth. "I fought it so hard. I fought it with everything I had. But all my fighting only brought us there, backed up against the wall, trapped, with no choice. He begged me to do it. We knew – Ebisu had told us – that the only way to save everyone was to sacrifice him. So I..." I shuddered.

"Go on."

"I killed him."

I'd said it now. Dad had made me say it. There was no going back. Out of the corner of my eyes, I saw the strange symbols carved into the walls begin to glow with a vivid blue light, but none of it really registered. My dad's face was very still.

When he stepped forward, I jerked back, unable to bear the thought that he would reach out, try to comfort me. It would break me, and I couldn't. I just couldn't.

"I ... drove the blade through his heart. I ... watched him ... fade away." I raised the sword between us, like an offering. "He's trapped in here. In the darkness. The cold. I don't know if he's even aware of me, if he can hear me, or if he's completely lost. He's as close to me as my own heartbeat, but I can never touch him again. *I* did that. I loved him – and I killed him."

Cracks shot through the ice walls, ringing like machine-gun fire. Ice crystals the size of my fist showered down on us, tinkling musically as they fell.

"No," my father said, shouting above the sounds of the glacier. "He was already bound to the blade – bound hundreds of years ago. You didn't do this to him. You said that he begged you. He made his own choice, and it was the right choice. It's not your fault!"

"Yes, it is!" I screamed. The tortured groaning of the cavern was the sound of my pain and guilt. The floor shuddered underfoot. "I started this – me. There had to have been another way. I should have figured it out, I could have figured it out, but I *didn't*. I—"

"Izanagi started this! Our ancestors did! Your grand-father forced you into it when you were just a child. You are not to blame."

"My hand was on the sword. I drove the blade in. It was me. *I killed him*."

The floor quivered. A wide crack arrowed through the ice under my boots and disappeared beneath the wall. Before it had finished, another crack laddered the ice, running in the opposite direction. I stumbled and landed on one knee. My father fell back against the opposite wall. We stared at each other, shocked out of the emotional trance that had blocked us from seeing what was happening.

The place was breaking apart around us.

On top of us.

My father's face blanched. "Go left!"

I didn't stop to question him. I just flung myself to

the side, as hard as I could. A thick shard of ice speared down into the place where I had knelt. Overhead, where the cavern narrowed, the walls were bristling with hundreds more enormous ice splinters. They vibrated and shuddered with the mourning howl of the cavern – just waiting to break free and fall.

I staggered to my feet and darted across the fracturing floor to my father. "We have to get out of here!" I yelled, seizing his hand.

He pushed away from the wall. A knife-sharp splinter forced itself free of the ice behind him and barely missed stabbing his arm. Our eyes met and his fingers tightened around mine like a vice.

"Run!" he yelled.

Together we ducked, wove and dodged, struggling to keep our balance on the floor as it heaved like a ship caught in a storm. Splinters of ice plunged down like swords amongst a thick powder of snow that nearly blinded me. The floor ahead exploded upwards into a jagged mound that cut across our path. My father's hand was all that kept me on my feet as I skidded around the obstruction. He twirled me away from a trio of falling icicles that speared down to our left.

Black fractures zigzagged across the walls as we bolted through the collapsing cavern. The low moans of the frozen water grew louder. And there was no sign of a way out.

The floor tilted underfoot. We both slid helplessly towards a shuddering section of wall that looked ready to give way at any second. My father let go of my hand and gave me a mighty shove. I tumbled away from him as the floor rose up in the middle, parting like the cargo doors on a ship. I hit the opposite wall with a thud that shook my teeth.

Terrifying whiplash cracks shook the cavern. The icy floor broke apart and disappeared, creating a yawning chasm between my father and me. Dad was stranded on a tiny ledge of ice – all that remained of the floor on that side of the cave. The gap was too wide for him to jump. And there was no water here to use to call Ebisu, if that would even work again. He was trapped.

"Dad!" I screamed above the cacophony of shrieking ice.

His mouth was moving, hands making frantic *Go!* motions.

The wall behind my father began to slip. It would crush him, spear him, or brush him straight off the ledge into the chasm.

I won't let go.

I reached back, seized the hilt of the katana and ripped the blade free. "Shinobu! Help us!"

For an instant, I thought I heard laughter echoing through the falling rumble of the ice.

Then everything went white.

CHAPTER 13

THE
LAST RESORT

With a quick, powerful tug of his hands, Hikaru pulled Jack forward and trapped her between his legs. Jack read the intention on his face and let out a little *eep* of protest, but before she could think of any way to extract herself painlessly, it was too late.

Hikaru was kissing her again. And not a quick smacker this time, either. A proper, full-on, let's-mack-on-the-bathroom-floor-baby kiss. He was surprisingly good at it. Or maybe it wasn't surprising, because he was five years older than her, after all. He'd probably kissed more girls than she had. And he wasn't aggressive about it, and he smelled nice, and his hands stayed in safe zones – one still gripping hers, and one on the small of her back. All in all, it could have been worse.

She thought she might be sick.

I should have told him, I should have said something,

why didn't I tell him, oh, HELL…

It took Hikaru about ten seconds to realize that something was wrong and pull back – which was also to his credit. He hung onto her hand, though, and his face was sort of soft and happy in a way that made her stomach lurch.

"What's the matter? Am I going too fast?"

There were a million gentle, tasteful, careful ways to break the news. Jack couldn't think of any of them right then. Better to just get it over with.

"I'm a lesbian."

"A what?" Hikaru asked. He looked genuinely puzzled.

Well, that's a first as far as reactions go.

"Um. OK. I'm only attracted to people of the same gender as me. Girls. You know, romantically. I really like you – I do – I just don't feel that way about you, and I should probably have told you before, but – but we can still be friends, right?"

Hikaru's eyes narrowed a little as he worked his way through it, and then his expression lightened. "Oh, I get it. This is one of those weird human sex hang-ups."

Jack extricated her hand from his none-too-gently. "I'm not weird."

"No, no, I didn't mean it like that! It's just, for Kitsune, gender is… It's different. We don't have, like, a fixed identity that way. It's kind of hard for me to understand the way it works for humans."

"So … you guys are all bisexual?" That was kind of

cool. Very cool, if it meant he hadn't just called her a weirdo.

"I don't know what that word means," Hikaru said doubtfully.

Jack rumpled her hair thoughtfully. "It's just the human word for... You're into boys *and* girls, right?"

"I suppose you could put it that way," he said, even more confused.

"But you're still a boy, see? You identify as a male; you have the boy-equipment—" She froze, horrified, as she realized she might have just shoved her foot straight into her mouth. "Oh my God, is that what you're talking about? Kitsune don't have any equipment? But you said you can mate with humans!"

Hikaru snorted with laughter. His shoulders shook so badly that he had to hang onto the edge of the toilet seat to keep from sliding off. Jack sat down on the floor with a thump and crossed her arms. This was not the way this sort of conversation usually went. This was not the way any conversation usually went.

"You can stop laughing at any time now," she said after a minute. "Any time."

"Sorry. Sorry. No, I really am. It's just ... er..." Hikaru shoved his hair back. "I'll show you."

"Show me *what*?" she asked, scooting backwards. Her shoulders hit the wall. "You keep those pants on, Furball."

He barked with laughter again. "Just sit there for a minute, and don't freak out."

"I can't possibly get any more freaked out," she muttered.

Once again, Hikaru proved her wrong.

A tornado of copper and white light enveloped his body, compressing his long form down into a much tinier one. Between one instant and the next, Hikaru had become a fox, a sleek and beautiful animal with shining metallic copper fur and a white blaze on his chest. His eyes glinted vivid green. He looked very out of place sitting on the olive toilet.

"This is a Kitsune's basic, original form," he told her, his human voice edged with a faintly foxy growl. "We can alter it a little, for example to camouflage ourselves when we're out in the mortal realm. But other than that, it's fixed. And it's non-sexual. We don't … um … you know, in this form. That would be … euw."

"No jiggy-jiggy as a fox. Got it."

He yipped – fox laughter. "Pretty much. Now, when it comes to our human forms…"

The vivid lights coalesced around his shape again, glittering and stretching him out. Human legs, clad in jeans, and a human torso, clad in a thin white tank top, unfolded out of it. Jack stared in silence for a long moment.

Then she shrieked. "WHAT THE EFF?"

"You said you wouldn't freak out," Hikaru reminded her, the voice altered again – a little higher, a little softer.

"I made no such promise!" Jack scrambled to her feet, pointing an accusing finger. "What *is* this?"

"This is me. It's still me."

Hikaru stood up, palms raised in a calming gesture. It *was* still Hikaru. Still the same height, the same slender, athletic body type. The same long copper hair falling down to the waist, the same green, slanting eyes. Undeniably the same person.

But this Hikaru was a *girl*.

The face was slightly more delicate, the chin a bit more pointed, the nose finer and tip tilted, ever so faintly. The lips were fuller and the cheekbones rounder. The neck somehow seemed long and swan-like without an Adam's apple bobbing in it. Hikaru's thin tank top showed off the same muscular arms, but with a slimmer waist, and gently curving hips. The shoulders were a little less broad. And instead of a firm, flat chest, Hikaru had …

… boobs.

Extremely nice boobs, Jack couldn't help noticing, before she ripped her gaze away.

"Kitsune naturally switch between different bodies all the time," Hikaru explained. "So we don't really care about whether the body is biologically male or female. There's no... It's not a big deal for us, individually, or when we get together. You refer to a person as whatever pronoun they were the last time you saw them in their human form – that's polite. Kitsune who are trying to have babies together obviously have to stay in one form. Other than that, some Kitsune do have a favourite, and they tend to show up as, say, a female in human form more often than not. Others go through phases. It's – I suppose it's kind of like deciding if you'll wear a skirt or a pair of trousers today."

"Huh," Jack said blankly. "What – what about you, then? You … I mean, you've never turned up … looking like *this* before now."

Hikaru nodded, tossing his – her – hair back over his – her – shoulder again. The gesture was one male Hikaru made all the time, but somehow now it seemed unbearably, even provocatively feminine. Jack twitched and folded her arms over her chest.

"Honestly, I don't have a strong preference," Hikaru said. "But I was male the first time I met you and since you were a girl – and I've watched enough human TV and stuff to know that human girls mostly go for human guys – that was just how I thought you'd like me best."

Jack thought her eyes might literally fall out of her face. "You stayed in a boy body for me?" she squeaked.

Hikaru shrugged. "It wasn't a big sacrifice or anything. If I'd known you liked girls better, I'd have done that."

"Oh my God. No, no, no. That's … that is so wrong. You – you can't be changing *your* body, *your* gender, based on what *I* like."

"But it doesn't matter," Hikaru said patiently. "I'm me regardless, Jack. This is me. The fox is me. The version with boy-parts is me. It's just how we are."

Hikaru's voice had gone slightly throaty as she pleaded

173

for understanding. Her face – still Hikaru's face, and Hikaru had always been kind of pretty, even for a boy – suddenly struck Jack as *beautiful*. Jack felt herself twitch again as a painfully strong pang of affection for Hikaru went through her body, tugging on her heart. It tugged on some other stuff in there, too, and that stuff was responding like crazy.

In theory, Jack thought that gender identity was a mostly cultural construct, and that no one needed to abide by binaries in the twenty-first century. But she had not been prepared for the issue to come up in her own life, and definitely not with Hikaru. It didn't help that her body seemed to have jumped straight into *Hot Chick Ahoy* mode when she needed time to think this through. It was dizzying. Literally.

Too much.

Jack took a step sideways and sat down on the edge of the bath, putting her head in her hands. Instinct was flashing like red lights in the back of her skull. Hikaru had just proved very clearly how little Jack really knew him. Her. How little Jack knew *her*. And Jack liked and trusted Hikaru as a friend, but … as more than that? When they were different species and lived in different worlds? When Hikaru would live forever?

When she would, inevitably, have to leave Jack and go back to her own people?

She liked Hikaru so much already. Too much. Maybe more than she would have *let* herself like Hikaru if Hikaru hadn't apparently been the wrong gender and … safe. This, now? This was *dangerous*. It could end up hurting a lot.

It was better just to be friends.

"I'm..." Jack began, eyes skittering away from the warm, hopeful look on Hikaru's face. "I—"

Ebisu's voice calling from below made them both jump guiltily.

"The mirror is working, children!" A short pause. "Oh, dear! That doesn't look good..."

"Crap," Hikaru blurted. "What now?"

Without another word they grabbed their damp clothes and shoes and ran for the stairs.

When I opened my eyes again, the world was dim and quiet. My head ached with a slow, throbbing beat and my eyelids seemed to be glued together.

Where am I? What happened? My breathing sped up as I remembered the tunnels under London, the iceberg palace. Dad and I were the only ones left. The cavern had been about to come down on top of us – on top of him. I'd pulled the katana from its sheath...

"Save him, Kusanagi-no-Tsurugi! Save him, Shinobu!"

The tunnel had exploded in a wave of flaring, prismatic flames. The blast slammed me into the ice again; my head had bounced off the wall with a dull thud. I saw, or thought I saw, the walls of the cavern begin to ripple away, like ice cubes attacked with a hairdryer. The very fabric of the dream world had warped under the blade's power. Falling snow and deadly icicles were melting into harmless water. The last thing I had seen was the pale blur of my father's face against the opposite wall, his lips making the shape of my name.

I forced my eyes open, blinking and squinting against a faint blue glow that seemed to come from all around me. Where was Dad? I pushed myself up into a sitting position – and looked straight into the empty eye sockets of a human skull.

A cry of pure animal terror ripped out of my throat. *No. It couldn't be. It couldn't be. No, no, not again, not again—*

Then I heard his voice, broken and ragged. "Mio! Oh my God, you're alive."

I scrambled up and turned in a circle, scanning the space for any sign of my dad. Dry things like chunks of shattered safety glass slithered and scattered all around me. Crystals. Powdery, crushed-up crystal. I was standing on a pile of the stuff, higher than I was tall. The skeleton – a head, spine and ribcage, nothing else – was speared grotesquely on a glowing blue spike of crystal that protruded from the wall next to me. There were more of the faintly glowing stones everywhere, sticking out of the walls and floor and ceiling of the round chamber. In fact, they *were* the walls and ceiling. The walls were layered strata of white, blue, purple crystals. I was in some kind of giant geode.

Holes had been hacked into the crystal walls – and in

the holes were skeletons. Dozens of them, their ancient, dry bones riddled with reddish cracks. But the skeletons hadn't been allowed to lie in peace. The crystals had kept growing around them, through them, forcing some of them out of their graves and caging others in diamond-sharp needles. There was a narrow opening in one of the walls, about a foot wide and a couple of feet high, and a clear turquoise stream ran out of it, pooling in the bottom and centre of the geode. The water was full of tangled ribs and finger bones and skulls.

"Where are you? I don't see you." My words trembled pathetically.

"I'm not in there, Midget," my dad said. "I'm up here. Follow my voice. Just follow my voice."

I closed my eyes, blocking out the disturbing sight of the strange graveyard around me, and tried to focus only on the sound. "Keep talking, Dad. Just ... keep talking to me."

He gave a choked laugh. "As the father of a teen-age daughter, I have to say I never expected to hear that request."

I climbed further up the towering heap of crushed crystals I'd been lying on and saw, about six feet overhead, a chink of light breaking through the roof of the geode. There was a hole, about the size of my two clenched fists. Through the gap, I could see my father's face.

He's all right. He's alive. Thank you. Oh, thank you...

"It's – it's really good to see you."

He laughed again, and I saw his hand swipe over his eyes. "Never thought I'd hear that, either."

"Are you OK? You're not hurt?"

"A bit banged and bruised, but nothing serious. What about you? You bashed your head pretty hard on the ice."

"I'm f – er – I'm OK, too."

"Vision blurred? Do you feel sick?" he questioned anxiously.

"No, Dad. I'm OK. Shush for a minute – just let me… I have to…"

Predictably, he kept talking anyway. I tuned him out as I climbed to the very peak of the crushed heap of crystals, trying to get closer to the gap where he was. I stretched out to my full height and searched for handholds in the walls, but their steeply concave shape and razor-sharp crystals made them impossible to climb.

Nursing my scraped and bleeding hands, I squinted up at the ceiling. I could jump. It wasn't that far of a distance for me, not any more. But there was nothing to grab onto up there. If I tried to anchor myself on the crystals, I could lose a finger. If I jumped too hard, they might skewer me. And the hole was far too tiny to jump straight out of. Maybe Dad could make it a bit wider from his side…?

"There has to be a way up," I muttered. "There has to be a way out."

"Mio, will you please *listen* to me? I tried everything

while you were lying down there unconscious. You wouldn't answer me, you weren't moving and I couldn't even see if you were breathing. I was desperate. I hacked at this wall with my sword, kicked it, punched it, tried to claw it apart with my bare hands. Nothing works. The rock on this side is like iron. There aren't any other openings."

I rubbed my pounding forehead, realized I was getting blood on my face and sighed. "I don't get it. How did I get in here while you're stuck out there?"

"The katana blew the cavern apart. It blew the whole glacier apart – I'm standing in the melting ruins now. The impact threw me back through the wall, but you went through the floor. Through this hole. By the time I could climb down, the hole had begun to close up again. It was already too small for me to get through, and it's still getting smaller. It's half the size now that it was fifteen minutes ago."

I tried to think through the pain and the exhaustion weighing my body down. "So this gap, the one we're talking through, soon it'll just close up?"

"I think so. Try using the katana again. It got you in there. It ought to be able to get you out."

"Right." I reached back to the saya on my back … and found it empty. "Shit!"

My stomach lurched. I whirled around, sending crushed crystals flying and nearly skidding off the heap.

I had been holding the sword when I bashed my head against the ice wall. He was in my hand. But he hadn't been in my hand when I woke up. Where had he gone? Dad didn't have him. He had to be here. He *had* to be here. I raked at the heaped-up shattered crystals with both hands, smearing the pale fragments with blood. In my blind panic it took me nearly a full minute to remember that I had the ability to summon the blade to me.

"Shinobu!" I shrieked. "Shinobu, where are you?"

The crystals shifted under me – and exploded in a whirlwind of powdery crystal dust. The katana's hilt slapped into my bleeding palm, fitting into place like a part of my own body. My spine went weak and quivery with relief, and I held the hilt in both hands, eyes closed, head bowed.

When I opened my eyes, I gasped.

"What is it? You found it, didn't you?" my dad called down.

"No – I mean, yes – but look!"

I held the sword up above my head so that my dad could see.

The katana had changed. The steel had somehow sheared off, or melted away, transforming the elegant, classic curve of the katana, with its single silver cutting edge, into something … different. The blade was no longer curved but straight – a dense black metal, marked with faint flame-shaped ripples that radiated out from the centre. Ragged silver cutting edges ran along each side, making the blade double-edged. Right above the familiar pierced circle of the sword guard, the blade was narrow, but it widened in the middle and then narrowed again at the tip, coming to a wicked razor-edged point. It was like a black and silver flame that had been caught and frozen in a metal shell. A blade like a flame... Why was the shape so oddly familiar to me?

The green blade flashes down in the red light—

I flinched from the memory – and felt my eyes go wide. Not a flame. A leaf. I'd always seen that green blade as a leaf. But it wasn't exactly alike. That sword, including the hilt and guard, had clearly been carved from a single piece of some blotchy greenish stone. This one was still metal, still had its black-silk-wrapped grip and tsuba. It just had the shape of the green blade—

The blade that Izanagi had plunged into Shinobu's chest.

"It looks almost like a Greek xiphos," my dad said incredulously. "Except that it's far too long. How in the world did the blade take that sort of damage without shattering? How did it take any damage at all, when it's supposed to be indestructible?"

"I don't think it did..." I said hesitantly. "Ebisu said ... he said that after Izanagi murdered Shinobu with the sword, after he bound Shinobu's soul to the blade, Izanagi laid the 'seeming' of an ordinary katana on it. He made the sword look like the Yamato katana that Shinobu carried into the battle with the Nekomata. It was another layer of protection, another reason for the Yamato family to cherish the blade, because it belonged to their fallen son. The magical blade – the one that Izanami wants so desperately, and Izanagi wants so desperately to hide – wasn't a katana. It was never really our katana. That was just its disguise."

Which meant the sword wasn't damaged. It was the *illusion* that had broken, or perhaps just begun to flake away, revealing the true shape of the legendary meitou beneath.

My dad swiped his hand over his face again. "Look, put that aside for now. The important thing is to see if the katana can make this gap wider so that I can climb down or you can jump up."

I knew the answer to that. The sword was already out of its sheath, already in my hand, already unbound … and its energy was barely a murmur. I'd used both its true names up there in the ice cavern. There was nothing else to call on.

Still, I had my father stand back from the rapidly closing hole in the ceiling and pointed the sharp tip of the leaf-shaped blade at it as I called both true names again – *Shinobu* and *Kusanagi-no-Tsurugi*. The hilt didn't even quiver in my grip. There was no spark of flame, no wave of energy, nothing. Nothing.

"It's not going to work," I said wearily. The hole was

the size of one of my fists now, and I could only make out my father's eyes staring anxiously down at me. "I can't get up there. You can't get down here. Is there anything – any kind of a path, or opening – *anything* up there that seems to be leading you forward?"

"I don't think…" There were some faint crunching noises. "No. Only the stepping stones."

I let out a long, deep sigh. "The dream realm separated us."

"What?"

"You know exactly what I mean. That's how this place works. Ebisu said that the only way we'd find the waki-zashi is by moving forward – but there's only one way forward now, and it's down here, where only I can use it. This wasn't an accident. The dream realm separated us. Dad, I think … I think you have to go home."

There was a long, tense pause, and I saw his eyes squeeze shut. A moment later his hand came through the hole in the ceiling, reaching down towards me.

He was too far away. We were never going to be able to touch. But I reached my free hand up to him anyway, closing my fingers on empty air and imagining his strong, bony hand grasping mine.

"I don't want to go," he said roughly, his hand withdrawing so I could see a little of his face again. "I promised I wouldn't leave you again."

"It's OK, Dad," I told him firmly. "There's nothing else

183

you can do. I must be close to the end now. I'll practically be right behind you."

I heard his long-suffering sigh – the same sigh that used to set my every nerve on edge, and which I was now so perversely fond of. "Use the water to call Ebisu if you have to, Mio. Don't kill yourself trying to find this wakizashi. We might need it, but it's still not worth your life. Nothing is."

"I know," I said quickly, hoping it sounded convincing. "I'll use the water if I have to."

"You don't have to prove you're a hero to anyone," he said quietly. "Not me. Not even yourself. I love you."

My throat closed up and the only reply I could manage was a choked grunt. I nodded, hoping he saw it. I heard another crunching sound above as he moved, and then the muffled sound of his voice speaking Ebisu's name.

Light flashed in the closing gap like lightning and left silence behind.

He was gone.

I eased myself down onto the heap of crushed crystals and stared up at the hole where I'd last seen my father's face. New crystals were rapidly spreading around the edges like blue frost. Soon you wouldn't even be able to see where the gap had been. The heaped-up crystals slipped and settled, as if they had a life of their own. It wasn't very comfortable sitting on them. I would get up in a minute. Just another minute.

My fingers trembled and then tightened around the familiar grip of the sword. In the beginning it had been just me and the sword in that attic. Just me opening the box. I had started this whole thing by myself. That was how the dream realm or its guardian wanted me to finish it.

The pile of crystals heaved beneath me, hard enough to send me tipping sideways off my perch. I jumped to my feet and scuttled back, instinctively bringing the sword up into a two-handed grip. Was there something in there? Another monster?

"Show yourself!" I said, my voice coming out high and sharp, just this side of panicked. "What are you?"

In answer, a hand thrust up out of the crystal shards. A human hand. There was a faint, hoarse cough. And then an impossible voice gasped, "Help!"

CHAPTER 14

HOMECOMING

Aiko had finally convinced Rachel to set her down on her own two feet about thirty minutes ago. She'd immediately regretted it, mostly because of the smart high-heeled leather pumps she'd chosen to put on this morning. They weren't at all comfortable to run in, and she thought she was probably getting blisters. If she'd known that she was going to spend her morning fleeing across London and dodging – dear Lord – a variety of mythological monsters, she would have worn trainers. This was what happened when people kept her out of the loop.

She leaned tiredly against the wall of the alley where Rachel had called a halt. "And none of you – not a single one of you – thought I might perhaps have needed to know any of this *before I came back to London*?" Aiko asked.

Rachel gave Aiko a quelling look over her shoulder. "Can you keep your voice down, please?"

"Oh, I do beg your pardon. Am I failing to take the news of the impending apocalypse calmly enough?"

A tiny grin curved one side of Rachel's mouth. "Now you sound like your husband."

Aiko narrowed her eyes. "You are grounded. All of you. So very grounded."

"If you say so, Mrs Yamato."

"Not Takashi, though. Grounding is too good for him. I'm still debating whether I'm going to kick his lying arse out onto the street or set all his clothes on fire." She paused. "Maybe I'll do both."

Rachel turned away from the mouth of the alley. "Everything seems to be normal out there, but after that giant spider-woman this morning, I just have a bad feeling. I think we should go now. We have to be quick, OK?"

Aiko sighed, whipped off her high-heels, and stuffed them into her shoulder bag. With the other hand, she arranged her house keys so that the sharp metal poked out between the fingers of her fist. She'd learned that in a self-defence class, and now seemed like a pretty good time to give it a go. "Fine. I'm ready."

Rachel cast a doubtful look at Aiko's bare feet. "You sure you don't want me to...?"

"No, thank you. Honestly, I can walk down my own street without help."

"Run," said Rachel with conspicuous calmness. "We're going to run."

She turned and stepped out of the gap between the two buildings. Aiko followed – and came to an immediate dead stop as she surveyed the carnage. Practically in front of her house there was some kind of giant, winged carcass, burned to a crisp, blackened bones poking out. Crushed and dismembered monster parts were littered everywhere, along with gooey spatters of rusty blood. Up and down the road, windows were barricaded on the inside. Someone had driven an old Ford Fiesta into the railings at the end of the street, and it had overturned and been abandoned there. Aiko had been trudging – occasionally running and quite often hiding – across London with Rachel for nearly two hours now, and she had witnessed some way-out and terrifying things. But seeing her own peaceful home turf transformed into a war zone out of some violent video game? That was shocking and heartbreaking in a completely different way.

"*Quickly*, remember?" Rachel said as she took a firm grip on Aiko's elbow and towed her forward. "I told you it was bad. Don't step on those spider legs – they're sharp. Watch out for the broken glass."

Aiko gave herself a shake, tore her attention from an eviscerated spider that was nailed to a wall with a shard of iron railing – had her little Mio done that? – and fixed her eyes on home. They scuttled down the street towards the sanctuary offered by her black-painted front door.

They were only a few steps away from safety when a

188

tinny crash to Aiko's right made them both jump. Rachel immediately pushed Aiko behind her, spinning on her heel to confront the potential threat. Aiko peeked over the younger woman's shoulder anxiously – then relaxed. It was just a stray dog, rummaging in an overturned litter bin. It was about the size of a Labrador, but shaggy-coated with splotchy black and white fur. Its scruffy tail waved frantically as it buried its head in the pile of refuse. It must have found something good in there.

"Phew," Aiko breathed.

"The poor thing," said Rachel softly. "I wonder if its owners abandoned it? The city is no place for a helpless animal to be wandering loose right now..." She took a step forward, making gentle kissy-kissy noises.

The dog lifted its head out of the rubbish. Aiko let out an involuntary noise of horror, and the dog – thing – whatever – responded with a deep, rumbling growl, despite the fact that it had the head, and presumably the vocal chords, of a human being.

"What is that?" Aiko squeaked.

"Back up. Just ... back up slowly towards the door," Rachel said, matching words to actions. She kept her body between Aiko and the thing, and never took her eyes off it.

The dog-creature continued to growl at them, the hackles rising all along its splotchy back as it stalked after them. Its human face was splotchy too – with dried blood. The awful thing was that it was quite a normal sort of face.

189

Rounded chin with a dimple in it, dark hair with a hint of a curl, and human eyes – eyes exactly like the ones Aiko looked at every day in the mirror, except that there wasn't a person behind them. There was an animal.

A very wild, very hungry animal.

Aiko was so focused on the creature that she was completely unaware of her own front steps creeping up behind her until her heel hit the bottom one and sent her sprawling backwards. Her rear hit the stairs with a thump and her keys and shoulder bag went flying.

Aiko's sudden movement seemed to enrage the dog-monster. It lowered its head and sprang right at Rachel. Rachel gave a shout and – instinctively, it seemed to Aiko – ducked.

The monster flew over her head towards Aiko. Its jaw unhinged into a great gaping maw filled with strings of drool and rows of sharp teeth. Aiko grabbed the handle of her shoulder bag and whopped the creature right between the eyes.

Miscellaneous items showered out of the bag as the monster yelped as it landed clumsily on the steps leading to the door. Aiko grabbed one of her fallen shoes and chucked it as hard as she could. The solid wooden heel got the monster right on the nose. It yelped again, turning at bay against the door, completely blocking the entrance to the house. Its lips peeled back over its teeth and Aiko could see its muscular back legs bracing for another jump.

Aiko's hand closed over another object from her bag. She recognized it by feel, brought it up, aimed, and depressed the top, spraying the monster's face with a concentrated dose of Chanel No. 5. The animal howled. It spun in a circle and then collapsed to scrabble at its eyes with both front paws.

Rachel was dragging at the back of Aiko's jacket. "Come on, quick. We have to go!"

"We can take this thing!" Aiko cried, on fire. She scooped her other shoe up off the steps and threw that, too, not even wincing when it missed and left a ding in the front door. "Just you find my keys. I'll kick this mangy mongrel's—"

"Aiko!" Rachel shrieked. "Will you shut up and *look*!"

Her pointing finger was aimed squarely at half a dozen new dog-monsters slinking down the road towards them. The lead one was twice the size of the whimpering creature on Aiko's front doorstep, and its off-white face and fur were almost pink with splashes of blood.

Wild dogs come in packs.

"Good point," Aiko said hastily. "Rachel, would you mind—?"

Rachel wrapped her arm around Aiko's waist and slung her over one shoulder in a single, easy motion. "Not at all."

They took off in the opposite direction as the half-human howls of the dog-monsters filled the street.

"Where are we going?" Aiko gasped. Houses blurred past her, but she could hear the yipping and barks of the dogs not far behind. "I think they're following – can we outrun them?"

"Probably for a little while at least," Rachel called back, answering the second question first. "I'm pretty fast. But don't worry. I know another place where we should be safe.:."

My sword hit the crystal floor of the chamber with a dry crunch. I stood, paralysed, not blinking, not breathing, and watched the hand in the pile of broken crystals close into a fist.

Then that voice again. "Mio?"

The spell broke. I fell on the crystals, clawing handfuls away, uncaring of the damage the crystals were doing to my unprotected skin or of the hacking sobs that shook my body. A second familiar hand burst out of the powdery mess. There was more coughing. I found an elbow, grabbed it and pulled. The pile slid, and suddenly a head and upper torso surged up, free.

"Shinobu?" The word broke from my lips like a pane of glass shattering. "Shinobu?"

He heaved his legs out with a furious kick and knelt up, leaning over me. An impatient swipe of a forearm pushed tangled hanks of hair back, and he stared into my face, eyes burning like black holes in his face. A line of moisture tracked down his cheek, washing through the dirt that coated his golden skin.

"Mio."

His shaking hands caressed my face, tilting it up to his, and there, covered in blood and dust, we kissed,

kissed, kissed again, hands entwining, sliding, clutching, until disbelief and grief and hope had burned away and all that was left was love.

"You are real. You're really real." I kept repeating the words, as if they were some kind of mantra that could fix him in reality.

"I am real. I am really real," he whispered back again and again, and maybe he was doing the same thing as I was, pleading and promising at the same time. "I was with you. I stayed with you. All the time. As close as could be. When you unsheathed the blade and called its name – my name – the sword's energy exploded through me again. But it was more this time. Stronger than anything I've experienced. I felt the prison, the cage around me, shatter and blow away, and I was blown away too. Back into my corporeal form. It must have knocked me out. The last thing I remember is seeing the roof of the ice cavern disintegrate. I woke up buried alive, and praying that you were all right, that you were near."

"Like when the Nekomata tried to pull the seals off the sword with its tail," I said slowly, working it out. "It stripped you away and you materialized. It makes sense. It does make sense. This is real."

"I promise," he told me, as if he could sense the cold slither of fear inside. He tucked the flyaway hair back behind my ears, his eyes searching my face. "I promise.

Believe me, Mio. This is real. I will not let anything separate us again. Where you go—"

"I will follow," I finished, knowing the right response as if it had been written on my heart.

"Always."

So I believed. I put my arms around him, and I *believed*.

We didn't move for a while. Didn't speak much either. I just had to hold onto him and feel him – warm and alive, breathing, heart beating – beside me. Then my leg went to sleep. It was unbearably tingly, and I had to let go so that I could massage my calf.

"Ow. Ouch. Wow, this is – this is definitely not romantic."

"Let me," Shinobu said, smiling his half-cocky, half-shy smile. The sight of it made my insides tingle too – but in a much nicer way. He pulled me back against him again and draped my legs over his. Then he went to work, big hands kneading at the muscles gently, thumbs circling and pressing with exactly the right pressure. I tried not to make any embarrassing sounds.

"We have to move on," I said reluctantly. "I don't know how much time is passing out there in the real world, or what's happening. We need that wakizashi…" I stopped as I remembered the way that Ebisu's unsheathing of the blade had felled Shinobu before. My fingers coiled up in the back of his hakama.

"We need it," he said firmly. "So we will find it. And this time we will get Ebisu to explain what it is and how it must be used. If it is dangerous to me and I must be fifty miles away when it is unsheathed, then so be it. I can come back. I won't leave you again."

I nodded, my hand relaxing to stroke down the muscular line of his back. He made a faint growling noise, almost a purr, and then looked mortified. His hands fell still on my leg. "S-sorry."

I couldn't help it – I snorted with laughter. "I love you."

He bowed his head over mine, glossy coils of dark hair falling around our faces. *"Aishiteru zo, Mio-dono."*

I didn't have to ask what he meant. I could feel it, like sunlight falling on my face after a long, terrible journey through darkness. His lips found mine.

CHAPTER 15

INTO
THE PAST

Finally we peeled ourselves apart. Shinobu stooped and handed me the sword – it didn't feel right to call it the katana, as it clearly wasn't any more – and as I took it in my hands I realized we had a problem. The shape of the blade had completely changed. The shape of the saya had not. How was I supposed to fit a straight sword into a curved sheath? And what the hell was I going to do when we got out of the dream realm and the Shinobu-free blade started talking to me again? I'd have no way to shut it out.

The sheer bliss of having Shinobu with me blunted my panic – but not completely. If there was going to be a future for us, I still needed to do my job. I had to free London from the attentions of the gods. With the sword constantly trying to wrestle control of my mind away, enslave me and destroy everything it saw, that task was going to be a *lot* harder.

"But you are stronger now," Shinobu said when I explained. "It is obvious in everything about you. My father would have called you a burned warrior. One who has walked through fire and not been consumed by it, only hardened."

I worried at my lip, unconvinced.

Shinobu touched my cheek. "Let me try something."

When I nodded, he reached over my shoulder and freed the saya from the leather rings of the harness. It looked exactly the same as before. Gently curving, gleaming with golden cherry blossoms set in black lacquer. Whatever transformation the sword had undergone, it had left the sheath untouched.

"The sword that we see is only an illusion. It has only ever been an illusion," Shinobu said in answer to my questioning look. He hefted the lightweight saya between his hands. "Yet the blade has always fitted within this saya. What is more, the saya has always had the ability to dampen the sword's energy – something no ordinary sheath could do. I think this is part of the same illusion that cloaks the blade, part of those seals that Izanagi laid on it to hide it and conceal its power. And if that is the case…"

"Then the blade should still fit," I finished.

Shinobu handed me the saya. I took it into my left hand as always, gripping it near the top, and carefully fitted the sharp point of the blade to the koiguchi – the mouth of the saya – and pushed.

The sword slid home smoothly. The guard clicked into place.

"It worked." I turned the sheathed sword over in my hands, hardly able to believe it. "My brain does not want to accept what my eyes just saw."

"A common state of affairs for both of us since we first met," Shinobu said, smiling. He took the sword from me – and it was a nice side effect of the dream realm that I felt no strong urge to rip it out of his hands – and fitted it back into the harness so that it rested between my shoulder blades.

"Let's get going then," I said, helplessly smiling back.

We splashed into the turquoise water of the pool, making strenuous efforts to avoid the rusty looking piles of bones at the bottom. I was braced for the water to be icy cold like the pool in the glacier, but instead it was strangely warm. Not quite bath temperature, but definitely a pleasant surprise considering that we had no choice but to wade through it up to our knees. It also had a faint, eggy odour that I hadn't picked up on before. I sniffed suspiciously.

"Sulphur," Shinobu said. "The water must come from a hot spring. We had them in our village. Everyone loved to bathe there, especially in the winter. We sometimes cooked eggs in the water, too, when we were children, and ate them. Onsen eggs."

I stared at his back. That was the second time he had mentioned his first life in the space of just a few minutes – and so casually, too, without even a hint of the painful hesitation that had always made me too worried to pursue the subject before. What had changed? Could something about this place be making him open up that way? My dad had certainly been a lot more forthcoming than usual in the ice cavern.

I silently tucked the little jewel of information into the treasure box in my memory reserved solely for Shinobu, and promised myself that I would try asking for more details later on, after we were out of the dream realm, and I could trust that Shinobu really *wanted* to talk.

He stepped to one side to avoid crushing a skull under his foot, and I moved past him, reaching the gap in the wall first. I crouched down to get a better look – and found myself being gently but firmly put aside by Shinobu.

"Let me go first," he said.

"Why? I'm the smallest—"

"Which means that if you go ahead of me, you may lead us down a passage that is too narrow for me to follow, and then you will have to back up. If I go first, we will only be able to take routes that we both may fit into."

His argument made perfect sense. It was also complete and total bull. He always insisted on going ahead of me, taking the lead and brushing me to one side.

And he did it for one simple reason: he was determined to put himself between me and danger. That same instinct had led him to sacrifice himself three times now – once at my hand.

No matter how many times I showed him that I wasn't some useless, fragile burden, the issue kept coming between us. Why did he have to wrest control from me, over and over? What was he trying to prove?

Why am I so much lesser than you, Shinobu? Why do you always try to leave me behind?

I felt as if he'd returned to me only to stab me in the heart.

"Mio-dono?" Shinobu's warm hand closed around my wrist. "What is it?"

The touch broke through my dark thoughts. The intense sense of rejection and betrayal disappeared, sucked away like dirty water swirling down a drain. I realized with a shock that my hands had clenched into knotted fists. I forced them to open so that Shinobu could take my hand properly.

"Sorry." I shook myself and looked up at him. "Sorry, I think I zoned out for a second there. I'm not sure…"

"Are you all right? You looked…" He stopped abruptly. His fingers entwined with mine, wordlessly communicating his concern.

I didn't care if Shinobu was protective. Did I? Maybe I'd rolled my eyes over it a couple of times, but it had always struck me as kind of sweet and old-fashioned. It was just a part of him. So why had it suddenly set me off that way? I hadn't even felt like myself for a second there – the feelings had been so strong. It had to be this place, messing with my head.

The sooner we got what I'd come for and left, the better.

"I'm fine – I promise." I squeezed his hand and smiled up at him. His face relaxed. He squeezed my hand back, then ducked down and bent himself double in order to squash into the tiny opening in the wall. I was hot on his heels.

The only way to move in the narrow tunnel was to crawl on hands and knees in the shallow bed of the little stream, which meant getting soaked in stinky water up to my chest. Ahead of me, Shinobu had no choice but to lie on his belly and use his elbows to pull himself along. The roof was so low that he could barely raise his head. I was very glad that we seemed to have left the last of the skeletal remains behind in the geode cave – there'd be no way to avoid them like this.

I could see light shining somewhere beyond Shinobu. It was different to the dim bluish glow of the crystals all around us. Moving in the cramped tunnel was so uncomfortable that it felt like we were in it forever, but in reality I think it was only five minutes or so before Shinobu made a sound of relief and disappeared through a small, round opening that had appeared ahead.

I popped out after him with a wet squelch, dripping water everywhere. "Euw, that must be what it's like to be born…" My voice trailed off as I took in the room we had found.

The walls and low ceiling were of the same purple-blue-and-white-striped crystal as the geode, but here the spiky crystals had been sanded down and shaped so that they blended into a smooth, shimmering surface. A sort of chandelier, made of polished blue gems, hung from the centre of the roof, providing more light. The stream we had crawled through to get here trickled out of the narrow tunnel mouth behind me and down into a shallow trench that encircled the room at the base of the walls, so that the space was filled with the low murmur of water. But what really caught my attention were the three doorways spaced equally around the curving walls.

These weren't roughly hacked-out openings or natural cave mouths. They were real doorways, with black lintels, and each one was blocked by a door of glowing crystal bound in iron. Inlaid in the crystal was curling script made of the same black metal. The first door, to my left, proclaimed PAST. The one directly ahead of me was PRESENT. And the one on the right was FUTURE.

"This is different from anything I've seen so far," I said with dawning excitement. "We must be getting close to the centre – close to the wakizashi."

"That means the hazards will be likely to increase," Shinobu said, eyeing the doors with caution. "Each of these possibilities would seem to present its own perils."

"Not a shocker. Which one do you think we should pick?"

He shook his head, giving me a serious look. "You are the sword-bearer. You should choose."

I blew out a long breath as I considered it. "I suppose … logically, if we have to face things that have already happened in our past, then that would give us an edge – because we've already overcome them once. We should know the answers. Does that make sense?"

"Yes – and I agree."

"Good." I grabbed the handle of the door marked PAST.

The cold metal of the rod-shaped handle shuddered against the skin of my palm. Then it warmed, perceptibly, like a blush creeping over a shy girl's cheek. The texture of the metal seemed to change in my grasp, and I felt silk wrappings and the solid rounded edge of a hilt ornament. It was like holding the katana's grip again for the very first time.

With a deep, gusty sound that was disturbingly human, the door began to swing open. Air swirled around me, tugging inquisitively at my hair and damp clothes and tickling my face and hands. Light spilled out of the widening opening, and I breathed in a sweet, heady scent that I couldn't quite place.

"Sakura," Shinobu said softly, behind me. "It smells like the cherry blossoms in my mother's garden."

I looked back at him over my shoulder, my hand still on the door handle that felt like a sword hilt. Words leapt to my lips, words I hadn't intended to speak out loud. "Maybe it's your dream we're heading into, Shinobu. Your past."

Shinobu's face changed. He reached out as if to pull me back – to step in front of me again. Answering an irresistible impulse, I shrugged his hand off and slipped through the doorway into the past.

He was right: it was a garden. A great, beautiful garden spreading out as far as the eye could see. And everywhere I looked, masses of fruit trees were in bloom, crowding the sky with cloudy mantles of pink and white blossoms, filling the air with that intoxicating perfume that somehow made me want to laugh, and dance, and sing. Carefully landscaped hills rose around me, topped with small Chinese-style pagodas of white and red and gold. The little stream of clear water circled my feet and then ran away to play under a series of crescent-moon-shaped bridges painted the colour of jade.

"Shin-chan!" A small figure – a little girl dressed in a red-and-white kimono – skipped through the spiralling cherry blossoms on the path ahead of us. The wind tossed dark, unruly hair around her head, and when she glanced back, I caught a glimpse of a pair of bright, laughing eyes. "Shin-chan, come and play!"

Shinobu was still hesitating on the threshold. Impatiently I grabbed his hand and dragged him into the garden. "We have to catch her."

"Mio – I…" His voice was choked.

The door swung shut behind us with a deep, hollow thud.

"Come on." I pulled at his hand as I scanned the garden for the little girl. She had disappeared around the next bend. She was playing with us. Hide-and-seek. Laughter bubbled up inside me. "She's waiting."

I tugged at his hand again and he came with me as I ran down the path. I barely noticed when my running strides turned into skipping ones, and then dancing ones.

"Where are you, little princess?" I called out. "Come out, come out, wherever you are!"

Childish laughter echoed around us. Drifting cherry blossoms caught in my hair as the wind shifted. One landed on my tongue and without thinking I swallowed it. *Sweet.* I squeezed Shinobu's hand and held it up above my head so that I could twirl in a circle. "Isn't it beautiful?"

I glimpsed a blur of red and white ahead of us on a low, rounded hill crowned by a massive cherry tree that towered over all the rest. The tree's gnarled, silvery trunk spoke of great age. "She's up there."

I let go of Shinobu's hand and raced up the hill, filled

with inexplicable, joyful anticipation – desperate to find the little girl and learn who she was and how she had got here. There was another fleeting blur of a flowered kimono and tangled hair as the child whipped away from me to hide behind the tree. The faint gurgle of her giggles would have given away her location even if I hadn't seen her.

"I've found you, little princess."

Resting my hand on the bark of the tree, I circled its trunk, expecting with each step to find the girl. But there was no sign of her. I circled the tree again in the opposite direction, still looking. Her laughter had fallen silent now.

"Where did you go?" I whispered.

Where did you go, little princess? The echo of a voice. The echo, not the sound. Deep inside, something stirred…

I heard footsteps rustling in the grass and turned to see Shinobu walking up the hill towards me. The wind caught at his unbound hair and dark clothes, sending them billowing around him like black clouds. Cherry blossoms spiralled in the air around him, and I felt that strange echo again – as if I was seeing him for the first time. As if I saw him through new eyes.

Shin-chan! Come and play, Shin-chan!

The echo of forgotten voices, of familiar laughter, rang through me again. An echo of recognition – of memory.

In my mind I could feel something unfolding,

moving, coming to life. Dancing through my memories like the little girl had danced through the falling sakura. A dance I knew so well. One I had learned when I was a child and practised each day when I was grown. The kata for katana that my Ojiichan had taught me... No, that my *father* had taught *us*, taught us together...

"The sword is a part of you. Part of your body. The edged extension of your own flesh. The blade is your will moving through the world. A true warrior reveals his own soul with every flash of his sword."

Remember.

I remembered dancing with Shinobu in a room filled with sunlight, on bare wooden floors, in bare feet. Dancing the kata. We flowed together, our bodies tensing and shifting effortlessly in the rhythm that we knew as well as breathing. Turn. Extend. Left foot. Right. Forward. Back. Turn.

Remember, little princess.

Shin-chan! Come and play!

I saw the little girl again, in my mind.

She stood by the side of a tall woman with a kind face, beneath the spreading boughs of a cherry tree in bloom. A man, plainly dressed, his silver-streaked hair neatly drawn back into a topknot, approached. A little boy walked behind him. A little boy with golden skin and dark eyes filled with reflections of the cloudy blue sky above. He moved stiffly, his tense shoulders telegraphing both fear and pride.

This is your new son, my dear. Mio, this is your new big brother. Shinobu, say hello.

The little girl smiled. *Shin-chan.*

Shinobu, the boy corrected gravely.

The little girl shook her head, and strands of hair fell into her face. She brushed them back with an exasperated sound. *No, you are Shin-chan, and we will be best friends.*

The little boy's small hands clenched into fists. The little girl only smiled wider – a wicked, mischievous, irresistible grin. After a moment, as if he couldn't help it, a shy smile twitched at the corners of the boy's mouth. He reached out and tucked the little girl's hair carefully behind her ear. *Perhaps we will, Mio-dono.*

Shin-chan! Come and play!

I saw the boy and girl running together through fields of long, waving grass, shrieking with laughter, collapsing in the shade of a red Japanese maple. Behind them, the brown thatch of a long, low house baked gently in the sun.

I saw the girl and boy sparring with wooden swords under the watchful eye of the same older man – his hair was more silver than ever now, his beard almost completely white.

I saw the boy and the girl kiss, for the very first time, in the garden under a cherry tree.

I saw the girl stare at the boy as if she didn't know

him, heartbreak and betrayal on her face. I saw her fling her hand out towards him. *Go then. Go without me. But don't bother coming back – you are nothing to me any more. I hate you, and I never want to see you again.*

I saw the girl in the garden at dusk, alone, with a black-and-gold katana clutched to her chest. She slumped to her knees on the ground, her back and shoulders jerking with sobs that seemed hard enough to rip her apart, thin fingers turning yellow and red with strain around the saya of the sword. *Shinobu... I didn't mean it. I didn't mean it. I should never have let you go...*

Where was the little girl? Where had she gone?

Who was she?

But I was only asking myself those questions because the realization, the flood of memories, was so overwhelming, so impossible to absorb and believe. I knew the answer already.

She is me.

I was the little girl.

I was the young woman.

I was the one who Shinobu had loved and lost five hundred years ago.

And I was the one he loved now.

I am Mio.

In my mind the dance of memories slowed and came to a halt. I found myself standing in the shelter of Shinobu's body, my head resting on his chest. His hands were pressed into my back, holding me as if he was frightened I would fly away without their restraint. The sakura-scented wind sent pink petals fluttering around us. I opened my eyes, but kept them trained on the black fabric of his hakama.

"How?" I asked.

CHAPTER 16

OUT OF THE PAST

He didn't reply. Beneath my hands the muscles of his body were rigid with tension.

"How?" I repeated.

He took a deep, shuddering breath. "I do not know. I do not know, Mio-dono."

Mio-dono. The name – his pet name for me, the special name that only he ever used – set off a new cascade of remembrance. The little wooden doll he had carved for my birthday when I was eight. The first time he had sent me flying when we sparred, and his horrified, anxious face. The first time I had beaten him and how I had crowed and gloated. The first time he had whispered to me, *Aishiteru zo, Mio-dono.*

I could feel that other Mio's shape, like a new skeleton inside me that was slowly sinking into place. A different me. One who had been raised in a completely different time and place, in another culture. One who had been bolder and fiercer in some ways – quieter and more thoughtful in others. One whose temper flared at things mine didn't, and whose humour lit at jokes I didn't get. One who had loved and trusted and known Shinobu completely, because he had been the most beloved part of her whole life.

A different me. But still me.

"You knew," I whispered.

"Not at first," he said. "I did not … did not dare to believe, at first. I felt something – recognition – the moment that you held the sword for the first time as a child. But you were so different. The Mio I knew before was … delicate. *Frail*. A summer cold could nearly kill you. Sometimes you couldn't eat for days without being sick. You burned all the more brightly for that frailty. You fought to prove you were as fast, as strong as me. I feared that you would kill yourself trying to prove it."

"She was – I was beautiful, though." I remembered the visions. That glowing girl-child blossoming into maturity. The lovely, sharp-boned little face.

"You have always been beautiful to me."

I shook my head. "When did you *know*, Shinobu?"

He hesitated. "I guessed that day at your parents' house. When we danced the kata together. No one else could ever move with me, lead and follow me, the way she – you – could. Like being the two halves of one person. I was sure then it had to be you."

I stared up into his face. "You knew all the way back then? That was – that was the first day we met!"

He looked away, his hands like stones pressed into my back. "You did not remember me."

"But from the second we met the connection was there. Sometimes I thought I was losing my mind – and you let me think it. Why?"

He still wouldn't meet my eyes. I could see a muscle jerking in his jaw, as if he was grinding his teeth.

"You didn't want me to remember, did you?" I shoved away from him, putting distance between us.

Finally he looked at me, his eyes pleading and conflicted. "I could not tell you. I could not take the risk."

"What *risk*? You can't lie to me, keep things from me, and then claim that it's somehow for my own good. Tell me the truth. Why did you want to keep my other life – *our* other life, everything that we were to each other – a secret?"

"Because you hated me," he whispered.

"I – what?" I stuttered. Out of all the things that he could have said, I'd never expected that one.

"I lost you. You hated me then, and I knew that if you remembered you would hate me again."

Me hate Shinobu? That couldn't be right! I would never – I would *never*... I searched the confusing jumble of memories, like turning out a box of mixed-up puzzle pieces, trying to make sense of what he'd said. There had been an argument. I had cried – I remembered that. I'd … I'd said that I hated him, yes. But I hadn't *meant* it.

Had I?

"Explain," I mumbled, my mouth suddenly dry. "What went wrong?"

"*I* did." He straightened, his shoulders jerking into that suddenly familiar stance of fearful defiant pride. "I betrayed you. You were onna bugeisha. You were everything. And I left you behind."

"I was – I was what? A geisha?" The term was familiar, but I couldn't find the meaning among the splinters of remembrance in my head.

He shook his head wearily. "Onna bugeisha. You know this – you know what you were. A woman of noble birth trained in the way of the sword so that she might defend her honour and her family's honour. Your father taught us together, side by side, as soon as we were old enough to hold the practice swords. He said that as long as we fought together nothing could ever best us. We would always be safe, our family would always be safe, as long as we were together. Where you went, I would follow. Always."

He made a sudden choked sound between his teeth. His legs seemed to buckle, and he dropped to his knees, bowing his head in misery. His body shuddered as he dragged in a deep breath.

"When the Nekomata came, and it was decided that we should fight it… Of course, you were to fight with me. That was the way of things, the way we were. The long sword and the short sword. A matched pair. *Daishō*. We fought together or not at all. But I was a coward – I was frightened of losing you. I went to your father. I manipulated him. I reminded him of how frail and small you had always been. I made him swear that he would keep you from the battle and let me fight alone."

I froze. "You … left me behind?"

"I would have hurt you less had I taken out my blade and stabbed you through the heart. You begged me not to do it. You, who had never begged anyone for anything your whole life, begged me…" His voice broke. "But I did not listen."

I backed away from Shinobu, struggling to keep my breathing even. A new flood of emotions – memories – broke inside me. I remembered this. I had needed to fight to protect those that I loved. To protect Shinobu and my family. Had needed it every bit as much as he had. It was my right, and what I had trained for since I was a child. And my father and my own beloved Shinobu – Shinobu, whom I had trusted completely – had turned against me. They had plotted behind my back to exclude me, as if my training and strength and courage counted for nothing.

As if I was nothing.

Shinobu looked up at me with dull resignation, like

a man waiting for his execution. "You had given me your heart, your trust, your honour. I shattered it all. When you said you would never forgive me, I knew it was the truth. I left the house to go into the forest and face the beast – but before I went, I stole your blade. Your katana."

"Mine?" I whispered. "The katana was mine?"

"The cherry blossom blade, we called it. It was a gift from your father. He had it made especially for you. You loved it, and I suppose … I wanted to bring a tiny part of you with me into that fight."

One of my hands went back to touch the hilt – that black-silk-wrapped hilt that had always felt so familiar and right in my hands. Strange to think that perhaps it wasn't all magic and compulsion. To think that some of my love for the sword was just … love.

"You remember now, don't you? I can see it in your eyes." Without waiting for an answer, he climbed back to his feet, turning away from me. He stared out at the sea of dancing cherry blossoms with loathing. His hands knotted into fists, but he didn't say anything else.

I rubbed my hands over my face, pressing the heels of my palms against my forehead as I struggled to make sense of all that I now knew. I remembered the feelings of unbearable betrayal and heartbreak as if they had only happened yesterday. But I also remembered something else.

I had let him go.

My father had broken his promise. He couldn't bear to lock me in as he had said he would, though he ordered me strictly to stay behind. He knew, after all, that there were no locks or bars that could have held me, had I been determined to get out.

I could have gone after Shinobu. I could have refused to be left behind. But I had been too proud and too angry and too hurt. I had let Shinobu go without me.

I had let him go.

And he had died.

I'd had to live with that. I lived with it for five years – five endless, terrible years without him – until a winter fever took me from the world. Then my soul had torn free of my withered body and tried to fly to Shinobu, but it couldn't find him. Something – Izanagi, I now realized – had kept us apart. For five hundred years. Him trapped in the sword, in the dark and cold. Me trapped in some blank, empty space between life and death. Both of us waiting for the chance to be reunited. Reborn.

Redeemed.

That awful day, when I had seen Izanagi emerge from the forest carrying Shinobu's sword, my sword, and had known he was gone, I would have done anything, given anything, to go back in time – to change my own choices, and run after Shinobu without pride hobbling my steps. To change the last words I spoke to him into words of love instead of hate. All that time I had floated, barely conscious – a disembodied soul yearning for existence, like a butterfly stifling behind dusty glass – hoping to see him again and put things right. And he, too, had been carrying that guilt all this time. It had been five hundred years since that fight, since pride and fear had torn us apart.

My rebirth should have been impossible. *I* should have been impossible. But somehow I had escaped and found a new life as the descendant of one of my own younger brothers, and everything, everything that happened afterwards was … inevitable.

We were meant to be together. Our bad choices back then couldn't change that. Hundreds of years couldn't change it. Even the gods couldn't keep us apart, not forever. We were just human beings: fragile, flawed and finite. Yet our frail, human hearts had kept on beating for each other all this time.

Where you go, I will follow. Always.

It took more effort than it should have to take the two steps towards him. My arms were like lead weights as I lifted them. But the moment I wrapped them around him, the heaviness – the sorrow and regret that I had been carrying unknowingly all my life – fell away.

I pressed myself into his back, feeling him tense up with surprise. "It's all right," I said, leaning my forehead between his shoulder blades. "It's all right now. We're together again."

One of his hands brushed mine tentatively. "But I – I lied to you. I hurt you so much. Then and now."

"You deserve a second chance," I said softly. "We deserve a second chance. Shinobu, I forgive you."

His shoulders shook, and then his hands grasped mine and squeezed them desperately, painfully tight.

The wind swept across the sakura blossoms, making the treetops toss like foam on the crests of a stormy ocean. The hill undulated under our feet.

"What is—?" Shinobu began.

Before he could finish his thought, there was no hill any more.

We dropped with twin yells, forced to release each other as we hit the water. Our epic splash was drowned out by the boom and hiss of the waves as they rose up around us. The garden was gone. We were in the middle of a seething grey sea. The sky above us was low and leaden, almost black, streaked with veins of gold.

The water threw us upward and then tumbled us down as if we were on a rollercoaster. Shinobu grabbed the arm of my hoodie and pointed with his other hand. "There! Dry land!"

I saw it. A pale, sharp peak, wreathed in a veil of white clouds, standing up out of the water. It was shining silver-blue-grey, radiating light even in the stormy darkness. More ice? Or more bloody crystals? Was it huge and far away, or close and tiny? No way to tell. There was no way to judge perspective out here. No other options, either. I nodded, treading water.

Shinobu let go of me and we struck out towards the pale mountain, riding the surging tide when it took us that way, fighting when it tried to turn us back. The salt water stung my eyes and plastered my hair to my face. Shivers of cold wracked my body as I forced it to find the rhythm of the front crawl, struggling to keep my head above the water. I longed to reach back and check on the sword, but I couldn't stop swimming for long enough – a second's hesitation and I would be left behind. The only points of reference I had were the shining shape of the mountain in front and Shinobu's soaked otter-sleek hair to my left. I had to keep my eyes on one or the other.

A wave buoyed me up and suddenly I could see a narrow strip of beach ahead of us, shadowed by a pale, glimmering cliff-face. "Almost there!" I shouted and saw one of Shinobu's hands flash up in acknowledgement.

The water shunted me forward. Two more mighty pulls with aching arms and my feet hit soft, sucking sand. I heaved myself out of the water, sagging as I took my weight and the weight of my sodden clothes. After a quick check of the sword, I turned to see Shinobu land behind me. He took my hand and helped me upright, and we trudged up the shallow slope as quickly as we could. I, for one, was afraid that the sea would change its mind and try to drag us back.

When we reached the high-water mark where the sand was pale and dry, we both collapsed. Shinobu leaned against a glittering blue-grey rock. I pulled up my knees and rested my head on them. It was hot – almost uncomfortably hot to my clammy skin after the shocking cold of the water. Our clothes and hair were already steaming.

"What was that, do you think?" I rasped. "A punishment from the dream realm for being unbearably emo?"

"You are too harsh upon yourself." The deep, rumbling voice echoed all around us, impossibly vast. "In fact, it was a shortcut."

The rock against Shinobu's back stirred and stretched. It wasn't a rock.

It was a claw.

Shinobu shot forward so fast that he cannoned into me. I caught my balance and stood up, turning in a circle as the sand along the beach – no, the beach itself – began to shift and loop upwards. The sand slithered away into the water, and great coils of a reptilian body lifted up from beneath it to reveal radiant silver scales the size of dinner plates. A five-clawed foot, at least nine feet long, emerged next to me, flexing luxuriantly.

There was nowhere to go. Even the sea was blocked from us now. A scaled coil had emerged behind us. We stood on a small patch of sand no more than four feet square.

"You might have kept on wandering for days more,"

the voice rumbled on. "Some people walk here for whole lifetimes before they can be brought to honestly face their own mistakes, confront their deepest, most secret selves. Some people never can."

I looked up to see the whole shining cliff-face and the silvery mountain above it unravelling from around an unremarkable stony crag. An immense head with a slender snout, two slim, pointed ears and a crown of floating, glowing blue filaments like captured lightning slithered down the side of the crag towards us. The chin came to rest on the clawed foot in the sand. I looked into a multifaceted, almond-shaped eye – an eye wider than I was tall – swirling with lustrous darkness and shifting colours: a night sky filled with the aurora borealis.

"Dragon…" Shinobu breathed.

CHAPTER 17

SILVER FANGS

Shinobu went fluidly to his knees, bowing over hands pressed flat to the sand. Shock, disbelief and a hefty dose of pure terror kept me upright. Myths and legends cycled through my head – all that I had learned in two lifetimes about dragons and the things they did to humans. The bit of me that had grown up in Japan knew that dragons were wise, mostly benevolent celestial messengers. The part that had grown up in Europe was equally sure that they were psychotic man-eaters. A quote I'd seen on a T-shirt once drifted through my head: *Meddle not in the business of dragons, for you are crunchy when fried and good with ketchup.*

Should I look it in the eye? Would it hypnotize me if I did? Should I bow like Shinobu? Or refuse to bow and show it that I was strong? My hands twitched with the desire to reach back for my sword and I only just managed to control myself.

"This one is polite," the dragon said, looking at Shinobu before turning its huge, swirling eyes on me. "Are you being rude? Or are you just in shock? I have some difficulty reading human facial expressions."

"Er … shock, I think. Sorry 'bout that," I managed to croak.

"No apology is required," the dragon assured me. She moved her snout a little closer and sniffed. The suction dragged me forward a step and made my eyes water. "You are Beautiful Cherry Blossoms Tied with the Red Thread of Fate. And this must be your mate, Stealthy Man Who Remembers and Endures. I am currently female, and my name is too long for a human to remember, but some of my friends call me Sharp Silver Fangs of the Crescent Moon. You may do the same if you wish."

"Hello?" I said faintly.

The dragon tilted her head back and chuckled. The noise shook the sand under my feet and rolled through the air like thunder. Between her lips I caught a glimpse of pearly fangs as tall as Shinobu that spiralled like unicorn horns. Her breath smelled of jasmine.

"Beautiful Cherry Blossoms Tied with the Red Thread of Fate, dragons do not eat humans. In fact, we *like* humans. That is why I guided you to me. I have something for you."

I remembered the voice I had heard when I first

stepped through Ebisu's portal, the distant sound of laughter when I unsheathed the katana and Ebisu's warning. The dragon had been watching us the whole time. She was the guardian of this realm.

"Honoured Grandmother," Shinobu said reverently, lifting his head to look into the dragon's enormous face. "You have the wakizashi?"

"And you know everything that's been happening?" I said. "In the human realm, with the sword and the gods, and—"

The dragon lifted a claw, silencing me. "I was born in the centre of the first star that lit this universe. I have sailed on the milky winds of time and drunk from the ruby-red depths of nothingness. I know everything, human child, that there is to be known."

I blinked. "That would seem to … answer that question, yes."

"The first thing you need to know is the name of the final seal upon the sword. Its original name, the one it was born with, is *Ame-no-Murakumo-no-Tsurugi*, or in this tongue, the Sword of the Gathering Clouds of Heaven. To free the blade's full power, you will need to use this name. You must also have the wakizashi."

Shinobu and I exchanged a look. Ebisu hadn't said anything to us about unsealing the sword's full power. Did we actually *want* to do that? And what about—?

"Honoured Grandmother, may I ask, what exactly do

we need the wakizashi for?" Shinobu ventured, reading my mind.

"An excellent question. When Izanagi cast his enchantment upon the meitou to conceal and constrain its powers, he made one mistake. He did not realize that the katana he was using to disguise the cosmic blade did not belong to the human whose soul he had captured. Because your soul sensed that the katana did not truly belong to it, you did not fully bond with it or the meitou, as Izanagi-no-Kami had intended. A splinter of your spirit broke free and instead merged with your own blade, the one you had carried into battle – the wakizashi."

I nearly slapped myself on the forehead with exasperation. In every vision I'd had of that terrible, fatal confrontation between Shinobu and the Nekomata, I'd seen Shinobu fighting in his personal style, with a blade in each hand – katana and wakizashi. But somehow I'd never bothered to look at the short blade, or even wonder what had happened to it. *Idiot.*

"Ebisu," said Sharp Silver Fangs of the Crescent Moon, "who had been spying upon his father for centuries hoping for the chance to bring him low, saw what had happened. When Izanagi walked away and left the wakizashi discarded on the battlefield, Ebisu darted in and took it, hiding it within the fabric of his own body.

"It took Izanagi a little while to notice that his seals upon the blade were imperfect. The sword's power was leaking, creating a much stronger connection between it and the Yamato family than he had ever anticipated. A faint scent of the sword's power was also perceptible – enough that Izanami would know it was still in the mortal realm and keep searching for it.

"Izanagi realized then what must have occurred. But the wakizashi was gone, and all he found in its place were traces of Ebisu's magic. He sought out his son and demanded that the younger Kami give up the wakizashi. Ebisu refused. Enraged and frightened, Izanagi placed a fearsome ward upon his son, imprisoning Ebisu within the energy of a natural nexus so that he could take no action without Izanagi knowing it, nor speak of what he knew. Most especially, Ebisu could not speak of the wakizashi."

"I still don't understand," I said. "Well, I mean, obviously if some of Shinobu's soul is trapped inside it, then the wakizashi is important – I get that – but why do we need it for the fight against Izanagi? What am I supposed to *do* with it?"

"Free him," Silver Fangs answered, nodding in Shinobu's direction. "Free your mate from his binding to the Sword of the Gathering Clouds of Heaven. When the wakizashi is unsheathed, the fragment of your mate's spirit that was trapped within it will return to him, breaking Izanagi's spell finally and completely. He and the sword will both be unbound and returned to their original forms. The sword's true power will be unleashed at last – and in your mate's case, he will become a fully corporeal, fully human being, exactly as he was in the moment that Izanagi imprisoned him in the blade."

Shinobu's face lit up with wonder and happiness – and my stomach lurched. What had happened at Avalon Books when Ebisu began to draw the wakizashi from its sheath? Shinobu had collapsed in agony, hands at his chest, bleeding. Just like in my vision of the battle with the Nekomata.

"He was dying," I said abruptly. "When Izanagi trapped him in the sword, Shinobu was already bleeding to death. If breaking the seal returns him to how he was the moment before that happened, then..."

The animated happiness drained from Shinobu's face as he realized the implications. "No," he said hollowly, looking at me. "Not again. Not when we have only just..."

I reached out and our fingers entwined. "No," I agreed firmly. "Shinobu, Ebisu is wrong. Breaking the final seal and unleashing the full powers of the Sword of the Heavenly—"

"Sword of the Gathering Clouds of Heaven," the dragon broke in.

"Yes, that. It's the last thing we want to do. I know that it's the last thing Izanagi wants as well, but that isn't a good enough reason to just go ahead and do it – not for us, even if it is for Ebisu. Izanami would go ballistic if she sensed the sword's full energy in the mortal realm again. She'd send everything she had after us, and if she managed to get hold of the sword, she'd be able to break out of Yomi in a finger snap. Then it would be bye-bye to our world. We *can't* break the last seal. We mustn't." I met Silver Fangs' glowing gaze and forced myself to hold it. "I'm really sorry, but Ebisu's plan doesn't work."

"You have misunderstood," said the dragon, and somehow her vast eyes seemed kind. "Think back to the tales you were taught as children and you will see. Izanami does not want freedom. She has never wanted to leave Yomi. All Izanami has ever desired is for her husband to keep his promise. She will never stop fighting – the war in the mortal realm will never end – until that promise is kept. Izanagi must be sent back to Yomi."

"But he wouldn't stay there," Shinobu objected. "Yomi is not for gods. It is for denizens of the Underworld and for the dead—"

I let out a choked sound – half gasp, half sob. My hands flew up instinctively, concealing my expression from Shinobu as I frantically worked it through in my head.

"Mio?"

I get it. I get it. Oh, God, I finally understand.

Shinobu caught my shoulders, supporting my weight as I sagged. "What is it? Mio, talk to me. Tell me what is wrong."

My hands curled into fists against my face. I slowly let them drop and forced myself to look up into the smoky depths of Shinobu's eyes. "They want me to use the sword to send Izanagi to the Underworld. For good. They want me to kill him."

CHAPTER 18

THE
RED THREAD

"**A**re you out of your mind?" Shinobu demanded of the dragon, low and furious, all his deferential respect burned away. "Even Ebisu admitted that gods cannot truly die – and certainly not at the hands of a mortal."

The cloud of feathery blue filaments shifted around the dragon's ears as she tilted her head. "The Sword of the Gathering Clouds of Heaven is unlike any other sword. It may do what no other weapon can. It is a god-killing blade. This is why, when Izanagi tired of his wife's creatures hunting him, and it, he chose to place it in the hands of a human family. After all, he believed, no mortal would ever be able to use it against him. No ordinary human could face a god in battle and win. Yet your mate has carried the sword with her and fought with it many times. Her ancestors absorbed particles of the sword's energy for generations. The sword has already bonded with her and has apparently chosen her to be its bearer. She is no ordinary mortal."

"He will kill her!" Shinobu snarled.

"One way or another, the battle would end in her death," the dragon agreed calmly. "Even should she succeed, the terrible forces set free by the death of a god would destroy anyone standing within range. Certainly anyone who was touching the blade. That is inevitable."

Shinobu stared at her in horror. "And you – you would ask her to do this?"

"No," I said, finally finding the strength to speak up. My voice came out strangled and I had to clear my throat as I disentangled myself from Shinobu's embrace, placing the tips of my fingers on his lips to quiet him when he would have spoken. "She's not asking me to do it. Are you? That's why Sharp Silver Fangs of the Crescent Moon hasn't given us the wakizashi yet. She's giving us a choice."

"Of course," the dragon said, as if surprised. "This war is between gods. It is born of their selfishness, fear and insanity. No human should ever have been dragged into it. You have both already suffered greatly and for five times the proper span of even the most long-lived mortals' existence. If you wish, you may remain here in the dream realm, and you will be safe from the Kami. You will never grow old. Never be parted again. In a few decades or so, you will develop the ability to control your environment with your minds and shape it to your will as I do. In the meantime, you may stay with me, and I will protect you and provide you with all that you need."

"That's very kind of you," I said quietly.

"Not at all. I will enjoy your company."

"So that is our choice?" Shinobu said, half speaking to himself. "To stay forever in the land of dreams while the human realm burns, or return home, fight Izanagi and die."

The dragon didn't answer. She didn't need to.

Shinobu took both my hands in his and stared down at them with glittering eyes. When he spoke, his voice was hollow. "Why does fate keep bringing us together, only to tear us apart? Why is there no other choice but this?"

I couldn't answer. I stared at the familiar shape of his jaw, the glossy mess of his drying hair, the lines of his brow, and longed to comfort him. That was all. Just to be able to comfort him.

"Do you remember," I said, slowly, "when we were little and Hitomi the kitchen maid told us the story of the red thread? How some people are born tied together by a long scarlet string that no one can see? The red thread is fate. People joined in this way would always be searching for each other, always moving towards each other, even if they never realized it until the moment they met.

Remember she said that the red thread may stretch, or tangle, but never, ever break?"

A pained half-smile twitched at one corner of his mouth. "You stole the red silk from your mother's embroidery box and tied our little fingers together."

"Which only lasted until bath time, when Father very firmly cut us apart again." I stroked his left little finger with mine. "I still believe in that thread, Shinobu. I know it's there. I can feel it, even if I can't see it. We were always meant to be together. But maybe … maybe we weren't meant to be together forever."

"Mio-dono…"

"Shin-chan." I forced myself to smile into his anguished eyes through the welling tears. "If none of this had ever happened, if Izanagi and the Nekomata had never come to the village, if we had grown old together in my family's home the way we dreamed, we would have chosen this, wouldn't we? To be together as long as we could. And, when it was time, to die together. After all these years, we finally get our wish."

He whispered, "You have already made up your mind, my love."

"Haven't you? Where you go…"

He raised my hands and pressed them to his heart, then kissed each palm. "I will follow, always."

"Humans are incomprehensible," Silver Fangs said. "You are each given a stretch of years shorter than the

234

blink of one of my eyes, yet some of you are willing to sacrifice even that tiny shining gift of life in order to save others."

Probably there was some grand sentiment that I ought to produce in answer to that, but I was all out. "Can we have the wakizashi now?" I asked instead.

Silver Fangs let out a deep sigh that sent a mini sand-devil whirling around us. Our still-damp clothes and hair dried instantly in the heat of her breath. She lifted her massive foot off the sand and uncurled her fifth and smallest toe. The wakizashi lay there, plain, battered and disconcertingly ordinary looking against her glowing scales.

The instrument of our victory – and destruction.

I reached over, picked it carefully out of her grasp and held it out to Shinobu. He hesitated for a second, then took it from me and carefully attached it to the white sash at his waist. He rested his hand on the rubbed-silk wrappings of the hilt.

"Strange," he murmured. "It feels good to wear it again."

Silver Fangs lowered her head to look directly at us. "Time grows short in the mortal realm – noon has come and gone, and your sun is beginning its journey towards rest. Tonight is the winter solstice, the longest and dark-est night, which increases the power of Izanami, goddess of all dark things. She will bring all her strength to bear on the mouth of Yomi and force it to yawn open in your realm, so that her most terrible creatures may spill free and hunt for the blade. It will happen at midnight. Izanagi will be drawn there, to the mouth of Yomi, and so will the god-killing blade. Let the sword lead you, and when you reach the place where Izanagi stands, you will have found your battleground. You must kill him there and force him into hell."

I nodded. "I understand."

Shinobu took my hand again. "If you will move a little, Honoured Grandmother, and allow us access to the sea, we will call on Ebisu to bring us home."

"There's no need for that," Silver Fangs said. "I can transport you, if you do not mind riding on my back?"

Even after everything we had just learned, nothing could prevent the tiny thrill of primal excitement that ran through me. "I would *love* to."

"Climb up behind my mane, then," she said, uncoiling further and sliding her chin down to rest on the sand at our level. "Try not to kick me too much. You'll leave scuff marks on my hide, and they take an eon to come out."

I let out a tired, feeble little laugh. Shinobu made a cup of his hands and boosted me up.

Silver Fangs' scales were soft, like the butteriest, most expensive suede ever. I found purchase in the fluted edges of one massive scale and cautiously clambered up to sit at the back of her neck, just behind where the slim ears grew out of her skull. The drifting light filaments of her mane bobbed around me. Where they touched my skin, it tingled pleasantly. I leaned down to offer Shinobu my hand, and he climbed up to sit behind me, then nestled my body into his as if we were riding pillion on a horse.

"Ready?" Silver Fang asked, her voice vibrating through her body and shaking me right down to the bones. "Hang on."

Without further warning her head began to lift, shooting smoothly up, up, up, carrying us hundreds of feet into the air in less time than it took for me to draw in an awed breath. The g-force of her acceleration slammed us firmly against the ridged scales of her neck, but as if to be sure of our safety, the filaments of her mane wound around my wrists, and their tingly, tickly touch secured me in place. They found Shinobu's hands, resting on my waist, and wove around them too. A magical safety belt.

Below us, the dragon's massive body uncoiled like a reel of silk ribbon – boneless and fluid against the frothing grey sea. The black sky pressed down on us. Silver Fangs aimed at one of the narrow golden veins that crisscrossed the dark clouds and undulated her body into a corkscrew, threading herself deftly through it. We flipped in the air. For a heart-stopping moment both of us were hanging upside down, held in place only by our knees clamped against hot dragon scales and the grasp of those deceptively fine blue filaments. I let out a wild scream of mixed fright and exhilaration. Silver Fangs opened her jaws and trumpeted back, her voice rocking the sky.

Then we were surrounded by warm golden light. The tranquil sky around us was filled with towering cloud castles bigger than the Palace of Westminster and tinted with all the fiery shades of sunset. She plunged straight into the nearest cloud edifice. As we flew further into the mist, it changed colour, from red-gold to a deep blue-silver that nearly matched the shade of Silver Fangs' scales. Finally we broke out of the cloud – into darkness. There were no stars and no moon, and I couldn't see anything but black below us. When I craned my neck back, I realized there wasn't a sky above us, but a ceiling – a massive ceiling of sandy-coloured stone that stretched as far as the eye could see in all directions.

"Nearly there!" Silver Fangs carolled. I could hear the joy of flying in her voice. It made her sound eager and almost young. "Brace yourselves for the next part!"

She pointed her nose directly at the ceiling blocking our way and surged upwards, her body straightening into a vertical line like an arrow. We shot towards the stone – the individual blocks looming larger and larger at an alarming rate.

That was when I realized she was intending to fly headlong into the ceiling.

"Oh, shiiiiitt!" I screamed.

Silver Fangs' nose hit the stone blocks – and

disappeared, gliding smoothly into them as if they were completely insubstantial. Her face, ears and mane all followed. The ceiling hurtled towards us. Shinobu tightened his grip on my waist, curving his larger frame around mine to protect me – as if anything could protect either of us from an impact like that.

We hit the stones.

I think the impact knocked me unconscious for a second. The next thing I knew, the dragon's warm scales were no longer beneath me, and my hands were free. I opened my eyes to see a swirling blue sea above me, then realized it wasn't real water, but paint. I knew that paint job.

We were on the floor of Ebisu's shop. I was sprawled on my back with Shinobu beneath me. Both of us were breathing and in one piece. Silver Fangs had known what she was doing – of course. Jack, Dad and Hikaru made a semicircle around us, apparently frozen with shock.

I started to sit up, and the sword, lying against my spine, roared to life in a blaze of energy that set my back on fire. I jerked involuntarily and put a hand on the ground to steady myself, holding in a groan with an effort. *Oh, God. It's awake.*

I could feel its energy stretching, testing out the limits of the last, flawed seal that still partially bound it. Its vibration was deeper and stronger. I could almost hear its voice. All at once I knew that there would be no unsheathing the blade, no fighting with it, until I was face-to-face with Izanagi. It was already too powerful. I wouldn't be able to control it. When the time came to go up against the god, I would just have to rely on the sword's craving for destruction to do the job that needed to be done. And once I had succeeded or failed, it wouldn't matter any more.

The sword wouldn't be able to enslave me if I was dead.

All this played out in my mind in a split-second. I met Shinobu's eyes and mouthed the words, *Don't tell them.*

Shinobu gave me a tiny, discreet nod, and I knew that he had understood.

Then the moment of shocked stillness was over — and everyone piled down onto us at once. Jack grabbed me into a hug, locking her arms around my neck. Hikaru caught Shinobu by the front of his hakama and kissed him full on the lips. "You're alive! I never thought I'd be so glad to see you, Tall, Dark and Gorgeous!"

Something struck me as slightly different about Hikaru, but before I could figure out what it was, or decide if I needed to rescue Shinobu, who looked shell-shocked, Jack was talking to me.

"That was hands down the coolest thing I've ever seen!" she squeaked. I'd never heard her voice hit that pitch before. "A dragon! You actually rode on a real, live dragon!"

"Wait a minute." I struggled out of her grip so that I could breathe. "How did you know about that?"

"That was my doing." Ebisu's familiar voice made me look sideways, over the top of Jack's head. The old man was seated on his stool next to the till, drinking tea, with his cane propped against his knee. He looked, if possible, even more shrunken and rumpled than before. In the few hours – no more than, what, six? – since I'd left the mortal realm this morning, he seemed somehow to have lost mass, and his eyes in his sallow face were surrounded by purplish shadows. He might be unkill-able, but the effort of helping us seemed to be taking a pretty awful toll regardless. Still, he gave me a little wave, then pointed behind me. "We've been watch-ing you in my water mirror. Just watching, mind you. There's no sound."

My face must have betrayed complete horror. Watching us? The whole time? What if they'd read our lips, what if they'd worked out what Silver Fangs had said? They'd never let us go!

"Don't worry," my father said dryly. He gathered me into one of his trademark awkward dad-hugs. I could feel him shaking a little bit, and he, too, looked drawn and tired. "I looked away during all the personal moments. Frankly, it was that or lose my breakfast."

"And I made Hikaru look away," Jack said. "Although, seriously, at one point I was starting to wonder if you two were just going to stay in the dream realm and mack forever."

I saw Shinobu's lips twitch at that. I was so relieved they hadn't rumbled us that I managed a sort of feeble giggle. Dad gave me a pat on the shoulder, then stood and held his hand out to Shinobu, who took it and let Dad pull him upright. The rest of us followed. At which point I got my first really good look at Hikaru and felt my eyebrows jump up and try to hide in my hair.

"Hikaru ... um ... did you ... make kind of a *change* since I last saw you?"

Hikaru sighed. She – yes, clearly and very definitely she – reached out to hug me. "It's a Kitsune thing. Can we just leave it at that?"

I took that to mean I should shut up about it. My eyes shot to Jack, who was wearing a slightly guilty, conflicted expression. Then I checked Shinobu. He seemed entirely unphased. That probably meant gender-change was an accepted part of folklore about fox spirits – which would explain quite a lot, now I came to think of it. Interesting. And the most interesting thing of all was that Jack didn't seem happier about it.

I hugged Hikaru back. "Of course we can, Friendly Neighbourhood Fox Spirit. But no more kissing my boy-friend on the mouth, though."

"Why?" she asked. A reckless light danced in her eyes, and her grin turned slightly manic. "Jealous? I can always give you a little smooching, too, to even things out."

Jack's glare could have sterilized a tray of my parents'

dental equipment. "Is that all you think about, Furball?"

"What?" Hikaru asked innocently, spreading her hands. "I'm just trying to be fair."

My father stepped forward, deftly inserting himself between Hikaru and me and Jack's death stare. "So, we finally have the wakizashi. What now? I assume that the dragon told you how you're supposed to use it?"

Out of the frying pan into the fire. I hesitated, trying to work out how to play this, but before I could formulate an answer, Ebisu put his teacup down and picked up his cane. He eased himself to his feet with a muffled groan. "I think that we are about to have visitors."

Shinobu was by my side in an instant. "Is it Izanagi?"

My hand shot back to the sword's hilt. Its fierce vibration jumped up a notch at my touch. It was yearning to be freed. I let go quickly. *Damn.* I couldn't fight Izanagi yet. I had to wait until midnight and the opening of the mouth of Yomi. "Should we run while we have the chance?" I demanded, my eyes heading to the STAFF ONLY door at the rear of the shop.

"No, it is not Izanagi," Ebisu said. "And I wouldn't advise you to flee, although one of your number may wish that he had in ... oh, about ten seconds..."

"What—?" Jack began.

The door of the shop flew open with a jangling of the bell. Rachel and my mother stumbled inside.

They were grubby, rumpled and clearly exhausted.

Mum had somehow lost her shoes. Rachel had a glistening trail of vivid-green slime all across her front and down one leg.

"Oh. Good." Rachel's eyes drifted over all of us, and she nodded. "You're back. Happy to see you again, Shinobu. Nice that you're not dead or whatever. I'm just going to…" She sat down on the floor, then laid flat and closed her eyes. "Wake me if the world ends."

"You!" Mum snarled. She dropped her shoulder bag, stalked across the shop to where my father stood and punched him right in the gut. He doubled over with a hoarse wheeze.

"You slimy, arrogant, lying *rat*! How dare you hide the truth about my *own daughter* from me? If you ever, ever try to exclude me in this way again, I swear that I will rip out your deceitful tongue and beat you senseless with it. Are we clear, Takashi? *Are we?*"

"Clear. Absolutely," Dad gasped, straightening up. "Never again."

"And another thing—" she began.

I brushed past Shinobu and my dad and flung myself at her.

CHAPTER 19

REUNION

"**O**h, sweetheart," Mum said, giving me the world's best hug. One of her hands rubbed my back in the same gentle rhythm she'd been using to comfort me since I was a baby. "I'm so sorry I wasn't here for you. It's OK now. You're OK. Everything is going to be fine."

It wasn't. It was going to be the exact opposite of fine. The clock hanging on the wall behind her said that it was just gone two, which meant that in less than ten hours, I would have to face Izanagi at the mouth of hell. I would watch Shinobu fall again – this time truly and forever – and then I would have to fight a vicious, evil god. And then I was going to die.

Held in Mum's arms, I was suddenly ambushed by memories of Okaasan. My first mother. Mum smelled of Chanel No. 5 and dry cleaning. Okaasan had smelled of sandalwood-scented soap and the herbs that her silk

245

kimonos were packed in to keep moths from eating them. Okaasan would never have embraced me in public this way, or argued with my father, or raised a hand to him.

Okaasan was – had been – so very different from Mum. A perfect yamato nadeshiko, the spirit of Japanese womanhood. She had been taller than me, quiet and thoughtful and gentle. Graceful in everything she did. She never made a hurried move, and never raised her voice – not even to me and Shinobu and my two younger brothers. But she was as strong as iron underneath her beauty, and my proud warrior father had asked for and listened to her advice in all important things.

I remembered Okaasan crying over me as I tossed and turned in that final awful fever that took my life. She had held my hand and I had felt the cool drops fall onto my burning skin like snowflakes. It was one of only two occasions in my entire life that I had seen her cry. The other was when Shinobu did not return. When I heard her sobs, I knew I was going to die. I knew I was going to break her heart.

Mum cried all the time. On the right day of the month, a commercial with a puppy in it was enough to set her off. When she was really upset, though, she didn't cry. She got angry. And she got things done.

Two mothers, centuries apart, without a thing in common except one. Me.

Mum was about to lose her only daughter, exactly as Okaasan had.

I'll leave our world better and safer than I found it this time. You will be OK, Mum. I promise. You will.

My shoulders shook once, convulsively. But my eyes stayed dry. I'd run out of tears, and I was glad of it. Finally, I eased away from her and forced my mouth into a smile.

"I'm really, really glad that you're back. Even though I kind of wish you were still safe in Paris."

"Yes, well I wouldn't mind being in a nice little cafe somewhere drinking fabulous coffee and eating ridiculously expensive chocolates, either," Mum admitted. "But only if you and your numbskull of a father were there with me. Mio, why didn't you tell us the truth and ask for help?"

"I didn't know how. I didn't think you – anyone – would believe me. And I thought Dad would blame me and hit the roof."

"She was actually right about that," my dad confessed. "Although I got over myself quite quickly, to be fair. Shinobu threatened to gut me if I upset her any more."

I looked at Shinobu in surprise. "You did?"

His cheeks darkened, and he looked down at his feet.

"So this is Shinobu," Mum said, letting go of me fully and stepping forward. She looked him slowly up and down, a process which he endured better than I did.

I whined, "Muuuum…"

"Shush, honey. You're really five hundred years old?" she asked him doubtfully.

"Not really," Shinobu said in his grave, thoughtful way. "I have only lived seventeen years in the real world."

"Rachel did say something about that. Come here; let me look at you." Mum gestured imperiously, and after a moment's hesitation, Shinobu bent down so that she could cup his face in her small, delicate fingers. She stared up at him, dark gaze piercing. He stayed still, but behind his back I saw his hands find each other and his fingers lace together, as if it was an effort not to fidget. I didn't blame him.

"Rachel also says that you helped save her and did a lot of other heroic things. I think you must have a great deal of character to have survived everything that's happened to you, Shinobu, and I'm very grateful for all that you've done for my family. But I'm fully aware that you've been hanging out in my house with my underage daughter completely unsupervised the whole time I've been gone. I will be keeping my eye on you from now on."

Shinobu nodded respectfully, not moving out of my mother's grasp. I couldn't stand it.

"Mum! Shinobu's been a – a perfect gentleman!"

"And I was there at least some of the time," my father put in.

"There is no such thing as a perfect gentleman, Mio. And you don't count, Takashi. You can never tell when

Mio's lying about anything." She fixed her eyes back on Shinobu. "I'm not saying that I don't approve. But if you're the sort of young man that I want for my daughter – and I think you are – you won't have a problem with me looking out for her. When this mess is sorted out, we can get to know each other properly."

Shinobu nodded again. Mum smiled at him and slid her hands down to pat his shoulders, and he smiled back, his expression a little dazed. *Damn. Dazzled by Mum Power.*

"'This mess' being … the imminent apocalypse?" my dad asked, apparently unable to leave well enough alone.

Mum ignored his tone magnificently. "Yes, that. Now, could anyone else murder a sandwich and a cup of tea? Because I've had a heck of a day."

Jack and Hikaru, who'd retreated to the till area with Ebisu during the family drama, crept out. Jack raised her hand. "I'm starving."

"Me too," Hikaru said.

"Ah, the appetites of the young," Ebisu said, smiling serenely as he limped towards my mother and offered her his hand. "It is a pleasure to meet you, Mrs Yamato. You are almost exactly as I had imagined. Let's go upstairs to my flat and see what we can find to eat, yes?"

"You might want to put me in charge of that," my dad said, hurrying after them. "She's a terrible cook."

"Stuff it," my mum retorted as Ebisu led her away.

"I'm still not talking to you."

And just like that, our motley crew had another member. My mum.

Sweet baby Jebus, how did this happen?

"Sorry about that," I whispered to Shinobu.

"Your father – your first father – was a great deal harder on me when I approached him to ask his permission to court you," Shinobu replied softly. "I do not think your mother will require me to beat her to a standstill in a kenjutsu match."

"What?" Rachel suddenly jerked upright. "Who? Where? Is the world ending yet?"

"It's me, you're in Ebisu's shop and don't panic – world-ending is off the lunchtime menu," Jack said, crouching down next to her. "You OK?"

Rachel rubbed her eyes. "Yeah. Just a bit wrung out. Mrs Yamato is … well, she's definitely a handful."

"Thanks for taking care of her," I said. "Although – why did you bring her here? I thought you were going back to the house."

"Ah." Rachel made an apologetic face at me as she climbed to her feet. "Um. Bad news there, I'm afraid. The house is surrounded by a pack of wild-dog things that apparently really like the taste of human. I only just got your mum away from there. I'm not saying that you couldn't fight your way in, Mio, but … London is a war zone right now. And it's getting worse all the time."

We sat on the floor of Ebisu's shop on a blanket that my mum had spread out to catch crumbs, while everyone – Jack and Rachel, Hikaru, Shinobu, Ebisu, my parents and I – sat on cushions to devour a meagre selection of cheese slices, slightly stale crisps and nuts from Ebisu's kitchen. It was … bizarre. The oddest thing of all was how downright normal it all seemed. Just a jolly indoor picnic with an immortal fox spirit, a trapped god, a five-hundred-year-old warrior boy and the rest of the gang. You know. The usual.

"Well, I suppose it's better than nothing. I'm kind of surprised you even have food in your kitchen," Jack said to Ebisu around a mouthful of peanuts. "Do you actually need to eat?"

"Jack!" Rachel elbowed Jack, ignoring her sputter as she choked. "I apologize for her manners. She wasn't raised in a barn, honestly."

"Oh, that's all right," Ebisu said placidly, sipping yet another cup of tea. "I do need to eat, but not what you would call food. We eat energy. The ambient energy of the universe, generally, although other kinds of energy will do. The nexus here keeps me quite well fed. But that doesn't mean I can't eat human food, or enjoy it. Sadly, however, I haven't had time to do my Internet shopping this week."

"This is perfectly fine, thank you, Mr Ebisu," Mum

interrupted tiredly, pinching the bridge of her nose. "Can we get back to the subject at hand, please? I'm – I'm really trying to make sense of this."

"Sorry, Mrs Yamato," Rachel and Jack chorused.

"Mio, I – you were telling me that you're going to need to find some random location in London, where hell – literally, hell – is going to be … *unleashed*, and that once you're there, you'll break the spell, or whatever it is, on the sword – which will free Shinobu and turn him back into a normal human – and then you're going to have *an actual fight with Izanagi-no-Kami*, Father of the Gods, and – and somehow force him into the Underworld." She stopped and looked around as if for support. "This … doesn't strike anyone else as a bad plan? The worst plan. I mean, the absolute. Worst. Plan. Takashi?"

"I'm not exactly doing cartwheels of joy over it," my father said. He rubbed Mum's arm soothingly, and she let him, displaying her usual inability to cling to a grudge.

"Well then, say something!" she demanded. "This is our little girl. I'm sure… I mean, there has to be some other way?"

"There isn't," I contradicted flatly.

"Mio…"

"Sweetheart, I've seen Mio fight," Dad said soothingly. "She's … formidable. Amazing. She'll have the sword, which protects her and makes her stronger, and she'll have all of us. I believe she can do this. It may have been what she was born to do."

Jack chimed in, very obviously trying to lighten the mood. "Seriously, until you've seen Mimi fly through the air, do a backflip off a wall and decapitate a demon in one swipe, you're not really going to get it."

"It is pretty impressive," Rachel agreed.

"And what about that time when she summoned the sword's power with its true name and caused an earthquake in the spirit realm?" Hikaru said enthusiastically. "That was great! I'll never forget my Aunt Midori's face!"

My mum looked at them, then stared at me as if she wasn't sure she even knew me.

I put both hands up to soothe my burning cheeks and block out her expression. "Can you all please stop talking about me like I'm not here?"

Shinobu ran one finger tenderly down the line of my spine, telling me without words, *I haven't forgotten you're here*.

"Look, Mum," I said before she could start ranting again. "I understand this is a lot to take in and you're freaking out. But this isn't up for debate. We don't have any other options. If Izanagi isn't sent to Yomi, Izanami will never stop pursuing him – or the sword. You've seen what it's like out there. And Izanagi will keep hounding me, too, and I don't even know what he'll try to do to me if he catches me again. The Yamato family have been enslaved by the sword's compulsion for five hundred years. The sword has already ruined so many lives – it nearly ruined Dad's." I saw a telltale glimmer in her eye at this appeal to family feeling and knew I was on the right track with my argument.

I swallowed, then pushed on. "I'm going to have kids someday, Mum. I don't want to have to go through what Dad went through. I don't want them to have to experience what I have: fighting and killing and fear and nothing to show for it but living to pass the curse onto the next generation. It has to stop. I have the chance to make that happen today and I'm going to take it. Nothing that you or anyone can say will stop me."

Mum stared at me for a second, speechless. Then her eyes welled up and she turned her face into Dad's shoulder. "Oh my God, she grew up. When did that happen? Did we give her permission to do that?" she asked, her voice muffled.

"Nope." Dad patted Mum's back, turning suspiciously shining eyes away from me.

Jack mimed gagging and Hikaru let out a foxy snort-laugh that she hastily turned into a cough when Rachel glared at her. Because I knew it was expected, I gave them all the finger. They thought I was just doing my thing – spinning the situation to get my own way like I always did. I had no way to tell them how much this hurt – or how much I was going to hurt them all by tomorrow morning.

I didn't even dare look at Shinobu. I suddenly wondered how he felt about kids. For that matter, how did I feel about them? I'd never get the chance to find out now, would I?

Mum pulled away from Dad, sniffed briskly and wiped her face with a paper napkin. "All right, fine. You have to do this. But – but I'm coming with you, Mio! And so is your father. You're not heading out on this – this mission alone."

"We're coming, too," Rachel said seriously.

"Duh. Like you needed to tell her that," Jack said. "She knows we wouldn't kick her out to fight on her own."

"In it together," Hikaru agreed with a decisive nod. "From beginning to end."

But she was wrong about that. In the beginning it had been just me, the sword and Shinobu. In the end, that was how it would be again.

Pushing aside doubts and sadness, I gave Hikaru a serious look. "We're going to need the Kitsune to make this work, though. We have to talk to your king."

"I wish I could help with that," Ebisu said sadly, shifting on his little stool. "But I'm afraid the Kitsune wards on the spirit realm are too strong for me to break. I can't open a rupture for you."

"Should we head back to our house and use the rupture under the mulberry bush?" Jack asked.

"That's not a good idea," Rachel cut in before Hikaru could answer. "There is a lot of bad stuff sitting between us and the house, believe me. We almost got swallowed by some kind of giant slime-lizard thing at the end of this road. Isn't there somewhere closer?"

Hikaru ran her hands through her hair distractedly. "We have rupture sites all over London, but the house is the closest one by a long way. Damn, if only I was old enough to open my own."

"Aren't you?" Jack asked.

Hikaru stopped tugging on her hair and stared at Jack. A strange look passed between them – almost like Hikaru was asking for reassurance. Jack quirked her eyebrows and nodded.

Hikaru took a deep breath. Then she squared her shoulders. "Maybe. Maybe I am. But I need, like, greenery. Soil. Something to anchor to. Anyone got any ideas?"

"I think I can help," Ebisu said. "Come with me."

He limped his way to the STAFF ONLY door and into the tiny lobby filled with bundles of piled-up newspapers. Instead of heading back up the rickety stairs, though, he pulled open the outside door to reveal a glimpse of a dingy courtyard floored with cracked concrete that was stained vivid green with algae. He stepped to one side, leaning on his stick, and gestured Hikaru outside.

I hung back at the STAFF ONLY door with Shinobu, Rachel and my parents behind me, as Hikaru went out into the courtyard with Jack and looked around. Her copper eyebrows crimped together. "I guess this counts," she said. "But normally beginners use something really solid and alive. Like a big tree or a hill. This would be more tricky."

"Could Hiro or Araki do it?" Jack asked, naming the two other fox spirits that we'd met and fought alongside. Both of them were over three hundred years old. *What is Jack up to with this?*

Hikaru rubbed her hands together anxiously. "Maybe? Yeah, I think so."

"Then try," Jack said. "If you can't make it work, then we'll think of something else, OK? But I think you can. I really do."

When the fox spirit still looked anxious, Jack reached out – apparently without thinking – and put her arm around Hikaru's shoulder for a quick hug. Hikaru's expression conveyed shocked pleasure. I felt my eyes widen. Rachel let out a huff of surprise. Jack wasn't a hugger – or much of a toucher at all, really – except with people that she absolutely trusted and felt close to. As far as I knew, that was her mum, her sister and me.

And now, apparently, Hikaru.

Jack turned away from Hikaru to look at the rest of us. "Come on outside, everyone. We'll give it a go, just to see if it works."

Hikaru was gazing down at her sneaker-clad feet, but I could see just the faintest quiver of a smile. Sadness pierced me as I realized that I wasn't going to get to see whatever happened next between these two. By the time they got their act together, I would be gone.

"OK, Mimi?" Jack asked. I looked up and realized that everyone else had filed past me into the garden – apart from Shinobu, who was hesitating on the threshold with a concerned look.

"Yep, sorry. Just thinking." I went forward quickly, brushing Shinobu's hand with mine to reassure him.

There wasn't really enough room in the courtyard for all of us, even with Ebisu staying inside. We jostled around, trying to find places to put our feet without stepping all over each other or brushing against the slimy green concrete walls. Mum drew me towards her so that I ended up standing between her and Dad, and Shinobu stationed himself on Dad's other side.

Looking back at the shop, I saw a half-dead-looking vine of some kind clinging tenaciously to the battered white render around the door. That meant Hikaru would have a little bit more to "anchor" to than just the algae out here. That was good. Probably. Well, I hoped so, anyway.

"Are you all as far back as you can get?" Hikaru asked.

A couple of us shuffled a bit to show that we'd done our best. She rolled her eyes. "Fine. All right then. All right." She turned back to stare at the doorway. "Brace yourselves, cupcakes. Time to go through the looking glass."

Behind Hikaru's back, I saw Jack cross her fingers.

CHAPTER 20

"OOPS" IS AN UNDERSTATEMENT

Hikaru shook out her hands and pressed them together, palm to palm. Her tail lashed once, then began swishing rhythmically, making wide figures of eight in the air behind her. Tiny sparks trailed from the tail, lingering like the light patterns left behind by a sparkler. She began that deep, musical crooning low in her throat, and I felt all the hairs on the back of my neck jump to attention.

My mum grabbed my hand and squeezed it. Her eyes were wide with a combination of apprehension and excitement. On my other side, my dad stood solidly, gaze riveted on Hikaru. His shoulder brushed mine. I would never admit it to anyone, but this was sort of … nice. Having them both with me now, just for a little while, before…

Slowly, tendrils of fizzing white electricity began to

squirm to life against the wall of Ebisu's shop. They wove into place around the drooping vine, sprouting as we watched, growing into a new plant – a glowing rectangular vine of electrical magic that encircled the door. Ebisu, who was still standing in the doorway, tilted his head to one side as if listening, then smiled at Hikaru. He bowed a shallow, stiff bow to all of us and stepped back, pulling the door shut behind him.

I guess that's goodbye from him, then.

"It's working," Jack said. "It's working!"

Hikaru's mesmerizing song grew louder. Her tail swished faster, blazing with sparks. The electric vine around the door brightened. The light was so intense now that it was hard to look at it. But I had to look, because Jack was right – it was working. The space inside Hikaru's vine was beginning to fade away into darkness.

Hikaru's tail lashed upwards, the white fur tip alive with electricity. A jagged spear of lightning jumped from it and hit the glowing vine. She shouted something – a phrase in some strange language that I didn't know. The words boomed through the little courtyard, making us all stagger as a deep grinding shook the concrete underfoot.

Then silence. Hikaru dropped her hands. "Wow. Huh. That … that actually wasn't so bad after all," she said, panting a little.

"You nailed it!" Jack jumped up and down and

punched Hikaru on the shoulder. "I knew you could! In your FACE, Midori! Whoop!"

"Thanks," the fox spirit said, laughing as she gave her arm a quick rub. The look in her eyes when she smiled at Jack was almost painfully obvious. Jack seemed to see it a second after I had. Her exuberance drained away, and she bit her lip.

Hikaru's face fell. She sighed and made a gesture towards the rupture. "Well, everyone pile in, then."

The doorway was narrow, so we went in two by two: Jack and Rachel entered the darkness first, followed by Mum and Dad. When Shinobu and I followed, I immediately found myself squashed up against my dad's back.

He tried to make room for me, but there wasn't really anywhere to go. In front, Jack made a little squeaking noise, as if she was being crushed.

"Right, this is the trickiest bit," Hikaru said. I felt her cram herself into the rupture directly behind me, and Shinobu grunted as if she had maybe stood on him. "Sorry. Give me a minute."

The light from the courtyard opening snapped off, leaving us in total darkness.

"Hmm," I heard the fox spirit mutter. "Might as well go for it, I suppose. Geronimo!"

A deep rumbling sound shook the narrow space around us. I put my free hand out to the side for balance and felt the dry soil and whiskery roots trembling under my palm. Tiny bits of earth pattered down on our heads.

"Ick!" That was Rachel. Jack shushed her.

Somewhere ahead of me, a tiny shaft of light suddenly broke through the blackness. The light grew, widening slowly into a circle, like a pupil dilating. Hikaru was leaning into me now, and I could hear her harsh breathing. I braced myself and took her weight. The rumbling deepened, and the hole grew even wider.

"Is it … wide enough … yet?" Hikaru asked raspily.

"Yep. It's perfect," Jack called back cheerfully. Actually, peering between my parents' shoulders, I could see that we'd all probably have to step high and duck a bit to get out – but it seemed cruel to quibble. I kept quiet, and so did everyone else.

The rumbling stopped. The circle stopped growing. Hikaru let out a relieved sigh and straightened up. "All right, it's fixed."

Jack and Rachel trooped forward, followed closely by Mum and Dad, who were clearly eager to escape the cramped, earthy cave of Between. I was about to congratulate Hikaru when I heard a muffled scream – Mum – and an angry voice shout, "Halt intruders!"

Behind me, Hikaru whispered, "Oops."

I bolted forward and leapt out of the entrance – only to plough into the back of my dad for the second time. This time I didn't stop to say sorry. I zipped around him and shoved my mum behind me into Shinobu's arms, knowing he would keep her safe.

We were in the heart of the Kitsune Kingdom, at the bottom of the deep natural amphitheatre of mossy turf that the fox spirits used as their court. High above us, crowding around the rim of the amphitheatre, were ancient trees with trunks so vast that four people standing with their arms extended couldn't encircle one of them.

Hikaru had opened the rupture in the small, smooth hillock that sat at the centre of the court.

The king's throne.

It was difficult right now to make out the rich green-gold of the tree trunks, the silver canopy of leaves that formed a roof high above, or even the rows of grassy steps lining the walls of the amphitheatre which the Kitsune usually sat on when the court was in session. The whole place was enveloped in dim twilight. The last time we'd been here, thousands of glowing fox lights had drifted among the trees, providing light that was as clear and steady as the sun. At the moment there were only four fox lights, bobbing just above our heads. They belonged, I guessed, to the extremely well-armed and very pissed-off looking pair of Kitsune guards, in human form, who were ranged in front of Jack and Rachel.

Jack and Rachel, wisely, were standing completely still, with their hands in the air.

"What are you doing here?" one guard demanded.

She was a three-tails, and she held a modern composite bow. The nocked arrow was aimed directly at Rachel. "How did you appear in our realm this way?"

"Did you come to spy, humans? To steal?" the other guard – a two-tails – hissed. He held a long wooden spear with an angular metal blade, and as he spoke, he jabbed at Jack's face. She flinched back instinctively.

Crap, this is bad.

Rachel's hands shot out and plucked the spear from the guard's grasp, then snapped it in half across her knee. "Don't point. It's rude." She dropped the pieces contemptuously on the ground.

Aaand now it's much, much worse.

As one, the guards took a wary step back. There was a flare of light: both sets of tails had gone up defensively and were crackling with electricity. The male guard's tail let out a purplish spurt of panicked lightning. He caught it one-handed, letting it spike between his fingers in place of his broken weapon.

Keeping my hand away from my sword hilt with an effort, I eased forward, urging Jack behind me and hip-checking Rachel to force her to let me through when she resisted. I searched the guards' faces in vain for a sign of recognition. They didn't know who I was, and I didn't know them, either. *Damn.*

"Listen," I said, showing them my empty hands. "This isn't what you think. I'm sure you've heard of me – I'm

Yamato Mio-dono, the sword-bearer. I am a friend. We're all friends here."

The female guard stared hard at me for a moment, then lowered her bow so that the arrow pointed at the ground. "I've heard about the sword-bearer."

"Don't *believe* them!" the mouthy male one cried. "They're *humans*!" He jerked his hand back as if to let the ball of lightning in his hand fly—

The amphitheatre flooded with vibrant light, as bright as day. I looked up to see a whole constellation of pale blue fox lights filling the space under the silver leaves.

"The sword-bearer's powers seem to be evolving at a prodigious rate, indeed," said a familiar voice. It echoed with ancient power that betrayed its light, youthful quality and, as always, made my knees go slightly wobbly.

The guards drew back from us – the un-thrown lightning bolt in the male one's hand snuffed out like a candle – and prostrated themselves on the grass as the king stalked into view.

She was in her human form, a slender young girl, shorter than me, with pale skin and a light dusting of freckles. Having now met Hikaru as a girl, I saw that the resemblance between them was really striking, even though Hikaru was much taller and more athletically built. They could have been sisters. The king's copper hair was piled on top of her head in a mess of corkscrew curls, and she was swathed from neck to ankle in what I was sure had to be the fanciest dressing gown in this or any other realm – scarlet velvet with a stiff mandarin collar, huge bell-shaped sleeves and yards and yards of winking golden embroidery. Her great fan of tails – nine in all, showing that she was at least a thousand years old – was currently lit up with a sizzling glow of blue fire, tiny bolts of lightning leaping from tail to tail.

I caught a glimpse of acid green eyes blazing with tumultuous emotions that I couldn't identify and looked away hurriedly.

"Your Majesty—"

She cut me off. "This rupture punched through our protective wards as if they were tissue paper and opened my own personal gateway, in the middle of the night" – *oh, crap, that's right: day and night are reversed in the spirit realm* – "without any prior warning. How is this possible? And how on earth did you imagine that I would allow you – even you – to get away with it?" Her voice was icy, but beneath the ice I sensed something else. Unhappiness. Almost fear.

The king? Afraid? Of … what?

"Grandmother." Hikaru was suddenly right next to me, haphazardly brushing soil off her hands. I only just controlled a startled jump. I'd almost forgotten about her: it had taken her long enough to turn up. But, of course – she'd had to close the rupture behind us before she could do anything else.

The king seemed to turn into a statue as she stared at her youngest descendant. Her gaze turned glassy. It was as if she couldn't believe her eyes.

I heard Hikaru gulp. "Grandmother, this is my fault. Please don't blame Mio or the others – they didn't know that I was going to bring us here. I apologize deeply for using the throne gateway without permission. I never meant to offer you any disrespect. I honestly wasn't even sure that I could open a rupture at all, let alone lift the wards to let us in, and I didn't stop to think of the consequences."

Great. Now you tell us.

"You did this?" the king whispered, her face still immobile with shock. "You're not even half a century old. Great and little gods, you must be the most powerful Kitsune to be born since…"

"Since you, Grandmother?" Hikaru finished when the other fox spirit's voice trailed off.

The king's face lit with fury. She marched towards Hikaru and dealt her a ringing blow upside the head.

"You thoughtless, reckless child! How dare you dis-appear without a word to me or anyone, sneak into the mortal realm against my express instructions, enter a battle with a swarm of Shikome *and then not even bother to let us know you are alive*?!"

"I – I thought – your scrying mirror…" Hikaru said weakly, clutching the back of her skull.

"The power explosion from the sword shattered it. Scouts went out to look for you and found the city awash with monsters and no sign of you. I was worried out of my mind, Hikaru!"

On the last word her voice trembled, and the next thing I knew she was hugging Hikaru fiercely.

"I'm sorry," Hikaru said, in a completely different tone to her formal apology earlier. "I really am. I didn't realize… I didn't know you'd worry."

"Well, you should have! Perhaps I have not always been the … the most demonstrative of grandparents, but you must *know* that I love you, child. Never put me through such an ordeal again."

The king sniffed hard, then stepped back from Hikaru and took the younger Kitsune's face between her hands in a gesture that reminded me uncomfortably of my mother. Her expression grew steely. "And now, hear this. If you defy me a second time there will be consequences, Granddaughter. The only reason I am not punishing you is that it's a first offence, and I'm too bloody relieved. Once more, and you will be in exile. With your Aunt Midori and the lovely Miyako-san. Think on that."

Hikaru gulped again. The king let go of Hikaru's face, shook herself and seemed to remember that the rest of us were still there.

"You two! Get up!" She prodded one of the guards, who were still lying on the grass, with a small, bare foot.

"That may be how things are done in the Old Kingdom, but if you dive headfirst onto the grass every time you have the honour of being in my presence, you'll end up with indelible grass stains on your foreheads."

As the guards got sheepishly to their feet, she turned back to me. I thought that there might be the slightest hint of an apology in her voice when she said, "I am glad that I was not mistaken in you, Yamato Mio-dono."

"I am glad that the misunderstanding has been cleared up, Your Majesty."

"Who are the new people that you have brought to meet us?" she asked. Then her gingery eyebrows went up. "Surely not... Are these your parents, sword-bearer?"

I nodded. "This is Yamato Takashi and Yamato Aiko. I brought them here to be safe, since London is under attack by denizens of the Underworld."

Shinobu let go of my mum's shoulders and stepped out of their way. My parents – not being idiots – said nothing, just executed twin deep bows. Normally the king expected newcomers who hadn't yet been awarded a status to do a dive onto the grass pretty much exactly the way that the guards had done, but since she was apparently not in the mood for that, I let Mum and Dad get on with it.

"The family of the sword-bearer is, of course, welcome," the king said, with a gracious wave of her hand. "Given what we have observed of the state of the city, and taking into account Hikaru's somewhat precipitous actions in bringing you here, I assume that you have at last come to claim the boon that I granted you?"

"Yes, Your Majesty." But I couldn't spill the beans about that just yet, so I quickly changed the subject. "I finally know what the sword is and where it came from. It is a god-killing blade, and tonight, at midnight in the human realm, Izanami-no-Kami will open the mouth of Yomi and unleash the Underworld on London in order to try to retrieve it. If I'm to prevent the destruction of the city and perhaps our entire world, I must fight Izanami's former husband, Izanagi-no-Kami, and send him back to his wife in hell."

For once, I saw the king look thoroughly disconcerted. Her eyes flicked to the hilt of the sword protruding over my left shoulder, and then back to my face, and then, surprisingly, to my parents. "I ... see. Go on."

"We don't know where the mouth of Yomi will open, or where the battle will take place. London is already a war zone. By tonight it's likely to be even worse. I need to know that I – and everyone I've brought with me here – will be able to get to the fight in time, and in one piece. Can you help?"

"This fight concerns the fate of an entire plane. I will willingly place my soldiers – the Kitsune that you fought alongside at Battersea – at your disposal. But they are only a small force. I fear it may require more to guarantee your safety and the safety of your friends." She pursed her lips. "It is against my principles to *order* my Kingdom to war. Many of my people are not fighters by nature, nor trained warriors, though they all possess the natural weapons of the Kitsune. If that is the boon you wish to claim...?"

"It isn't," I said quickly. "There's something else that I want to ask of you, something even more important. But it would be great to convince more of your people to fight with us, if we can. Do you think some might volunteer, if we explained the situation to them?"

"It is possible," she conceded. "I have made you an adopted daughter of the Kitsune, and you therefore have the right to speak in court, as we all do. If you wish to address my people to plead your cause, I can arrange it."

"Address your...?" It took a moment for her meaning to click, and then I quailed, remembering the intimidatingly packed amphitheatre on my first visit here. Most of the Kitsune had looked like they wanted to eat me for breakfast. No way could I get up in front of all those fox spirits and get them to take me seriously. They'd laugh in my face, if they let me speak at all...

The king arched an eyebrow. "If you do not wish me to order my people to fight, there is nothing else I can do in the matter. As a ruler, I can command, but not beg. You have the power to ask, which I do not." She hesitated for a second, then added, "If any human can convince them to take up this battle, it would be you, Yamato Mio-dono."

When she put it like that … it was still terrifying. But maybe – maybe she was right. I might be able to win at least a few of them over. The worst that could happen was that they'd say no.

That, or you could expose your pants to them all again.

I cleared my throat. "We don't have much time."

"Then you must make up your mind swiftly. I can summon my people almost immediately if that is what you want."

I sighed. "Yes, please."

"Very well. Guards! Rouse the Kingdom. Tell my people that the sword-bearer wishes to address them and does so with the king's blessing and favour. Attendance is mandatory. Then alert my soldiers and have them ready themselves for battle." She paused. "And when you've done all that, for the love of heaven, one of you bring me a cup of tea."

CHAPTER 21

DAUGHTER OF THE KITSUNE

The amphitheatre was full. I thought there were more Kitsune here now even than the first time. The grassy steps that ran around the walls of the steep bowl were jostling with foxes of every description. Classic red-and-white foxes like Hikaru and the king. Sandy-coloured foxes with huge, pointed ears and dark eyes. Tiny white foxes with black-tufted fur. Grey foxes, brown foxes, black foxes. Foxes with every number of tails possible, all the way up to eight. The whole of King Takahiro's Kingdom had turned out for this. Their curious chattering voices blended into an overwhelming tide of sound, and they were all staring at me.

I took deep, slow breaths, trying to calm my heartbeat and suppress the queasy simmering in my stomach. I had fought and survived a nine-tailed vampire-cat-demon, swarming Shikome and the worst that the dream realm had to offer. No way was a little speech going to make me ralph in public.

Right?

The king – in fox form now, and firmly back in control – approached me where I sat on the lowest tier of the steps. I was surrounded by my mum and dad and Jack and Rachel, with Shinobu's arm wrapped comfortingly around my shoulders. Hikaru had disappeared a short while ago with a promise to return before I started.

"Everyone is now present," the king said. "It is time for you to speak."

I tried to respond, but my voice came out as a squeaky whistle.

Shinobu tucked my hair behind my ear, his expression serious. "You are Yamato Mio-dono, onna bugeisha, the bearer of the god-killing blade. You are the equal of anyone in this place. You can do this."

"Listen to him, honey," Mum said warmly, as if that list of weirdness was completely normal. "We believe in you."

My dad patted my shoulder bracingly, and Rachel backed them both up with a firm nod.

"Knock 'em dead, She-Ra," Jack said. "But keep your trousers on this time."

My parents both stared at her in shock. Somehow I had managed to avoid mentioning that part of the story to either of them. I glared at her, and she gave me a help-less shrug.

With a sigh, I got to my feet and reached back to draw the sword, still sheathed in the saya, from its place in the harness. Maybe it was wrong of me to take comfort in that scorching pulse of power, like the heartbeat of a living nuclear bomb in my hand. But at this point, did it matter? The blade wasn't going to interfere with this – I was doing exactly what it wanted. *Everything* that it wanted. Soon, it would be unbound and free to attempt to destroy Izanagi, the one who had imprisoned it. The sword was *happy*. Its energy purred with the contentment of a sabre-toothed tiger about to feast on the guts of easy prey.

The king led me back to the centre of the bowl and the low green hill that was her throne. It struck me that Araki or another of the king's servants really ought to be doing this little escorting job. The fact that she was walking with me herself was a rare and pretty amazing honour. She was letting everyone within the court see that she considered me worthy of the personal attention of their ruler.

She might not be able to stoop to asking her people for their help, but it seemed she wasn't above flinging a fairly hefty hint at their heads.

We reached the base of the hillock and circled it. For the first time I saw the back of the throne. Steps like the ones in the wall of the amphitheatre, but on a much smaller scale, had been set into the smooth curve of the grass to allow someone in human form to ascend easily. That was good, because otherwise, knowing my luck, I'd have slipped in the scramble and ended up doing a face-plant in front of the entire court.

Before I could start up the hill, the king turned to me and sat, her tails fanning the air behind her gently. "Since we have a spare moment, perhaps you would enlighten me as to the nature of the boon that you intend to claim from me?"

It was framed – politely – as a request, but clearly it was a command. She was done waiting. This must have been bugging her since I'd turned cagey about it in front of my parents. Maybe even since I'd asked to hang onto the debt instead of claiming it right after we'd slain the Nekomata.

I looked around cautiously. No fox spirits sat directly behind the hill – not surprising, since you would struggle to see what was going on from that angle. The height and width of the hill blocked us from most of the amphitheatre. But Kitsune did have really acute hearing…

"I have blocked us from my people's eyes and ears," the king said. "Our conversation will be private."

Might as well get it over with.

"You … know, don't you?"

Her eyes narrowed a little. "Know what?"

"What's going to happen to me." I was surprised at how steady and matter-of-fact the statement came out. "I could see it in your face when I told you about my plan – the way you looked at my mum and dad. To succeed in sending Izanagi to hell I have to kill him. I'll never survive that, and if I don't manage to kill him, he'll slaughter me anyway. One way or another, things aren't looking that great for me past midnight tonight."

She sighed. "I'm glad you're aware of the consequences of what you intend to attempt. I was afraid it might fall on me to inform you."

"No, I know what I'm doing. But the thing is ... what you couldn't realize ... is when the sword's greatest power is summoned, Shinobu will also ... lose his life." Now my words croaked a bit, but I forged on. "That means, whether I win or lose, my friends and parents will be left alone when the battle ends. The boon that I'm asking of you is to take care of them. If Izanagi walks away and Izanami continues her assault, then the city is going to be overrun with Yomi creatures. My family and friends will need sanctuary. If I win, there will still most likely be dangers to face and they might not be fit to defend themselves. I need you to promise me that whatever happens, you'll keep them safe once I'm not here to do it."

The king stared at me, motionless, eyes wide. "Out of all the favours that I have the power to grant you, you would choose this? Didn't it occur to you to request that I shelter you from the blast of Izanagi's power? Or even to ask me, as an immortal, to fight in your place? The debt that we owe you is immeasurable. I could not turn you down."

Well, that explained why she had been so desperate to know what I was going to ask for. I looked away from her, trying to put my feelings into words.

"Your Majesty, ever since I took my grandfather's sword from its hiding place, I've had this odd feeling that came and went. I kept imagining that … that these immense forces were swirling around me, changing the universe while I stood, helpless, at the epicentre, feeling it all shift. But I had it wrong, and I realized that today. There is no great power controlling the world and forcing me to walk a predestined path. There's just me. The reason I felt the universe changing was that I was changing it. These choices, these terrible choices that kept altering the fate of the world – they were *mine*. Today I came to this moment, this choice that literally put my world in my hands, and I had the chance to walk away, and I couldn't." I looked back at her. "This is my fight. My responsibility. I know what I have to do. I just need to know that my loved ones will be safe when I'm done."

The king's whiskers trembled. She looked down at her paws, and her head lowered until her muzzle almost touched the grass. At first I didn't understand. Then I gaped like an idiot. She was bowing. She was actually bowing to *me*.

"I will grant what you ask. I do so swear, on the name of my line and the honour of my people." She straightened up slowly and fixed her eyes on me again. Spellbound, I couldn't force myself to look away. "Your Shinobu spoke the truth, you know. You are truly the equal of any in this realm."

While I struggled to come up with some reply to that, she climbed to her feet and pointed her nose to the steps. "Go on now, Yamato Mio-dono. Walk the path you have chosen. May the gods learn to fear your wrath."

"Right," I muttered. "No pressure then."

I began the short climb to the apex of the hill. The Kitsune didn't fall silent as I came into view on the crest of the throne – if anything, they got louder. I wished I had a megaphone, or my father's ability to emit a piercing whistle that threatened the eardrums of anyone within fifty yards. How was I supposed to convince them of anything if I couldn't even get them to shut it?

I saw movement on the hill a little below me. It was Hikaru. She stood up, threw her shoulders back and bellowed, "Silence!"

Her voice, magically amplified, echoed off the walls like thunder. The gossipy chatter of Kitsune voices cut off instantly. I wasn't sure if that was shock, interest or sheer affront. But they did stay quiet.

Hikaru looked up at me, gave me a thumbs up and then disappeared into a tangled whirlwind of copper and gold and white. A second later she reappeared as a fox, sat down and turned her face up to me, waiting.

Show time.

My hands clenched around the hilt and saya of the sword. It responded with a deep crackle of energy that flamed out of the mouth of the saya in blinding, rainbow-white flames. Quickly I lifted the sword into the air above my head. I held it in both palms so that all the fox spirits could see the glow of its power and recall what had happened the last time I unsheathed it here. That should keep their attention.

"You know me," I said. My words boomed, and I jumped. I sounded like that guy releasing the kraken in the *Clash of the Titans* movie. Hikaru was magically increasing my volume. I glanced down again and saw her widen her eyes at me. *Just go with it.*

"A few days ago, some of your number marched with me to fight the Nekomata at Battersea. I killed the monster and brought every one of your people home alive. And since then, I have defeated and banished the Shikome, whose taint is fatal to you, and been named a daughter of the Kitsune by your great king."

Damn, now I just sound like a big-headed prat. Where am I going with this? Some of the Kitsune stirred restlessly as the silence lengthened, and I hurried back into speech.

"In just a week, the mortal realm has seen more of the terrors of the Underworld than in a thousand years before that. None of these events are unconnected. They are the opening..." *What's that word? What is it...? Ah!* "Salvos of a deadly battle in a conflict which has raged for centuries, and which is about to break into open war and spill into the human world. A war between the father and mother of the gods. And it will be terrible."

I paused for breath and to organize my thoughts. This time the fox spirits didn't fidget.

"Tonight, Izanami and Izanagi will clash somewhere in London. In their madness and their fury, they will turn the city into a smoking crater. It will not be long before the entire human world is swallowed by shadows and blood..."

The blade let out a fierce buzz in its saya, flaring with new light. Several Kitsune startled visibly. My arm was aching. I lowered the sword, feeling its flames caress my skin as I held it diagonally across my body, as if I was ready to draw the blade at any moment.

"You might ask, what has this to do with you? The human realm is not your realm. Humans are not the business of the Kitsune. But your people are already a part of this battle. You have already fought against the Nekomata, and you have lost some of your own to the Shikome's taint. We may inhabit separate realms, but none of us are isolated. The first time that I visited the Kitsune Kingdom, one of your people explained to me that what happens in one realm inevitably influences the fate of the others. And tonight, the future of the entire world of humans hangs in the balance.

"If the mortal realm is turned to ashes, what will happen to the beautiful spirit realm? Do any of you really know? And when Izanami and Izanagi have finished breaking our world and can find nothing else to destroy there, what will prevent them from bringing their war here?

"We have one chance to stop them. One chance to prevent the destruction of London. Tonight, we can march into battle and teach the gods to fear us, as they have forced us to fear them for so long."

The blade buzzed once more, sending out a starburst of fire that danced around my body. I sucked in a deep breath, raising my sword into the air again. *Who will fight with me?*

I stood still, breathing hard, as the flames slowly died away around me. There was complete silence. If a single fox spirit had scratched a flea, I swear I would have heard it in that moment.

"I will," said Hikaru, standing. Her voice rang out, beautiful and lonely, like a heron crying in a wilderness.

A long pause. Then a deep brown fox, with a grey-streaked muzzle and four tails, stood up on the bottom tier of steps. "I will." I recognized her voice and belatedly realized that it was Araki.

Another fox, a three-tails with smoky-grey fur and a

splotchy white bib on his chest, stood up. I recognized him at once: Hiro. "I will!"

Well, it was nice to be supported, but Hiro and Araki were both soldiers. They would have fought with us anyway. *Anyone else? Anyone? Come on...*

On the step directly ahead of me, the king slowly and gracefully got up onto four paws. Her tails crackled with blue lightning as she lifted her muzzle and cried, "I will!"

A shock wave of reaction travelled around the curved walls of the amphitheatre.

Below the king, a red three-tailed fox jumped up. "I will!"

"I will!" A large black fox with five tails.

"We will! We will!" Three creamy-coloured foxes, right at the top of the bowl – a two-tails, a six-tails and a seven-tails.

"We will!" The voices filled the green bowl. Everywhere I looked Kitsune were standing. More than two thirds of the fox spirits were on their feet. My mum and dad were up, too, holding hands. Jack hopped around furiously, air-punching, while Rachel grinned. Shinobu's face was grave, but his dark eyes shone.

I did it.

We had our army.

When we returned to the spirit realm after defeating the Nekomata, the Kitsune had celebrated our victory with music, food, dancing and general revelry. It turned out that, when they had time, they traditionally celebrated the decision to go to war in exactly the same way.

In the few moments it took the king to transform back into her human form, they'd spread out colourful, beautifully embroidered cloths and fat silk cushions on the grass, and conjured up heaped silver trays and crystal bowls of delicious food and steaming golden goblets of drink. Faerie dancing music, sweet and liquid, invited even the most heavy foot to tap. Dozens of Kitsune took up that invitation, in both human and fox forms, twirling into wild, intricate shapes in groups of three or six or nine, between the picnic blankets and up and down the tiers of the amphitheatre. The bright fox lights that had bobbed high among the silver leaves of the trees had been dimmed and summoned down to hang in the air just above everyone's heads, like Chinese lanterns strung up at a party.

I thought it was a shame that Ebisu couldn't be here to enjoy this. It cast the little picnic on the floor of his shop into a pretty sad light.

The fact was we had just over seven hours to kill before we walked out into the mortal realm to fight. Nowhere was it written that those hours must be spent in my current preferred pastime of quiet brooding. It was likely at least that some of the Kitsune would die with me tonight. Die clearing a path for me, watching my back, or protecting my family from harm. They could go wild if they wanted.

I just couldn't quite summon up the energy to take part.

I sat a little way back from the rim of the amphitheatre, close enough to hear the festivities, but hidden from them by the peaceful shade of the spirit realm's trees. Everyone was well taken care of down there. When I'd slipped away, Hikaru had been exerting every foxy wile to get my dad to dance with her, and my mum had already given in to Hiro's flirtatious ways. Jack and Rachel were happily stuffing themselves with food.

And Shinobu…

"Here you are," he said, sitting down beside me, cross-legged. "This feels familiar."

Right on time. I turned my head and looked him over. "You didn't bring me Kitsune wine and peaches this time."

"No. If you want to eat and drink, I think you should join your family down there," he said.

I shrugged. "I'm not really hungry."

He shifted a bit closer, without quite touching me. A cackle of giddy laughter – whose, I had no idea – echoed up to us, and made us both smile.

"They're having fun."

"But you are not. Are you already letting go of them? Of life?" There was no judgement in his voice, only sadness and curiosity.

"I don't know. I have a lot of feelings right now." I reached out and ran my little finger lightly along his, where it rested on his thigh. "Jack and I were supposed to go to the ice rink next week. I was looking forward to that, even though I can't skate for toffee. And now I won't get to find out what that surprise Christmas present that my dad was teasing me about is. I hope they'll still have Christmas this year, even after … you know. I haven't bought any presents for Dad, because I was angry, and now I won't get the chance. You always think you'll have time." I shook my head at myself. "I sound like an old lady."

Shinobu touched my hair. Silence stretched between us, made all the louder for being full of words we didn't say. Just when it was about to become unbearable, Shinobu broke it.

"Will you dance with me?"

I blinked at him. "I … what? Like a sword dance? You think I ought to practise for the fight?"

"No." He grinned suddenly. "A real dance, like the others down there. The music is playing; we are alone; we have a little time. We have never danced a real dance together, you and I."

And if we don't now, we never will.

Again, the words were unspoken, but I could see them in his eyes.

"Um. OK." I got to my feet and brushed off my legs

and the seat of my leggings, watching awkwardly as he did the same. My hand went back to check the hilt of my sword, and then I caught at the release of the harness to pull it off, before leaning down to carefully place the blade in a little notch in the mossy earth.

Shinobu's grin widened. "You are nervous."

"*Pfft.* No."

"You are. Why? You love to dance."

I jerked my shoulder. "That's different. It's not … not like couple dancing. I don't know how to do that stuff."

"I have never danced with anyone else. We will learn together."

He held out his arms to me and I went into them, arranging us based on my not-very-extensive viewing of "Strictly Come Dancing". His left hand went to rest on my waist, and I put my right on his shoulder. Our free hands clasped and I held them out to the side. "I think that's about right."

Shinobu twisted his arm, bringing our clasped hands to rest against his chest, fingers entwined above his heart. "This is better."

He stepped back and I followed. He turned and I turned with him. Moving on instinct, anticipating each other the way we would in a sparring match, we drifted into a quirky kind of waltz, turning, turning, almost floating around the stillness of the massive trees. The music seemed to grow louder, the sound of pipes and violins rippling around us. It was as if we had our own private, invisible orchestra. Our bodies moved as one, melting together like thunderclouds in a storm.

My head drooped to rest on his shoulder. "This is nice," I whispered into his neck. He shivered.

He drew me closer as I kissed the base of his throat and then the pulse thundering under his jaw. We kept dancing as I found his lips and kissed him. We danced on as our arms went around each other. Our feet tangled and our breathing grew rough. Still dancing.

Suddenly my back came to rest against the warm, smooth bark of one of the trees. Shinobu's entire body pressed against the whole of mine, the slow movement of the dance somehow translated into another kind of movement. Something urgent. Unstoppable.

If we don't now, we never will…

"Mio," he whispered into my mouth as our lips met and parted and met again, breath mingling, hands stroking and clutching, hearts pounding like one heart. "My beautiful Mio. My love…"

I gasped his name as I slid one hand into his hakama and the other into his hair and pulled him down with me to the soft, mossy earth between the twisted tree roots. "Stop talking."

CHAPTER 22

TICK TOCK

Okaasan and I sit on the smooth cedar of the porch, in the shade, surrounded by piles of young willow branches and dried rushes. Summer's heat is coming, and the long sleeves of our light cotton yukata are tied back to keep us cool and free our hands to work on intricately plaited willow baskets. My hair straggles untidily around my face in sweaty strands. Okaasan's face shines with moisture, and now and again she stops to dab at it, but her hair and serenity are as flawless as always.

I will never be like that, *I think.* I will never be perfect in any way, let alone every way. Why would someone want an impatient, scrawny, bad-tempered girl like me? No wonder Shinobu—

A piece of willow snaps between my tense fingers. I swear loudly as the sharp fragment whips across my palm, leaving a slowly deepening welt.

"Where did you learn that word?" Okaasan's voice is dry. "Or need I ask?"

Otousan sometimes gets a little impatient when he instructs me in kenjutsu. Right now I can hear the muffled echo of his shouted instructions to Shinobu in the dojo, the familiar sound mixing with the peaceful whirring song of the cicadas and the rhythmic drip and pock of the bamboo tipping fountain.

"Let me see." Okaasan takes my hand in hers and inspects it. Her soft white fingers are like silk compared with my tanned, scarred skin. "No damage done. This time. Be more careful. Your father will cry if you cannot hold a bokken."

He is more likely to bind up my wound and tell me to fight through the pain like a true warrior. But Okaasan does not need to know that. She already thinks that Otousan takes my training too far.

"What is the matter?" she asks, taking up her basket again as I pluck restlessly at mine, trying to pull out the damaged part without ruining the rest. "Are you and Shinobu-kun at odds over something?"

I sigh. How does she always know? "He does not want to approach Otousan about... He says I am too young. He is only a year older than I am!"

"Nearly two years. And perhaps you are both too young. You are not yet sixteen, Mi-chan. You both have a whole life-time ahead of you that you have not yet glimpsed."

"We won't change our minds," I say. "Not about each other. And not everyone lives to be Old Hoshima-sama's age! I want to know happiness as soon as possible, and make the most of it – for however long or short a time that may be."

She smiles faintly, her eyes on the pattern she is deftly weaving around the basket rim. "Have you fought about this?"

"No." I pause. "Not really. You know how he is. He just goes all stubborn and refuses to talk. Like a rock. A big stupid rock."

"Such sweet words for your beloved." Okaasan's voice trembles with laughter.

"It is best to know your future husband's flaws," I say with as much dignity as I can muster.

"I am sure that Shinobu-kun will speak to your father when he thinks the time is right – and in the meantime," she goes on before I can interrupt, "you will increase both his and your father's respect for you if you act with grace and patience, like a good daughter, instead of hissing like a feral cat whose mouse has been stolen."

I glower down at the wreckage of my basket. If I were ever to act with grace and patience, both my father and Shin-chan would check my forehead for a fever.

A drop of sweat rolls down the side of my face and I swipe at it with my forearm. Warm wind stirs the cherry trees – only just bare of the last of the sakura – and sends their leaves sighing overhead.

The noise of sighing gets louder, taking on a strange, eerie note. Okaasan works on, undisturbed, but the basket drops from my fingers and I rub at my arms, feeling gooseflesh rise.

I never had a mother, a soft, singsong voice murmurs.

All around me a dense, grey mist begins to rise. It rises from the wood of the porch, from the trees, from where my mother sits finishing her basket. The very fabric of the world – no, of my memory – is dissolving. The golden light of the early summer day grows dim and dark as if storm clouds had swallowed the sun in an instant. The sounds of the insects, my father's voice, the smell of my mother's soap and my own sweat … everything fades away, wrapping my senses in empty darkness and cold.

I know what is happening, *I realized.* This is a dream. A dream of a life long, long ago…

I stared at my mother – my first mother – for as long as I could, trying to fix every detail of her beloved face in my mind. "Farewell, Okaasan. I love you."

Then she was gone.

The chill sank into my bones. I pulled off the cloths that bound the sleeves of my yukata and pulled the sleeves down to cover my arms. Grey fog boiled up around me. It choked my throat, sharp and grainy like crystals of ice.

I never had a father, either, *Izanami whispered.* I was born from the dust of the universe, and the light of the moon, and the whispers of the stars. All I ever had was Izanagi. He was my brother, my husband, my everything. We were everything to each other. And then he left me behind. He left me all alone…

"I understand. I know what he did. It was terrible." I looked around me, straining to distinguish anything in the

billows of grey fog. Her voice seemed to come from ... every-where. Where was she?

Soon be better now. No more waiting. No more alone. Tick tick tick tock! *A clear, tinkling little laugh, like broken glass raining down.*

"*You were ... you were very angry with me last time,*" I said.

I have been angry for years. Centuries. Millennia.

A shadow – a vast, rippling thing – emerged on my left, looming over me. Were those wings? A cloud of hair, stream-ing in some wind that I couldn't feel? The shadow swooped towards me. I ducked – but before it reached me it was gone, melting back into the fog.

It will all be different soon. Everything will be all right soon. I am coming to fetch him. Soon everything will be as it should be, should be, should be. Tick tock! Not long now!

The looming shadow spun through the fog to my right. I jumped, following it with my eyes, trying to keep it in sight. Its movements were jerky and somehow repellent, but ... familiar?

She was dancing. Izanami was dancing in the darkness.

You are going to help me, little birdie, aren't you? Now that you understand? You will bring him to where he should be, very soon, tick clock, twelve on the clock.

"Yes," I promised. "Yes, I will. But if you know that, then why don't you call your monsters off? Leave London alone?"

My teeth were beginning to chatter. I clenched my hands together.

But then he might not come. Or you might change your mind, little birdie! I cannot allow that. No, no, no – not when I have waited so long, so very, very long, all alone!

I gritted my teeth, rocked back by the rising wail of her voice. "All right! All right, I get it! I'm going to fight him. I'll do everything that I can. I'll do my best."

Oh, yes. You always do your best, don't you? *Another glassy giggle that sent chills slithering down my spine like worms. For an instant her shape was clear. Hands raised, hair flaring around her bleached white skull, she twirled almost close enough to touch.* You will do your best for me. Remember that, for I will be with you soon. Tick tock. Time is running away, and soon, so soon, I will be with you…

I opened my eyes. I was back in the spirit realm, lying on soft, warm moss beneath a canopy of silver leaves.

"What is the matter?" Shinobu stirred next to me and ran his big, warm hands up and down my bare arms. "You are cold. Did you have a nightmare?"

"I … I saw…" I said. My lips were numb. "Another true seeing. Izanami. She knows what we're going to do. She's all – hopped up – excited and jittering, like a little kid. She's waited thousands of years for this chance. She'll throw everything she has at the mortal realm tonight. And if we fail, she'll rip it apart."

The words rang like some kind of terrible prophesy and then dried up, leaving me panting, shuddering with cold. Shinobu wrapped himself around me. He murmured comfortingly into my hair – endearments in English and Japanese.

"Sorry," I managed after a minute. "That was a hell of a wake-up call for you."

"I woke with you in my arms. Nothing else matters."

I took his face between my hands and kissed him. "I'm sorry," I said again, in a completely different tone. "I'm sorry I couldn't think of a way out of all this for you. I'm sorry I wouldn't stay in the dream realm. I'm sorry I let you go after the Nekomata alone—"

"Don't," he murmured. "Don't. Where you go—"

"I will follow."

"Always. We have loved one another as the night sky loves the stars. A love great enough to defeat time, and the gods, and even death itself. I will not allow anyone to say it was not enough. Not even you."

"All right," I whispered, nodding. "OK. We – we should probably try to tidy ourselves up. We've been gone a long time."

The scramble to find all our hastily flung-away items of clothing, get the twigs and bits of moss out of our hair and identify all the grass stains in unmentionable places made me relax a little, and smile, and then laugh. Shinobu was right. I wasn't going to be sad. Not in this tiny, precious gift of time when I still had everything I loved.

Shinobu turned me around so that I faced away from him and carefully refastened my sword harness over my shoulders. The blade buzzed contentedly against my back.

"There. Ready for battle once more," he said, nuzzling the nape of my neck. The most delicious shiver – nothing like the Izanami-induced ones – worked through me. I sighed, my hands reaching back.

"Guys? Guys!" Jack's voice broke the spell. Shinobu and I both jumped, pulling apart guiltily an instant before her manic hair popped around the side of the tree trunk. Her eyes widened as she looked us over.

"Crap. Your mum is looking for you, Mimi, and if she finds you looking like this, together, death will be upon you with swift wings." She grabbed my hand and dragged me away from Shinobu. "You'd better skedaddle, Shinobs. Go braid your hair or something."

"Wait a second!" I protested. I turned back and kissed him quickly. "OK, now you can leave."

He caught hold of my top with one hand and held me still, leaning down to give me a sweet, lingering kiss that might have got completely out of control if Jack hadn't still been clutching my other arm. She pulled me away, making impatient noises.

"*Now* I can leave," he said. With a flash of his cocky-shy grin, he whisked out of sight behind another tree. I had no doubt at all that the next time I saw him, he'd look as neatly sober as an archbishop at a royal wedding.

"Come here," Jack said. She finger-combed my hair, tugged at my clothes to straighten them out and then pulled a wad of tissues out of her pocket. "You cannot pull off the gothic-grunge look, believe me. Spit."

"Euw! What are you, someone's granny?"

"You have grass stains on your face, doofus. Spit or die. Your choice."

I spat. She scrubbed at my chin, put the tissues away and stepped back to survey me again. "Get that dreamy look off your mug! You might as well have a neon sign saying 'Got Some' on your forehead."

"Oh, God." I sat down on a fallen branch that was nearly the size of a park bench. "Think unsexy thoughts. Think unsexy thoughts…"

Jack sat next to me. She nudged me with her shoulder. "That good, eh?"

"Jack, I'm trying to think about something else."

"Sorry, sorry. Try homework. Maths homework."

Eugh, maths. I'd seriously think myself lucky if I didn't get a D.

No. I wouldn't. I wouldn't get any grade at all. I was never going to hand my maths homework in again. Or any other homework either.

Just like that I came back down to earth. The bump was bruising.

Jack frowned at me. "I think you should stop now. You went from blissed-out to sadsack."

I ran my hands through my hair. "Don't worry about it. I'm just ... I'm all over the place right now."

"Shinobu looked 'all over the place'," she said, giving me a sly, sidelong look. "Roughed him up a bit, did you? Since your mum's not here yet…"

My cheeks caught fire. "Not a chance."

"Oh, come on! I'm your best friend! You don't have to tell me much – just a juicy detail or two."

I retaliated. "Only if you spill the beans about you and Hikaru."

Jack went poker-faced instantly. She fixed her eyes on a jewel-coloured snail the size of a jawbreaker that was slowly making its way over the fallen bough next to her. "We're just friends."

"Of course you are. Oh, by the way, Egypt called. They'd like their river back."

"Shut it. We're friends and that's all. I can be friends with hot girls. I'm friends with you, aren't I? Although not for much longer if you keep this up."

"Whoa." I sat back. "Hold up. You think I'm hot? Where's Shinobu – I need to tell him that I just got a better offer."

She snorted helplessly with laughter, her tense

posture easing a little bit. "I said shut it! Like you'd give that boy up. Even if he sprouted a second head. Or joined a boy band."

"Yeah, but if he ever dumps me, you're my number-one backup. Mum loves you already – total bonus."

Jack sighed, her laughter dying. I waited. She sighed again, more deeply this time, and her shoulders slumped. "I just didn't think of him like that. I liked him. I still like *her*. But I don't know if... I'm not like you, Mimi. I'm not brave. I don't want to put it all on the line and maybe get shot down in flames. Not yet. I'm not ready."

"You're one of the bravest people I've ever met," I said softly. I swallowed hard, then went on. "Not everyone lives to be a hundred, you know? Things happen. Chances slip away. People leave. Sometimes there's nothing you can do to change that. All you can do is grab hold of whatever makes you happy and hang onto it for however long it lasts."

Jack made a noise like a cross racehorse. "Did I ask for sensible advice? For all you know I might enjoy tormenting myself and being needlessly emo."

"Well, whatever happens, you know I've got your back, Maverick."

She put her arm around my shoulders in a sideways hug. "Oh my God, Mio. Don't you know *Top Gun* quotes are totally not cool?"

My mum arrived about three minutes later and found us giggling like pre-schoolers.

"I see you found her, Jack. Why were you hiding all the way up here on your own, sweetie?"

"I wasn't hiding," I said. "I didn't get much sleep last night, so I came up where it was a bit quieter and had a nap." One hundred per cent true. Although it had been quite a short one...

"Well, that was probably a good idea. But now you've had a rest, come down to the feast. You're missing out on dinner, and your father wants you to dance with him."

"*Dad* wants me to dance with him?" I repeated sceptically. "Or *you* want us to dance so that you can look on and smile mistily over the sentimental moment?"

"Both." She grinned. "It's time to shake your money-maker, kid."

I got up, grimacing. "Look, I'll go with you, but only if you promise never, ever to say that again."

"Deal."

So I walked down into the green bowl of the amphitheatre. I ate and drank with the Kitsune and my family. Laughed at Hikaru and Hiro's jokes. Danced with my dad, and Jack, and Shinobu, and then a whole bunch of Kitsune: some that I'd fought with at Battersea, and some who were complete strangers. Marvelled at Rachel's previously unknown jiving skills. Eventually ended up leaning dozily on Shinobu's shoulder, half-asleep. But most of all, I watched. I watched them all and stored these moments up – bright, warm fragments of life and happiness, of everything that was precious to me.

Because I could feel the clock counting down towards the moment when I would have to say goodbye to all of it – all of them – forever.

Tick ... tock.

CHAPTER 23

BEFORE
THE STORM

Eventually, most of us dozed off there on the blankets at the bottom of the amphitheatre. Even me. I was right in the middle of giggling with Jack at the sight of furry heaps of sleeping fox spirits, their paws in the air, tails sticking out all over the place, and then – wham. Out like a light.

I needed the rest, and it was a good one. If I dreamed at all, I don't remember it.

But when I woke up, the music had finished, the fox lights had drifted back up to the canopy of leaves and no one was dancing or laughing any more. The party was over. It was time to get ready.

The Kitsune opened up their enviable armouries and began kitting themselves out. We humans were led into the trees and Hiro and Araki, with the help of a couple of younger Kitsune, brought out selections of borrowed armour and weapons for us. This stuff was far from scruffy, tattered hand-me-downs. The odd battle scar showed, but each item had been lovingly polished and cleaned, and I strongly suspected that the Kitsune had some sort of grow–shrink spell that made anything they offered feel like it had been tailor-made for the wearer.

It was very reassuring to see my friends and parents re-emerge from behind the trees wearing tough Kevlar-plated coats and vests and steel-capped boots, and clutching a formidable array of knives, swords and, in Jack's case, a naginata. My mum and Rachel had both refused any kind of edged weapon, but Rachel claimed a weighted wooden staff, while Mum picked out a gleaming baton. She tucked it and some pepper spray into a Batman-style belt.

Shinobu gratefully accepted a new katana and my dad loaded himself up with every kind of sharp, pointy object on offer, from ninja throwing stars to wrist blades to a pair of long, single-edged tanto knives that he strapped to his outer thighs. I was surprised he didn't jingle when he walked, but I had no doubt whatsoever that he knew how to use all the hardware he'd chosen.

When it was my turn, I pulled on a white, long-sleeved T-shirt and a pair of snug-fitting black jeans, then a sort of stab vest made of toughened black leather that laced up my sides, under my arms. The vest had diamond-shaped metal studs dotted over its surface and lightweight, tough plates of armour underneath. It allowed me to twist and move without feeling restricted, and my sword harness fitted perfectly over the top. I also picked out a pair of black mesh swordsman's gauntlets which covered my lower arms to the elbow. They were reinforced with Kevlar on the backs of the hands and wrists, but were so fine over my fingers and palms that I barely felt I was wearing anything. They would help to keep my hands warm and my fingers flexible in the cold outside.

I kept my own footwear. It was the same light, ultra-comfy pair of boots that the Kitsune had given me after we'd fought the Nekomata, and despite all my adventures in the dream realm, they had never let water in or shrunk. I felt a sort of loyalty to them. Maybe they'd bring me luck.

Predictably, the moment that I stepped out, Hikaru, newly clad in the familiar white-leather ensemble from the Battersea battle, wolf-whistled me. Jack and Rachel began squabbling over whether my official code name ought to be Xena or She-Ra. I felt a headache coming on, so I shut them up by complaining that my hair kept falling into my face and bothering me.

As the best braider, Rachel took charge, sweeping back the sides of my hair and working it into two tight French plaits that ran from my temples to the back of my head. Fine strands immediately slid loose to tickle my cheeks, but it was still a vast improvement. Rachel shrugged off my thanks, but I thought she was pleased that she'd been able to contribute something.

A small part of me whined that all this was point-less. Some armour and a sensible hairstyle weren't going to pull me out of the fire. In fact, I could go out to fight in my teddy-bear pyjamas for all the difference it would ultimately make to my fate. I recognized that part of me. It was self-pity. The truth was that anything which increased my chances of getting to and taking down Izanagi increased my family's chances of having a world that was worth living in after I was gone. And I would have fought in my teddy-bear pyjamas if that was what it took to make that happen.

"Araki-san," I said, "could you do me a favour and escort these guys down to wait with everyone else? I need to talk to Shinobu in private."

"What about?" my mum asked, looking both worried and suspicious.

"If she was willing to tell all of us, then it wouldn't be private now, would it?" My dad put his arm around her shoulder and led her towards the rim of the bowl.

Jack discreetly waggled her eyebrows at me, whisper-ing, "Don't do anything I wouldn't do."

She and Hikaru went after my parents, and Rachel followed with a sidelong look that told me she shared Jack's opinion.

"They think we are going to … now?" Shinobu asked, torn between disapproval and amusement.

"I wish we were." I checked to make sure that they were all definitely out of earshot, then turned back to him. "I've been thinking about this fight, and how to make sure it goes down the way we want."

Instantly he sobered. "Go on."

"Izanagi is a coward. If I go strolling up to him with the Sword of the Gathering Clouds of Heaven already unbound and blazing with god-killing energy, I think he'll rabbit. He's already been running from the sword, and Izanami, for centuries: one more retreat won't bother him. And I don't exactly know what powers he has, but I have seen him disappear almost instantly – like teleportation – and if he does it again, we'll have no way of going after him. Our chance will be gone, and Izanami will…" My voice trailed off.

"I understand," Shinobu said, nodding. "What do you propose?"

"He's not scared of me. He's contemptuous, and he knows he can snap me in half with one hand. We need to use that, use the element of surprise." I touched the hilt of the wakizashi at Shinobu's waist. "Button up your coat over this so that he doesn't see we have it. I'm not sure how much energy it puts out, but with all the other powers that are going to be swirling around out there tonight hopefully he won't sense it. He won't know that we have the sword's final name, either. Let me fight with the blade as it is now – only partially unbound – at first. He'll see that it's changed shape and he'll think that's as far as we've got in breaking the bindings. With any luck it'll lull him into a false sense of security and he'll stick around to try to take the sword from me again. Then, at the last moment, when his guard is down and he thinks he's about to crush me…"

"I'll draw the wakizashi, and you will call the sword's last name to unbind it." Shinobu said it matter-of-factly, as if he wasn't talking about ending his own life. "He won't have time to run. But … he's going to hurt you, Mio. Badly."

I shrugged jerkily. "It's not like – I mean, it's not going to make any difference in the long run, is it? I just have to have enough left in me by the end to stick the sword in. And the blade will help me."

Shinobu stared into my face. "I will fight with you. Draw some of his ire. Take some of the punishment, until it's time."

"No," I said firmly, and kept talking over him when he tried to interrupt. "No, Shinobu. You have to leave it to me to keep him occupied. If he gets too close to you, he might sense the wakizashi and try to take it from us, or even attempt to put you back in the sword again, like the first time we went up against him. That's always been his ultimate goal. We can't give him that chance."

Shinobu looked away from me, jaw clenching. At his sides, his hands slowly curled into fists, straightened and then curled again. "This is hard."

"I know," I whispered. "For me, too."

We both reached out. Our hands entwined, and clung. We stood in silence for a moment, mourning each other in advance.

The green blade flashes down in the red light—
Don't let go!

I forced the flashback away. *It's too late for that now,* I told the part of me that was the first Mio. *It's not about holding on any more. It's about letting go together. You should understand that. It's all you ever wanted, really.*

"Yamato Mio-dono?" Araki reappeared over the top of the amphitheatre, and I reluctantly let go of Shinobu's hands. She bowed politely. "The king must know where she is to open the portal into your realm."

I blinked, taken aback. That was a good question, and I had no idea of the answer. It was all very well for Silver Fangs to say that the sword would lead me to the battle, but right now it was happily humming away and giving me no clues at all. "Um…"

"What does your intuition tell you, sword-bearer?" Shinobu asked with deliberate formality, seeing the clueless panic in my eyes.

My intuition wasn't talking. But common sense told me that I had no way of knowing the right place, and there was nothing I could do about it. So I might as well just pick a familiar location – somewhere that the Kitsune had a portal already.

"My house," I said firmly. "The blade will lead me from there."

Araki nodded. "That will make things easier. We are forming ranks now – will you come?" She moved away, and I put out a hand to stop her, not quite daring to touch.

"Araki-san, wait a moment. I just wanted to say that I – I'm very sorry for what the Foul Women did to that young Kitsune girl. I didn't even know who she was, but … it must have been awful for you."

Araki froze, then bowed her head. "Her name was Masaru. She was my niece."

"I'm sorry," I repeated, wondering if I should have brought it up.

"You will make the gods pay for it tonight, sword-bearer," she said. When she lifted her head, her eyes were flat and hard, like flint. "We will make them pay."

She bowed to me again, and walked away without another word. I hurried to follow, moving swiftly down the turf steps cut into the wall of the green bowl with Shinobu at my side. At the bottom of the amphitheatre, ranks and ranks of well-armed Kitsune were lined up, waiting for us.

The first group was the soldier fox spirits – the ones who had marched with us to Battersea. As I approached them, they stood to attention and saluted me. I could never pull off a salute that sharp. I nodded to them and lifted my hand in a gesture that was half wave, half blessing. Then we were past, walking between rows of volunteer Kitsune fighters. They didn't salute, but their eyes followed me. I nodded to them, too, trying to broadcast confidence and certainty. I didn't want them to feel scared. Even if they probably should be.

Ahead of me, at the centre of the amphitheatre, the king stood on her throne in her human form. Her hair was a crown of elaborate braids and she was dressed in shining white and gold. Tight white-leather trousers were tucked into soft golden boots, and a vest of chain mail washed in gold left her arms, clad in billowy white silk sleeves, free. Jewelled golden vambraces glinted on her wrists. A shotgun hung on one shoulder, and a bandolier of bullets was slung diagonally across her chest. Two huge unsheathed swords – not Japanese style, but exaggeratedly curved, like something you'd expect to see Sinbad the Sailor waving around – were secured to her wide golden belt. Blood-red stones winked in her ears. She looked like a modern-day, nine-tailed Elizabeth the First.

"I think I see where Hikaru gets her sense of style," I whispered to Shinobu.

"And certainly the love of tight leather trousers," he murmured back, smiling faintly.

A dark smoky-grey Kitsune – Tetsuo, the king's chief

advisor – also stood on the throne hill. The king was talking seriously to him, probably giving him instructions on how to run things while she was gone. Even though Tetsuo was an immensely powerful eight-tailed Kitsune, he wouldn't be fighting with us tonight. He was blind – but more than that, he somehow gave the impression of being fragile and ancient. The king was at least a hundred years his senior, but she seemed light-years younger. I wondered what his story was. I supposed I'd never get to find out now.

Araki quickly climbed the hill, and I went to my parents, Jack, Hikaru and Rachel, who were waiting in a little bunch just in front of the throne.

"That was quick. Did you have a good discussion?" Mum asked.

"We did," I said, bracing myself. "And now we're going to have another one. Here are the rules. You stay behind me, and you stay in the middle of the army. You let the Kitsune protect you, because they have lightning bolts coming out of their tails, and you don't. And none of you get carried away and run off alone trying to be a hero, no matter what."

"Well. That's told us, hasn't it?" my dad grumbled.

Jack folded her arms, looking unimpressed.

"That's the way it has to be. I can't do my job if I'm constantly looking back, checking on you guys, worrying about you. At the end of the day, no matter how brave and good at fighting you are, you're only human, and the things that we're facing out there tonight aren't. I know that you'll have Hikaru and Rachel watching out for you, but they can get hurt just as easily as anyone else, so don't make it hard for them. Got it?" I watched them for nods and shrugs. Then, as the silence became awkward, I sighed. "Do I get any kind of a hug in this situation?"

Smiles broke through. Worried, tense smiles, but still. We all scrambled to embrace each other, and Shinobu got caught up in it, too, getting a quick kiss on the cheek from my mum.

"You keep my daughter safe, now," she said softly. "After all, it's her birthday tomorrow. You don't want to miss the party."

"Mio does not need to be protected," Shinobu told her seriously, his eyes boring into hers. "But I will stay with her, Mrs Yamato. To the end."

Mum's expression clouded as she tried to decipher his words, but I didn't let it worry me. I smiled at him. I was proud that he'd finally got it through his head that it wasn't his job to guard me, but to fight with me. It had only taken him two lifetimes to accept it.

I noticed that Rachel was drawing Hikaru away from the rest of us, a little way around the side of the throne hill. I hesitated for a second, then took a couple of nonchalant steps back, tuned out the noise of the others talking and shamelessly eavesdropped.

"Er … so I guess we're the supernatural bodyguards, then. Good luck out there," Rachel said.

"Yeah, you too." From the corner of my eye, I watched Hikaru hold out her hand and Rachel shake it.

Rachel opened her mouth, closed it, then took a deep breath, and said, "Sorry if I've been a bit … you know."

Hikaru twiddled a strand of hair. "That's OK. Was it the species thing?"

"No!" Rachel said hastily. "I'm not a bigot. Or a hypocrite, since God knows what I am these days. It's just … you were a guy. And I could see that Jack liked you, and you liked her and … I don't know, I worried that maybe you'd try to push her back into the closet."

"Me?" Hikaru was clearly incredulous. "I couldn't push Jack anywhere she didn't want to go. Not even if I had a tank. I doubt anyone could."

"Well, you say that, but … look, Jack always knew who she was, and I was proud of her for that. But our dad made her life tough. He wouldn't take her seriously. He made fun of her, told her it was a 'phase' and that she'd 'grow out of it'. When he finally left, Jack took it hard. I've always been scared that she blamed herself, but she wouldn't talk about it. Then you turned up and I thought, 'Uh-oh.'"

Hikaru took all this in with a thoughtful expression. "You realize that I'm still male, though, right? I mean, that being a male is as much a part of me as being a female? I'm not all one thing or the other, and I don't want to be."

Rachel shook her head. "You don't need to explain. The point is that I realized things weren't so black and white – and that it was never really any of my business anyway, so ... basically, I hope that we can get on. Not just for Jack's sake. You're a cool girl. Guy. Person."

Hikaru shrugged and grinned her reckless grin. "Consider us pals from now on, cupcake."

I smiled to myself.

On the hill, the king finished conferring with Araki and Tetsuo and raised her arms. Silence fell over the court as the Kitsune turned their faces up to her.

"My people, the time is approaching. Tonight we will march into open war for the first time in almost a thousand years. There will be blood, and sacrifice, and loss – and in our hearts each of us must prepare ourselves for that."

"Great pep talk," Jack muttered. I elbowed her.

The king went on. "But there will also be bravery, glory and honour. Tonight we will defy the gods. For centuries to come, all Kitsune, all the people of spirit, will talk and sing and whisper of what we do now. When you step into the human realm, you will step forward as heroes. And no matter what happens, I promise that each and every one of you will be remembered as a hero forever."

The king's tails sent out a great crackling arc of blue lightning. The assembled fox spirits stamped in unison. The king walked slowly down the front of the throne, navigating the smooth, sheer slope as gracefully as if there were steps. She stopped directly before me, and placed her hands on my shoulders. I obeyed the pressure of her delicate fingers and bowed down so that my face was level with hers.

She pressed a firm kiss to the centre of my forehead.

"You will be remembered," she whispered, so quietly that I only felt her words as a breath against my skin. "Daughter of the Kitsune."

I blinked, speechless. She let me go, and I straightened up.

The king took up her position next to me and gestured to Hikaru, who came to stand on my other side. Shinobu, my parents, Jack and Rachel quickly fell in behind. Araki took the head of the column to my left, and Hiro the one to my right. Another column of Kitsune was forming behind me. This was it.

"What time is it in the mortal realm?" I whispered.

"Eleven thirty," Hikaru whispered back.

Half an hour to midnight. Thirty minutes. That was all we had. I took a deep, deep breath, pulled my gauntlets out of my belt and dragged them on over the sleeves of my T-shirt, flexing my fingers to stop them shaking.

The king nodded. Araki flung her head back and let

out a low, ululating cry. The massed fox spirits stamped again, shaking the amphitheatre and sending a handful of silver leaves spiralling down. Overhead, the fox lights began to flicker out one by one as the army and the king let them go, drawing all their lightning back to themselves. The court slowly faded into twilight.

On the hill ahead of us, three massive rings of light – each one the electric blue of the king's lightning and big enough for a Land Rover to drive through – sprang to life, flickering and snapping as they grew. The wreaths blazed, and within them the grass faded away. Darkness beckoned.

"Geronimo," I whispered.

"Geronimo," Jack, Hikaru and Shinobu echoed softly.

Thirty minutes before the storm breaks.

CHAPTER 24

SHADOWS AND BLOOD

There wasn't room in our back garden for the Kitsune army. Much as I would have liked to huddle there and stare at my home one last time, the tiny space filled up so quickly with fox spirits spilling out of the mulberry bush that there was no choice except to hurry forward, past the garage and out onto the street.

Cold silver moonlight illuminated the scene; the streetlights were unlit. One or two houses up and down the road showed a faint glow leaking out around the barricades on their windows, but it looked more like candlelight to me than steady electric light. The road was deserted. The quiet tramp of the fox spirits' feet as they flooded onto the tarmac and pavements completely failed to disguise the eerie absence of other sounds. No noises of cars, no tinny TV laughter, no drunken voices from the pub two streets down. A faint, faraway roaring in the distance might have been traffic, but then again – might not. I couldn't be sure.

A dog trotted into view ahead of us. My mum sucked in a sharp breath. "That's—"

One of the king's tails flicked. A lightning bolt sliced across my vision, leaving a blue after-image, like a scar, on the darkness. The dog yelped and fled, its fur smoking.

"Jinmenken," Her Majesty said calmly. "It is best to send them running before they bring their whole pack."

I opened my mouth to compliment her on her aim – and then something hit me.

It was like a meteor colliding with my back. The searing impact almost knocked me off my feet. I stumbled forward, holding a scream behind a cage of gritted teeth as I reached back to claw at the burning between my shoulder blades.

My hands found the hilt of the sword, and where they touched it, lit up with pain.

"Are you all right?" several voices asked at once.

"It's glowing!" Hikaru said.

I could almost hear the sizzle of my flesh and smell the stench of burning skin. I knew that if I opened my mouth, all that would come out would be shrieks of *Get it off me get it off get it OFF*. I clamped my lips together, grabbed the sword around the mouth of the saya and tore it out of the harness, still sheathed.

The moment that I brought the sword over my head

to my front, the burning stopped. The relief was so huge that I hardly noticed anything else – the others' worried, shocked faces, the fact that my gloved hands weren't blackened and blistered at all.

But I noticed that the sword was shining. There were no flames spurting from the saya this time. Just light. Pure, prismatic light, shot through with rippling rainbows, blazed around and through the black silk of the hilt wrappings, out of each golden sakura blossom on the sheath and from the pierced golden guard.

I couldn't hear the sheathed blade's voice in my head, but I barely needed to. It was communicating its desire to me loud and clear.

This way!

It was all I could do not to take off running. Instead, I let go of the hilt with one hand and pointed. My finger was as straight and steady as an arrow.

"That way?" Shinobu asked.

I looked at him gratefully and nodded. He took a step closer, his expression changing. "Mio-dono … your eyes…"

My parents muscled forward and stared too. "My God. Does it hurt?" my dad asked.

I didn't care what crazy crap the sword was doing to my eyes. I could see with them, and that was all that mattered. I just needed to move – now – before my skin split open with the scorching power of the sword's need.

I stabbed my finger into the air once more, then grasped the sword with both hands and started walking.

"Follow the sword-bearer!" the king commanded. Other voices immediately took up the cry. "Follow! Follow!"

The army spread out behind me as I stalked down the road. The sword pulled at me, tugging me forward like a giant ACME magnet from a cartoon.

This way! This way! This way!

I could feel its excitement glowing out of my pores. It was already happening. What the sword had always wanted. Even the saya could barely contain it now, and I was becoming saturated with its energy. Becoming a part of it.

Soon I wouldn't be Mio any more. I would only be the sword-bearer.

But not yet. *Not yet.* The time was still counting down. Until then I had to remain in control of myself and the blade. I'd had a lot of practice at this – compartmentalizing – over the past few days, and it paid off. Slowly but surely, I managed to clear a space in my head where I could function, and then I forced myself to think.

I was trotting. Almost running. That was stupid. I'd tire myself out before I even got anywhere. I dropped down into a walk. Then I looked around. The others were still with me. The king, Hikaru, Jack and Rachel were on my left, and Dad, Mum and Shinobu were on my right. The Kitsune were still on my heels. Good. OK.

Ahead of us, a chunk of buildings about three properties wide had been reduced to rubble and shards of glass. Underfoot, the paving stones and road surface were warped and cracked, as if they'd buckled upwards under some immense pressure. A manhole cover had somehow flipped up out of the ground and was now stuck out of a big electric sign on a shopfront; sparks rained down onto the pavement beneath it. A set of flickering traffic lights were twisted into demented spirals, and three trees planted next to the road had been reduced to splintery stubs.

Rachel and my mum had said it was bad, and I'd believed them. My own common sense and my encounters with Izanami had told me what must be happening out here. But still, I hadn't expected to see this. I hadn't believed, really believed, that my city, my home, could ever look this bad.

Abandoned cars were littered haphazardly across the main road and the pavement like discarded toys. Behind me, the army quietly split into smaller columns to march between the obstacles as I walked past a massive crater in the tarmac. Ahead of me, a white van and a red Mini had apparently collided on a traffic island between the two lanes. Another crater had been blown in the second floor of the building parallel to the island. Bricks, smashed window frames and cracked hunks of concrete had half buried the vehicles.

"Oh, God," Mum said. "Is he…?"

I followed her gaze and saw the body of a man mostly hidden under the rubble. His head, shoulders and one arm were visible.

My dad glanced at my mum's face and said, "I'll make sure."

The king's lifted hand brought the Kitsune behind us to a halt as my dad jogged off. In the twin glow of moonlight and my sword, it was very obvious to me that the man was long dead and past our help. His eyes were filmed over, unblinking, and his skin was the colour of chalk. But if checking would help Mum sleep better when this was all over, then it was worth a minute's delay.

This way! This way!

Shut up, I told the sword. *You'll get your chance soon enough.*

Dad reached the body, crouched by him and touched his neck. I guessed from his slight grimace that the man's skin was already cold. Dad shook his head, then stood up again, turning to face us.

"No pulse," he called.

The sword's vibration changed in my hand. My eyes shot up above Dad instinctively, to the hole in the building. I saw a giant wedge-shaped head – like a snake's, but covered in pink, soft-looking skin. I saw foot-long fangs, long whiskers like a cat's and glowing red eyes.

I screamed, "Get down *now!*"

My dad didn't stop to ask questions or argue. He flung himself flat on the pavement as the snake's neck suddenly stretched. Its head shot out of the broken wall like a tennis ball leaving a racket – but its fangs snapped shut on empty air instead of my dad's body. My mum let out a muffled screech, then clamped both hands over her mouth.

Half a dozen lightning bolts speared the thing's soft-looking hide as the Kitsune surged forward. My dad had already rolled and leapt to his feet, his katana practically flying into his hand. The snake-thing gave a savage hiss, arching back over the road. Its body – weirdly segmented and saggy looking, almost like a caterpillar, but with no legs – was still uncoiling. Twenty feet, now thirty, and still counting. Clear venom dripped from its fangs, its mouth gaping impossibly wide as the lower jaw dislocated. The lightning hadn't stopped it, only pissed it off.

"Aim for the eyes," the king instructed. She sounded as calm as if she was ordering a second slice of cake at a party. I did a double-take when I realized she had stepped sideways and folded her arms, observing.

Hikaru and another Kitsune – a dark-skinned, four-tailed man with spiky hair and a pierced nose – flung slender, sharp rods of lightning at the thing's face just as my dad hurled a ninja throwing star. Hikaru's shot hit the left eye dead on, and she whooped as the bulbous red orb popped like a balloon. My dad's blade buried itself in the right one an instant later. The monster let out a disturbingly human yell. A pink, rounded tongue flailed in its gaping mouth. It reared up even higher, the thickest part of its body flumping down into the road in a clatter of falling masonry. My dad and Hikaru jumped back out of the way.

I couldn't draw my sword. Not now, not like this. But that didn't mean I had to be useless. The thing was blinded now, but it could still hear and feel. I picked up a chunk of concrete and flung it at the monster's head. It bounced off the pink chin with a *thunk*.

"Hey, lizard-brains! Bite me!"

The monster hissed again, spattering the road with more venom. Its head lunged down, bringing the thinner neck section back into reach. Something dark flashed past me and suddenly Rachel – Rachel! – had hold of the snake's head. She wrapped her arms around it, small hands clamping down on its jaws and forcing them shut.

"I've got it!" She grunted, digging her heels into the ground, as it thrashed. "Oh, God, this is so disgusting. Someone cut its head off!"

Shinobu darted forward. His swords crossed in a silver zigzag of metal, and a deep gash opened in the monster's pink hide, exposing the shiny yellow of bone within.

"Jack!" my dad called. Jack tossed her naginata to him. He caught it one-handed, stepped forward and thrust the blade of the spear into the wound Shinobu had made, neatly severing the spinal cord. Rachel twisted her arms, and the head came off with a papery tearing sound. She tossed it away and wiped her hands on the front of her shirt, making *ick ick* noises.

The headless body flopped across the road, shuddering.

We all, even the Kitsune, stood still for a moment, just staring in mixed fascination and horror. Then Mum broke away, sprinted to my dad and gave him a smacking kiss on the lips. "You scared the life out of me!" She swiped one of his long knives. "I've changed my mind. I think I'll hang onto one of these, just in case."

"What *was* that?" Jack asked.

The king and Hikaru exchanged a look. "I'm not entirely sure," Her Majesty admitted. "Possibly a form of nozuchi, although I had not known they could grow so large."

"Izanami's pulling out all the stops for us," Hikaru said.

Jack waved her hands in the air. "Ooh, yippee."

"But!" The king turned back to the army. "It was also a lesson! Remember this: lightning cannot always be used as a method of brute force. Have your weapons and your brains at the ready, my people!"

The Kitsune shifted a bit sheepishly. The sword's desire pulled on me again, impatient. Without waiting any longer I moved forward, vaulting over the still twitching remains of the snake. The others poured after me.

"What time is it?" I asked as we continued down the road.

"Twenty to twelve," Jack answered. Her eyes were on the sky. The full moon shone just as brightly as ever, but all around it, thick clouds were beginning to gather. They were an intense, unnatural purple. Every now and again they pulsed with what looked like lightning – except that there was no answering rumble of thunder. And there was no wind to move them, either.

"She's getting closer," I said. *Twenty minutes.*

Twice more, strange creatures attacked our ranks. A tarry black liquid oozed up through the pavement almost under Araki's feet and tried to drag her and a couple of other Kitsune under the ground with it. They killed it with lightning. Then a bear-like monster with bamboo growing out of its back tried to take a chunk out of the last rank. They brought it down with bullets and a machete.

I broke into a jog again, and this time I couldn't make myself stop.

We began to see people. First, people's bodies. Even Mum didn't try to make us check on the desiccated husk lying in the mouth of an alleyway, although she made a sad noise at the sight of its long, shining blonde hair. But then living people began to show up as well. Scuttling away from us into spaces between buildings, fleeing in small groups. Some walked past us as if we weren't there, mumbling to themselves. With wide eyes and torn clothing covered in blood or other disgusting substances, they looked like refugees from some unspeakable war.

Which was exactly what they were.

I heard sirens in the distance, and screams. A couple of times police cars zipped in front of us at an intersection, and once an ambulance nearly mowed a couple of unwary Kitsune down. The roaring in the distance was getting closer, and louder, and eventually I realized what it was. After visiting the dream realm so recently I should have guessed it earlier.

Water. Churning, raging water.

The sword was leading us to the river – and the river sounded angry.

Above us, that great, bright moon seemed bigger than ever, its light taking on a strange, rusty tinge as the clouds got thicker and thicker around it. The sword was shuddering in my grip now.

This way! This way!

"Eight minutes to twelve," Rachel said. "Are we close?"

Rather than answer, I veered off the road and through a set of metal traffic bollards onto a paved pedestrianized area that was sandwiched between a modern glass building and a place built of ugly meat-coloured bricks. It was only when I glanced back to make sure the others were following that I saw the graceful dome of St Paul's Cathedral behind us. It took me a second to recognize it. At night, the building was normally lit up with blue or white spotlights, shining bright. It still was, in a way. Only now the lights were the wrong colour. They were red. Blood red. As the Kitsune streamed past me, I whipped around to look at the moon. Veins of dark crimson were worming onto the pale disc's edges, like threads of blood drifting in water.

THIS WAY!

I dashed through the ranks of Kitsune, streaked past my family, past Hikaru and the king. The sword thrummed in my grip and my feet hardly seemed to touch the ground as I shot out in front. "We don't have much time!"

Shinobu caught up with me almost at once, his face pale and set. The others took a few seconds longer to get it, but a moment later the army broke into a thundering gallop. The king and Hikaru were still right at the front, Jack and Rachel a little further back. Behind them my dad kept pace with my mum. That was all the attention I could spare. I turned my face in the right direction and sprinted.

We flooded into a tunnel. The road markings blurred into one continuous yellow line under flickering sodium lights; the sound of footsteps melded into a rumble like an approaching train. I shot out into the night and saw where we were. The sword dragged me onwards, even as behind me I heard exclamations of surprise and dismay at the sight ahead.

The great glittering black expanse of the Thames spread out before us, reflecting a nightmare in progress. Half the lights of the city were dark. Clouds of pale smoke drifted against the night sky, lit with the dancing light of fires – dozens of fires – burning on the other side of the river. One of them was The Shard. The iconic building was an eye-watering streak of white heat in the darkness – a flaming torch that turned the water below it to dazzling gold. The crushed and mangled remains of a ferry, a river-tour boat, drifted past, surrounded by debris. It looked as if a giant had tried to twist it into a pretzel and then dropped it in disgust when he couldn't get the metal to cooperate.

Almost directly ahead of us lay the slender, unmistakable curve of the Millennium Bridge.

Beneath the bridge, the river had become a whirlpool, stretching nearly as far as the banks on either side, with the bridge spanning its diameter. The liquid gleamed a rich, vivid crimson. I wasn't sure if it was even real Thames water any more, or if the power of Izanami's rage and madness had turned it into what it looked like: blood.

The entire structure of the bridge was caged with lightning – great pulsing veins of red lightning that speared up from the churning water below and peaked in a sharp arch, piercing the clouds above. Only the ends of the bridge, where it met the footpath on either side, were open. The red lightning licked at them, too, crawling over the empty space and then flickering away as if impatient to fill the gap.

That whirlpool was where the mouth of Yomi would open. There might as well have been a neon sign above it. But why there? Why choose there, in the river, under the bridge, of all places?

Then, in a sudden leap of intuition, I understood.

When midnight came, the lightning cage around the mouth of Yomi and the bridge would close. Whoever – whatever – stood on the bridge would be caught there within the lightning, unable to escape until Izanami chose to let them go.

Izanami had set a trap for Izanagi.

A trap for me.

The moon was almost entirely red now. The sword's pull had kept me moving, but shock had slowed my steps to a hesitant shuffle. I opened my mouth to ask the time again – and was drowned out by a scream.

A see-through blob the colour of vomit was crawling up onto the path behind me, oblivious to the bolts of lightning that the Kitsune flung at it. It had a horny black turtle shell on its back and black horns like a cow's. One of the fox spirits blasted it with a shotgun, but the bullets bounced off the shell with no effect. "Fire!" some-one shouted. "Set it on fire!"

Further back, a winged monstrosity – half bat, half lizard – swooped on the massed Kitsune. It scooped one up in a five-clawed foot. The Kitsune shocked it with a burst of lightning and it dropped her with a squawk.

We were under attack, but I had to keep going. I turned away and pelted towards the bridge.

"Form lines!" Her Majesty yelled. "Protect the sword-bearer! Protect the humans!"

Fox spirits surged around me, creating a living bar-rier, two people wide, between me and the water. An honour guard. I dashed past them, eyes fixed on the bridge and the swarming red veins that had almost cov-ered the moon. I had minutes, maybe seconds to get there. Shinobu ran beside me, eyes burning black in his face, his hand a knot around the fold of his coat where the wakizashi was hidden.

The bridge was only half a dozen steps away.

A huge sickly yellow tentacle, bristling with needles like a cactus, shot up out of the water. It swiped the Kitsune out of its way as if they were paper dolls, and then came at me.

Hikaru rugby tackled me, shoving me down. I hit the ground and rolled – and the tentacle seized Hikaru, scooping her off her feet. She let out a pained cry as she tumbled through the air towards the seething river.

There was a splash. Then she was gone.

Jack screamed. *"No!"*

Shinobu grabbed my arm and dragged me up off the wet pavement. I scrambled to my feet and risked one last look back. This was it. This was all I would get. An eye-blink image of darkness and terror, my parents' shocked faces, Jack screaming, Rachel stricken, the king reeling back from another monster as it lunged out of the water at her, and the gap where Hikaru should have been.

This was goodbye.

I turned away and flung myself onto the bridge with Shinobu. Our feet hit the walkway at the same moment, and we passed under the arch of flickering red lightning together.

There was a thunderclap and a fizzle of white light, and shining darkness unfurled at the other end of the bridge. Izanagi stepped out of it. His dark kimono glowed with golden embroidery, and his unbound hair lashed around his head. He stalked forward onto the bridge, energy crackling in his hands, eyes blank globes of searing white.

Izanami's voice – that eerie singsong voice, somehow a woman's and a child's at the same time – echoed up from under our feet, booming as if she was speaking into an Olympic sound system. "My beloved! The hour is come. Soon we shall be together again!"

"Give up, you crazed whore!" he snarled. "You cannot

get out. I will not let you out. Not ever!"

Through a gap in the lightning above, I saw the last of the moon's pale light disappear, eaten by blood. A deep, mournful sound, like some colossal temple bell, rang out over the water. Marking the hour. Midnight.

Time's up.

The red cage of electricity pulsed with new brilliance. In an instant, the openings at both ends snapped shut, sealing the bridge off from the outside world.

Trapping Shinobu and me on a bridge above the mouth of hell, with two mad gods.

Jack lost sight of Mio and Shinobu as they sprinted ahead of her, lost sight of the creepy red electric veins caging the bridge, the Eye of Sauron thing the moon was doing. All she could see was Hikaru's face, contorted in agony as she plunged into the water.

She shoved past the Kitsune that blocked her path to the river. "Hikaru!"

She can't be gone. She can't be gone just like that.

"Hikaru! Please answer me!"

Sobs choked her as her gaze searched the water, desperate for a sign of the stupid, brave fox spirit. The tentacle thing had disappeared without a trace. Did it have her? Was it holding her under water, slowly drowning her?

I have to go in.

Jack crouched, put her naginata down on the pavement,

334

and began to shrug off her heavy armoured coat.

"What are you doing?" Rachel demanded. Jack flinched. She'd all but forgotten her sister was there. "You can't go into the river! It's full of monsters. You wouldn't get two strokes without being eaten alive."

"She's out there! Someone has to help her," Jack said, struggling with the straps on her tactical vest.

"Then let me go, idiot!" Rachel sat down as if to take off her boots.

Something broke the surface. A sizeable chunk of yellow, prickle-covered tentacle floated past.

"Ladies," said a weak voice from below them. "No need … to fight. Plenty of me … to go … around."

Jack flung herself flat, thrust her arms over the side of the path and seized the pale hands that were scrabbling at the concrete blocks. With Rachel's help, she hauled a sopping-wet Hikaru out of the river, over the side of the bank, and onto the pavement.

"You nearly gave me a heart attack, Furball!" Jack yelled.

There was no answer. Hikaru lay stiffly, shuddering in Jack's arms. Jack stared at her friend with dawning horror. Dark blood oozed from a dozen puncture wounds where the tentacle's needles had gone through her leather clothes. Her breathing was harsh and laboured.

"Hikaru?"

"Hurts…" the fox spirit choked out. She turned her face

away from Jack – and went suddenly and terrifyingly limp.

"Poison?" Rachel asked urgently. "Those prickle things—"

"I don't know. Get – get the king, get Araki, or Hiro – anyone. She needs magic, a healing spell. Something. She needs help!"

Rachel scrambled to her feet and grabbed the nearest Kitsune. "Look after them! I'm going for the king!"

The Kitsune, a stocky girl with long blonde braids, stared at the king's granddaughter bleeding on the pavement and nodded wordlessly. She drew a machete from her belt and took up a guard position over Jack and Hikaru. Rachel disappeared into the seething mass of Kitsune fighters.

"Don't die, Hikaru," Jack whispered.

This is what Mio meant. You're never ready. You're never ready for loving someone – or losing them.

Why did I have to be such an effing coward?

Leaning down a little awkwardly, she kissed the corner of Hikaru's lips – and the sudden realization that this might be the last time she'd ever kiss Hikaru made a ragged sob tear out of her throat. "I like you, too. Please don't die. Please, please, please."

Hikaru shuddered, letting out a low, pained groan. But one of her clammy, bleeding hands lifted, and her fingers closed around Jack's.

Jack held on tightly.

CHAPTER 25

FRAIL HUMAN HEART

"This is useless, Izanami!" Izanagi screamed, face incandescent with fury. "You cannot keep me here once the hour of midnight is done. Your gateway will close, your powers will be cut off and you will sink back into your grave, where you belong!"

The shrill cackle of Izanami's laughter mixed with the deep roar of the water, sending chills down my spine.

"Answer me!" Izanagi's whole body flared with white light, on fire with the force of his anger. "Don't you dare ignore me, you rotting bitch!"

In my hand, the sword was rattling with eagerness. My fingers twitched with the urge to draw it, to fight – to end this. Our plan was redundant now. There was no need for the element of surprise. Izanagi couldn't escape me. I was ready.

"Shinobu." I turned to him.

He nodded, eyes fixed on mine. "It is time." He opened his coat and reached inside for the short sword attached to his belt—

Izanagi appeared in front of us in a flash of light. He ripped the wakizashi, still in its sheath, from Shinobu's grip and backhanded him with it in one smooth, deadly motion.

The terrible blow lifted Shinobu off his feet and sent him flying. He disappeared over the handrail of the bridge into the darkness below. Into the water, or into the portal itself, I had no way of knowing. It happened so fast, I didn't even hear a splash.

Jesus, Jesus, Jesus...

Suddenly I was all alone.

"So this is your plan, you stupid woman?" Izanagi shouted to his wife as I backed away warily, giving myself space. "To turn my own servants against me? Pathetic. You have only helped me – do you understand? You have handed me the item for which I have been searching. Did you truly believe that these weak human children could be a threat to me?"

"She is," Izanami shrieked. "She *is*!"

"She is nothing. A tattered old soul that I kept as a souvenir of my victory. She and her line are of no further use to me. I will bind the god-killing blade so tightly that you will never be able to find it or unseal it. You think that she can stop me? She should never even have been born."

"You're the one who should never have been born," I whispered. I ripped the black, flame-shaped blade from the saya and tossed the sheath away. "Shinobu! Kusanagi-no-Tsurugi!"

Power enveloped my body, driving down into my core like a spike. The sword caught light with a sharp crack. I couldn't even see its shape or colour – it was a fiery bar of pure energy, whistling in my hands. My skin burned with it, shining like mother-of-pearl. My eyes leaked tears of fire.

Let's kill him, the sword whispered.

"Yes."

I lunged at Izanagi. He flashed out of existence. The red lightning overhead sparked – was he trying to break out? – and a moment later he reappeared at the other side of the bridge, the sheathed wakizashi firmly clutched in his hand.

"Just as big a coward as ever," I taunted. I circled the sword forward and backward in my grip as I moved towards him, warming up my wrist. "What a shame you never had a mother. You'd have made a perfect mummy's boy."

He frowned in confusion, apparently realizing he'd been insulted, but not how.

Now! the sword said.

I jumped, and the power of the leap propelled me right into Izanagi's space. My blade flashed, quicker than the human eye could follow. Izanagi yowled as the blade cleaved him open from shoulder to waist. The wound flared with white fire.

He zipped into nothingness again.

Grating laughter sounded behind me. I whirled around to see him balanced on the handrail less than three feet away. The diagonal wound I'd inflicted was already gone, his kimono gaping open over a torso so smooth and unmarked it looked like wax instead of flesh. As I watched, the ragged edges of the dark cloth sealed together, mending the rip in his clothing. It was as if I'd never touched him.

"You are truly stupid, even for a mortal. No mere human can harm a god."

"Oh, really?" I sneered. "Cos that looked like it hurt to me. And if you're not shit-scared to fight me, then why do you keep running away? Or can't you help yourself? Yeah, I bet that's it. After a few thousand years of hiding from your own wife like a frightened little boy, it's just habit."

He flickered out of existence – and appeared again next to me, his arm already blurring into motion. I barely had time to register the knife of white energy in his hand before he thrust it into my side. The flaming blade cut through my armour as if it was tissue, slicing my innards with freezing fire.

I convulsed and coughed out a mouthful of blood, unable even to scream. My hands tightened into a knot on the hilt of the sword. I thrust it straight into his chest. The sword's power and the god's collided in a mini-explosion of sparks and heat, like plunging white-hot metal into ice water.

Izanagi shrieked. He yanked the knife out of me, and it flickered and disappeared as its energy was reabsorbed into his body. Blood gushed down my hip in a warm torrent. He grabbed me by the neck, lifted me off the ground – jerking my hissing blade from his heart – and threw me away like a scrunched-up ball of paper.

I hit the bridge on my left side and skidded several feet on my face and shoulder. My skull crunched, loud enough to deafen me. There was an agonizing pop as my arm dislocated from its socket. The world swam. Everything went black...

None of that! Wakey, wakey, the sword urged.

I was still lying on the bridge. I had passed out, but only for a second.

Half my field of vision was gone. I didn't know what had happened to my left eye, but it wasn't working any more. My left arm was useless too. Slithering and slipping in the rapidly spreading pool of my own blood, I flopped over onto my back and forced myself into a sitting position, biting down on a groan of anguish.

Izanagi loomed over me. I could hear Izanami's shrill screams as she watched her one chance of getting her husband back flush straight down the toilet. Izanagi still held the sheathed wakizashi absently in his left hand, fingers wrapped loosely around the worn grip. The wound to his chest – what should have been a death blow – was already healed.

"I don't get … it," I said, playing for time as I painfully transferred the sword from a two-handed grip to my right hand only. My words were slurred. I was pretty sure I had concussion. Maybe a fractured skull. If I took one more hit I'd be a goner.

I could feel the blade's energy working frantically inside me, struggling to fix the massive amount of damage I'd taken – maybe the bleeding in my side was already slowing down. If I could just stall him long enough…

"Get?" Izanagi repeated, reluctantly interested.

"You. Why do you even … want to live? What do you … have … to live *for*?" I asked, forcing the words out despite my lazy tongue. "Your wife is a … rotting corpse. You … murdered … or tried to murder … half your kids. The ones who tolerate you … now … only do it from fear. You have all this … power. And you do nothing … with it … but try to extend … your own … miserable existence. There's no being … in this realm, or any other … who loves you. You have *nothing*… Nothing worth living for… Why? Why fight … so hard?"

Izanagi's face jerked. The blank white eyes narrowed, and for less than a heartbeat I thought I saw something within them – something that might have been sorrow.

His lips compressed into a thin line.

"Do not seek to understand me, human. You have no concept of what it is to be a god. Your loves and joys are finite by definition, as are your insignificant lives. The gods are *infinite*. We are forever. We are eternal. And eternity is despair."

In his right fist, a long, curving blade of white energy slowly formed. I shoved myself backward, dragging myself away from him. But I couldn't get up. Everything below the waist was numb. Even with the sword screaming and smoking in my grasp, even with its power rippling out of my skin, I couldn't get my legs to obey me.

I couldn't get up.

"Noooo!" Izanami wailed. "No, no, no!"

"Be grateful for that which you are about to receive." Izanagi's feet splashed through my congealing blood. "I will end your suffering forever, and you will know what a blessing mortality is."

Izanagi's white blade rose above me. My sword's scream of rage filled my ears.

Behind Izanagi there was a flash of movement. A sleek black head rose above the bridge's silver handrail.

Shinobu.

With a heave of his arms, Shinobu flipped over the rail, water streaming off his clothes and hair, and landed silently in a coiled crouch. He was already moving as his gaze darted over us, flinging himself forward. In an

343

instant, Shinobu dived under Izanagi's left arm, both of his hands outstretched. He seized the battered black saya that hid the wakizashi.

Our gazes met.

Without hesitation Shinobu ripped the sheath away from the blade.

I sucked in a breath that seemed to take ten minutes to fill my lungs. The world stopped again. This time, instead of going black, everything seemed to brighten, to freeze, caught as if in a flashbulb photograph. Izanagi's expression of utter disbelief as he stared down at the unsheathed short-blade he was holding. Shinobu's deep, beautiful eyes, gazing into mine for the last time.

Goodbye again, my love.

Words burst from my lips:

"Ame-no-Murakumo-no-Tsurugi!"

The wakizashi shattered into a million pieces in Izanagi's hand. Fragments, nothing more than glittering metallic dust, rained out of the god's clutched fist. Shinobu dropped the empty sheath and fell, clutching at his chest. His back arched with pain. Blood spilled through his fingers, glowing red against his hands.

Izanagi let out a primal roar of anger and fear.

In my hand, the sword – the blade that had been my katana, my beloved, and the bane of my existence – detonated like a nuclear bomb.

A column of light erupted around me, stretching up

through the lightning cage into the heavens above, and down beneath me, through the churning water, to the very depths of hell. Power broke within the column like a tsunami and I screamed. And screamed. And screamed.

I was lifted up from my sprawled position on the bridge, suspended in a sea of pain and power. I kept on screaming as the blade's energy scoured through my body, taking possession of every fibre, every cell, every atom. My skull crunched brutally and my left eye suddenly worked again. My shoulder slid back into its socket with a hard *thock*. The deep wound in my side sealed up the way that a zip draws shut, the damage inside reknitting itself. Blood loss? Who needed blood when there was pure, liquid power running through their veins instead? I screamed and screamed as pain, doubt – emotion – burned away. Burned to nothing.

My screams cut off as if someone had flipped a switch.

Mine. Mine. All mine... the sword gloated gleefully. Its consciousness unfolded within my body with a sinuous stretch that straightened my arms and legs, unbent my back. At last, at long long last. Freedom.

Everything was clear. Everything was bright and new. I was the sword-bearer, the flesh-and-bone extension of the blade's will. I was the sword-bearer, and that was all. That was everything.

The sword's final form fitted into my hand as if I had been made to hold it, the hilt smooth and warm against my

345

palm. So elegantly simple and lovely. A leaf-shaped blade, carved from a single piece of priceless moss jade, the diamond-shaped pommel and angular guard etched with the twisting shapes of celestial dragons. To cover such beauty with a workaday skin of metal and silk had been a crime.

Izanagi's crime.

Where had he scurried off to? I turned, slowly drifting within the mantle of power. My eyes passed over the crumpled form of the boy – Shinobu – lying almost at the edge of the column of light. A tiny pang of sorrow touched my heart. I crushed it swiftly. No more of that. He was dead, or soon would be. What did it matter? Such meaningless things were beneath me now.

Ah, there was the little god, cowering on the other side of the bridge, as far away from me as he could get. Time to begin, then. The column of light narrowed into a shining corkscrew and sank into me like a sword into its sheath. Underfoot, the centre of the bridge and the concrete struts that had supported it disintegrated into glowing white ash, and the swirling red mouth of Yomi gaped directly below me. I walked lightly across the air, feeling it ripple against the soles of my feet, until I reached the edge of the hole and stepped onto the bridge again.

"Now," I purred, my voice a silvery, metallic mixture of my own human tones and the sword's inhuman ones. "What were you saying? Something about mortality being a gift?"

"Stay back," Izanagi ordered. Six-foot-long blades of energy – so crude, so … macho – trembled slightly in his hands. He swiped them through the air in a shining figure of eight. "Do not dare to approach me. I am a Kami. I am a god. You … you are nothing but a tool. A weapon. My weapon. You belong to me and you will obey me."

I yawned exaggeratedly, putting my left hand up to cover my lips. "Oh, sorry. It's just – I've heard all this before, a long time ago. Even then you couldn't hide the fact that you were afraid of me. That's why you imprisoned me and hid me away."

"I fear nothing," he hissed.

"Pull the other one, little man." The sword's laughter echoed out of my mouth, a delighted gurgle. "You are weak. A trembling coward with the powers of a god. It's some kind of cosmic joke! So let's see, shall we, how you fight against a real opponent? Let's see how you do against an enemy who can make you *bleed*."

"I do not fear you!"

"You will."

Izanagi flashed out of sight and reappeared directly behind me, his swords carving the air where I had stood. Except I wasn't there any more. I had already ducked beneath his strike. My blade lashed out almost lazily and I straightened as one of Izanagi's legs buckled beneath him. He crashed down and evaporated.

"Wave goodbye to your hamstring," I sang out merrily.

Izanagi flashed back into existence about twelve feet away – and fell to one knee with a whimper. He touched his leg, face twisting with disbelief as he saw dark liquid staining his fingers. "Impossible."

"Nope. I'm always right you know. So now…" I skipped and shuffled in place like a boxer. "It's time to fight for your life. Come on, give it your best shot. Impress me."

He zipped away, flickering back into existence behind me again. That seemed to be a favoured trick of his – the sneak attack. I stood still for him as he swung his right blade into a powerful overhead sweep, meant to slice my body in two.

At the last second, I twisted fluidly out of the way, my green blade snaking up to catch Izanagi's on its edge. There was a fierce sizzle, and Izanagi's white bolt of energy snapped. He dropped the other half with a yelp. I slid around him, too fast for him to dodge, and just kissed the crease of his left elbow with the blade. His arm jerked and his other sword fell, vanishing before it hit the bridge. "Annular and collateral ligaments," I told him. "That'll be hell on your tennis serve."

The blade flicked out, down, sideways, taunting and tormenting him, too fast for him to dodge. "Nicked your carotid. And your saphenous vein. That was your kidney, there. How do you feel about a pierced lung? Oops, too late!"

He whisked away into a cloud of writhing black and

gold filaments — his non-corporeal form. It surged and flowed like mist, trying to surround me.

"Funny how god anatomy is exactly the same as human," I told him. "I had a lot of time to think about anatomy, you know – learn about it, learn about the human jailors who should have been my slaves – while I was trapped within my metal prison. A lot of time to imagine the battles I could have fought, the lives I could have ended. I could have spent the last thousand years bathing in blood. If it weren't for you."

Wait. No.

"Shut up," I said savagely. "I don't have to listen to you any more. Now, Izanagi, just a word to the wise: you can hang about in your cloud form for as long as you like, but you won't heal. And you won't be able to escape me. Your lovely zombie wife still has thirty minutes of cage-time left. I wonder how many chunks I can carve you into before her time is up?"

A knotted rope of black and gold shot out of the vaporous cloud of Izanagi's power, its end sharpening into a gleaming spear-point. I caught it left-handed, an inch from my heart.

"Ah ah ah! I can't have you damaging my nice new body now – not when I've just broken it in."

A tortured scream echoed out of the coruscating blot of Izanami's power as I chopped the black and gold rope in two. The spear-point dissolved in my grasp and re-formed into a severed hand. The other end of the rope spurted dark liquid as it snapped back, withdrawing into the darkness. The black and gold cloud shrank into itself, boiling upwards off the bridge to hover just under the top of the red lightning cage.

"Ooh, that must have stung." I giggled. I considered the severed hand for a moment. "Should I keep this as a souvenir?"

This is sick. Stop torturing him. Just end it! Finish him off!

"Why should I?" I asked, smiling. "I'm going to play with him. I'm going to enjoy it. And there's nothing you can do to stop me, mortal child."

Izanami's voice wailed up through the gaping hole in the bridge. "Do it! Do it now! Return him to me!"

"You shut up, too!" I yelled back. "I don't take orders from you. I don't take orders from anyone. Wreck this wretched world if you like – devour it all. I don't care."

No. I didn't give my life for this. Shinobu didn't give his. We're supposed to end this and save everyone.

My arm twitched. Izanagi's cooling hand went flying out of my fingers into the hole in the centre of the bridge. I clenched my fist, staring at it in outrage. "How...? I am the sword-bearer."

You are a sadistic psycho and I won't let you destroy the world for kicks.

My whole body lurched, shuddering. "Stop! What are you doing?"

I'm taking my body back.

"No! No, this is my body mine, mine..."

Who are you, then?

"I am the sword-bearer!"

No, not your function. Your name. Who are you? Go on – answer me! You can't, can you? You don't exist. You're not a person. You're just a shadow of me that the sword is using to control my body, and I. Won't. Have. It.

My fingers and toes curled and, against my will, my head slowly turned from left to right. "Stop this! Stop – stop – stop!"

Suddenly I could hear it: the sword's alien voice chiming inside my head. The sword's voice? This was my voice – I was the sword-bearer... Wasn't I?

You are more than just the bearer of any sword, no matter how powerful. You are more than the servant of this blade. More than its puppet.

Images – feelings – began to surge up inside me, like waves washing over a stony cliff in great sprays of colour and warmth and life. The feeling of being hugged, a hand gently patting my back. A masculine whiskery scent and a deep voice saying the words *Midget Gem*.

My mother. My father. Your parents.

"I don't need parents!"

You do. And you need laughter, and friends.

Silly, uncontrollable giggling that came from a place of trust and happiness, a feeling that was somehow

streaked with pink and purple in my memories. A sense
of safety and responsibility and the image of a mug of tea
offered to me. A flashing, fey smile, the swish of a cop-
pery tail and the dry smell of ozone.

Jack. Rachel. Hikaru.

"Who are they? They are nothing to me! Meaningless
insects!"

*They're everything to you. Everything to me. You did all
this for them. You did it for him.*

Dark hair drifting around smoky, endless eyes. A shy,
cocky smile. The scent of bonfires and pine trees. A voice
that murmured *Mio-dono…*

"Shinobu?" I whispered.

Oh, God. Shinobu.

My gaze flew away from Izanagi's cloudy presence to
the other side of the bridge, where the boy I loved lay …
dying? Dead already? I couldn't tell. He was so still.

Tears spilled down my cheeks.

Shut up! Don't listen! You are me and I am you! We
are the night itself – we are the darkness hidden! We
are the Sword of the Gathering Clouds of Heaven! The
sword's energy shrieked, the green blade fizzing with
sparks, vibrating with rage in my hand.

We are all-powerful!

We are immortal!

We can destroy anything we want!

I sucked in a deep, shuddering breath and felt control

flow back into my own limbs in a tide of tingling pins and needles as I ripped the creeping tentacles of the sword's intelligence from my mind, my soul, my heart.

"My name is Mio Yamato," I told it grimly as my fingers clenched and loosened on the smooth stone grip of the sword. "I am not powerful. I am not immortal. And I don't want to destroy anything. *I just want this to be over.*"

I looked up at the shining gold and black vapours of Izanagi hovering above me, drew back my arm – No no no! the blade screeched – and flung the Sword of the Gathering Clouds of Heaven overhand like a spear with every bit of strength I had. The green blade screamed through the air, trailing white flames behind it.

It plunged home in the centre of Izanagi's non-corporeal form.

Black and gold lightning and pale fire fought around and within the dark cloud. Slowly, the human body of the god took shape. He hung in the air, lips gaping in a soundless scream, as he clutched the hilt of the jade sword that protruded from his chest. Dark liquid bubbled up around it, dripping over his one remaining hand.

His eyes. I could see his eyes, and they weren't white any more. They were brown. They were … human.

He dropped like a stone, falling past me, through the hole in the bridge and down into the swirling red river below. The sword's final high-pitched scream of fury made my ears buzz. Then the red waters closed over

Izanagi and swallowed him whole. Izanami's voice broke out in a choked, triumphant cry of joy.

There was a sound like a star collapsing in on itself, an indescribably vast, hollow *BOOM*. The water dimpled: sucked downward so fast that for an instant I saw the muddy bed, littered with rusting metal and trash. Then the water surged up like a fist.

The shock wave blew me straight off my feet. I felt the toxic radiation travel through me, claws of ice scraping out the marrow of my bones. Before I even hit the bridge again – my head bouncing against the path hard enough to make me see stars – I knew that I was dying.

I curled into a ball as the terrible forces raged around me, whistling and vibrating through the air like a steam cooker left on the heat for too long. The bridge heaved under me, letting out a series of deafening crunches and cracks. The waters rose, a great wave of blood washing over the bridge. With a groan, the whole structure rocked forward, then back.

And then, so suddenly that it was like a slap to the face … everything fell still.

I forced my eyes open.

I was lying on my back, one arm and the bottom half of my leg dangling down into the hole. Above me, the red lightning cage was gone. High, high above that, the sick crimson colour was draining away from the moon, leaving it silvery and clean again. The dense purple clouds were drifting away, shredding in some distant wind that I couldn't feel.

My poor struggling heart stuttered, defeated at last, failing. It should have hurt – it should have hurt like hell, the way it had last time – but it didn't. My grunting, choked breaths were a far-off, faintly annoying sound, nothing more. I'd already had so much pain. It was enough now. I was ready to go.

I was ready to go with him.

With a great effort, I rolled my heavy skull sideways. There. There he was, on the other side of the abyss. Shinobu. Lying so still, face turned up to the sky. His hands had fallen away from his chest. One curled just over the edge of the hole in the bridge, as mine did. It was as if we'd been reaching out to each other without even knowing it. Had he already gone? I supposed it didn't really matter. Whichever one of us was first would wait for the other to catch up.

My heart had finally gone quiet. My vision was narrowing: a black tunnel with a tiny pinprick of light at its centre. The dark blocked my view of Shinobu, but I knew where I would find him. I smiled as I mumbled, "Where you go…"

I will follow. Always.

I let my eyes close.

BITTERSWEET SIXTEEN

A faint, continuous beeping noise sounded to my left. It kept on, and on, slowly picking up speed. I could feel my eyebrows wrinkling in annoyance – which sent an ache echoing through my skull.

Wait.

Wait a second.

I'm breathing.

I peeled gluey, leaden eyelids open. Blue wall. Blue curtains. A hospital room. On one side, my dad, in an uncomfortable looking plastic chair, slumped over on the blanket by my feet with his head pillowed on his arms. On the other side, my mum, in a slightly less evil-looking armchair with her head resting against the wall by the window. Both asleep.

Fingers of syrup-coloured light crept under the curtains, touching my mum's hair, the floor, the wall.

Daylight. It was morning. It was … the morning of my sixteenth birthday.

I was sixteen years old.

I was alive.

Why?

"What happened?" My voice was a rasping croak that made me wince.

"The very question I have been asking myself," said a cheerful voice.

I jerked violently, inadvertently tugging on the IV drip taped to my arm, and winced again. My whole body protested against these movements, and it took a long while for me to persuade my watering eyes to focus.

Someone stood in the doorway. He had not been there an instant before. He was … jolly-looking. Early twenties, maybe, but already sloping gently into middle age. Chubby face, dimples, longish dark hair, and a neat beard. Like Santa in his uni years, maybe, if Santa was from Japan. Cute.

Then I met his eyes. Starry, infinite depths gazed back at me. I looked down and saw a battered old cane in his right hand.

"Ebisu?" I whispered.

"You don't have to keep your voice down. You won't wake your parents. You won't wake anyone."

I stared at my mum and dad. "You froze them?"

"No, my dear. I've just blessed them all with a nice,

357

deep sleep. They'll have beautiful dreams that they'll never quite remember, and wake feeling much the better for it. In the meantime, I think you and I should have a little chat. How do you feel about a walk?"

I blinked at him, head spinning. "Walk?"

"Well, I'll walk. You'd better stay sitting, I think. Yes? Good, good. Carefully does it…"

Without really understanding how it had happened, I was gently and competently detached from my heart monitor and IV drip, shoehorned out of bed and into a dressing gown, then tucked into a wheelchair with a blanket over my knees.

"Hold this," he said, placing his cane across my lap. "It won't bite."

I closed my hands tentatively over the cane to keep it from rolling off as he wheeled me out into the corridor. "You're … oddly good at this. Competent."

"I learned to care for humans as a child," he said matter-of-factly. "I grew up among them. The Ainu people found my sister and me drifting in the water after my father abandoned us, and took us in. They did not know what we were, only that we were helpless and alone. They taught me that simple kindness, human kindness, was the most valuable thing in the universe. A lesson I have always clung to, even in my darkest moments."

We rolled past a waiting room. I caught a glimpse of three familiar figures slumped together on a row of blue chairs: Jack, Rachel and Hikaru. Rachel's face was buried in Jack's shoulder – Jack's cheek rested on the top of Rachel's head. Hikaru was lying down, with her head in Jack's lap and her feet dangling off the edge of the last chair. She looked a bit pale, and I saw the edges of bandages peeking out of her clothes, but her lips were creased in a faint smile. One of Jack's hands was tangled with Hikaru's. The other rested protectively on Hikaru's head, as if she'd fallen asleep stroking Hikaru's long red hair.

The sight sent a pang through me. My stomach churned with it. I quickly looked away.

"Where are we going?" I asked.

"Not far," Ebisu said. He hummed under his breath as he pushed me up one corridor and down another. The hospital lay quiet around us, wrapped in a sort of peaceful stillness. The odd snore drifted in the air.

Ahead of us, a set of double doors swung open and stayed that way. The walls beyond were clear plastic from floor to ceiling, so that the whole of London seemed to spread out before me, bathed in the soft light of the low winter sun. It all looked so calm. So ... normal.

"Well?" Ebisu asked.

"Well, what?"

"It's still there. You did it. How do you feel?"

I opened my mouth. Nothing came out. There was a long, aching pause. Then I put my hands over my face, head bowing as my shoulders scrunched up. Tears squeezed out and plopped onto the front of my hospital gown. My whole body shook. I cried in near silence; sobs wrenched out of me like chunks of my heart.

"There, my dear. There." Ebisu's hand rested on my shoulder. His long, straight fingers seemed to radiate warmth. "It was too great a burden for anyone to carry, too great a sacrifice for anyone to make. But you did it all the same. And you survived."

"How?" I choked out. "How? I was supposed to die! This was all supposed to be over."

"Honestly, that has me in something of a confusion," he admitted. "Everything I knew told me that you could not survive. The knowledge grieved me deeply. Yet here you are. So perhaps I am not as clever as I like to think. Or perhaps…"

"What?" I demanded.

"You were the sword-bearer, Mio. You are a Yamato, and your family had bathed in the power of the blade for a very long time, you more than any of them. It's possible, just possible, that you are no longer – quite – human."

"Not human? What does that mean?"

"I can't tell you yet," he said. "But I'm sure we'll figure it out. Whatever the truth, I am glad of it, my dear. I am more glad than I can say that you are still here."

I wanted to shout, *I'm not!* I wanted to turn around and punch him. I wanted to throw his cane back in his face, stamp my feet, and scream, *I wasn't supposed to have*

to do this! I wasn't supposed to live through it. I wasn't sup-
posed to have to go on afterwards. Alone.

But Ebisu had lived for five hundred years as a pris-
oner in his own body, unable even to set foot outside his
front door. He had hidden the wakizashi, and kept the
secret, and each day he had suffered for it. He had helped
me. Helped us. He had been … kind.

He was the last person in the world that I could throw
a tantrum at over the bitter injustice of my life. So I swallowed the bitterness down, down, and nodded slowly.
"I'm glad … that you're free. I'm glad for you."

Ebisu patted my shoulder again. "You're a nice girl.
Come along now."

He wheeled me back the way we'd come. I assumed
the strange little interlude was over and held myself rigid,
determined to keep it together until he left me alone. But
at the big double doors he turned left instead of right.

"This is the wrong way," I said dully.

"Don't you want to visit?" Ebisu brought us to a stop
outside a door, and again, it opened untouched. The room
within was dark. A familiar beeping almost drowned out
the sound of someone's quiet, even breathing.

"Visit … who?" I'd already seen everyone.

"Your young man."

I sat like a stone, listening to the noises of life coming
from inside the room. It couldn't be. It couldn't be true.
I couldn't believe it, because if I did, and it wasn't real, I

would break and nothing and no one would ever be able to put me back together again.

My heart made a desperate, soundless plea. *Tell me! Tell me it's true! Tell me how!* Somehow, Ebisu heard it.

"His wound was fatal – absolutely fatal – five hundred years ago," he explained. "Nothing could have saved him then, I'm afraid. But in twenty-first-century London? Well, if someone got there in time to stop the bleeding, and then there was a good surgeon available at a good hospital, and after some fairly extensive stitching and patching up it was possible to give him a nice, fat blood transfusion … suddenly it wouldn't be fatal any more. In fact, all he'll have to show for it is a rather dashing scar. You won't mind that, will you?"

I didn't answer. I was already fighting with the blanket, hands fumbling, almost tipping myself out of the chair in my struggle to get free. Ebisu's cane clattered to the floor.

"Now, now, there's no need to be in such a panic," he said, calmly disentangling me and helping me to stand on noodle legs. He met my eyes and smiled his cherubic, joyful smile. "You have all the time in the world."

I staggered away from him, into the room. One step. Two steps. Three steps brought me to the bed. My eyes quickly adjusted to the gloom. I stared down at the boy lying there. I felt dizzy, lightheaded, as if I was under some kind of euphoric spell.

He was pale – deathly pale, almost grey. Dark circles made his bruised purple eyelids look sunken in his face, and his cheeks seemed gaunt. His hair was a tangled mess. His whole chest was wrapped round and round with layers of bandages. I'd never seen him look worse.

And he was alive. Alive, alive, *alive*.

By the time I thought to look up at the doorway again, Ebisu was gone.

"Thank you," I whispered. "Thank you."

Slowly I eased down onto the edge of the hard hospital bed, shaking fingers reaching out. The skin of Shinobu's bare shoulders was chilled. I pulled the blanket up over them. His eyebrows had furrowed in his sleep, and his eyelids were flickering as if he was having a bad dream. I smoothed the hair off his forehead and tucked it behind his ear, watching his sleeping face gradually relax.

"It's OK," I said softly. "I'm here."

Lying down on the narrow space next to him, I nestled my face carefully into its perfect place in the notch between his shoulder and neck, and breathed deep, cherishing the faint scent of smoke and pines underneath the hospital antiseptic. Cherishing the annoying, beautiful, steady blip of the heart monitor, and the shape of his body against mine. I would never say that I hated hospitals again.

"So. Looks like we have … another chance," I told him shakily, threading my fingers through his. "None of this epic star-crossed love crap this time, OK? No more monsters, no more magic. Just you and me. And we'll do so much better this time, I promise, Shinobu. This time … where you go, I will follow."

Maybe I imagined the soft, almost soundless breath against my hair that sounded like, "Always."

Then again, maybe not.

ACKNOWLEDGEMENTS

I'm strongly tempted here to just fill half a page with OH MY GOD I DID IT IT'S FINISHED HURRAY! Because there were many points when I thought that wasn't going to happen, and the relief in being wrong is truly overwhelming. If I had realized at the outset how incredibly challenging it would be to write a trilogy, I would probably have been too chicken to start. But the fact that this book – and this series – was completed, and is actually something of which I can be incredibly proud, is largely down to … well, all these people I'm about to name.

Boundless love and thanks go to:

Wonder Editor – Annalie Grainger – and Super Agent – Nancy Miles – for keeping me (mostly) sane through-out, and staying patient even when I inevitably began to babble about running away to herd yaks in Tibet.

The astonishingly talented and lovely Maria Soler Canton for, as always, blowing my mind with cover-tastic beauty (and Heather, for similarly delighting me with my American cover art).

Gill Evans, Hilary Van Dusen, Miriam Newman, Victoria Philpott, Paul Black, Sawako Shirota and all the multitudes of talented and hardworking folk at both Walker Books and Candlewick Press.

The Furtive Scribblers, who forgave me even though I neglected them horribly whilst embroiled in this book's clutches, and without whom I would never have had the idea for The Name of the Blade in the first place.

My online crew, including the marvellous UKYA bloggers, the Authors Allsorts and the YAThinkers, who sometimes were the only reason my laptop didn't take a flying journey out of a window.

My whole family, with a special mention to my nieces Esme, Alexandra and Clemence, whose dawning geekery has gladdened my days in particular recently, and who reassure me that the force is still strong in the next generation.

BC 9/15

Love The Name of the Blade series?
Love Zoë Marriott's other books!

Visit Zoë online at **www.zoemarriott.com**
and **thezoe-trope.blogspot.co.uk**
Follow her on Twitter, **@ZMarriott**